THE
WITCH
OF
WILLOW
SOUND

THE WITCH OF WILLOW SOUND

VANESSA F. PENNEY

Copyright © Vanessa F. Penney, 2025

Published by ECW Press
665 Gerrard Street East
Toronto, Ontario, Canada M4M 1Y2
416-694-3348 / info@ecwpress.com

All rights reserved. No part of this publication may be reproduced, stored in a retrieval system, or transmitted in any form by any process — electronic, mechanical, photocopying, recording, or otherwise — without the prior written permission of the copyright owners and ECW Press. The scanning, uploading, and distribution of this book via the internet or via any other means without the permission of the publisher is illegal and punishable by law. This book may not be used for text and data mining, AI training, and similar technologies. Please purchase only authorized electronic editions, and do not participate in or encourage electronic piracy of copyrighted materials. Your support of the author's rights is appreciated.

Editor for the Press: Jen Knoch
Copy editor: Crissy Boylan
Cover design: Jessica Albert
Cover artwork: © Teagan White / www.teaganwhite.com

This is a work of fiction. Names, characters, places, and incidents either are the product of the author's imagination or are used fictitiously, and any resemblance to actual persons, living or dead, business establishments, events, or locales is entirely coincidental.

LIBRARY AND ARCHIVES CANADA CATALOGUING IN PUBLICATION

Title: The witch of Willow Sound / Vanessa F. Penney.
Names: Penney, Vanessa F., author.
Identifiers: Canadiana (print) 20250215039 | Canadiana (ebook) 20250215047
ISBN 978-1-77041-842-4 (softcover)
ISBN 978-1-77852-502-5 (ePub)
ISBN 978-1-77852-503-2 (PDF)
Subjects: LCGFT: Gothic fiction. | LCGFT: Novels.
Classification: LCC PS8631.E562 W58 2025 | DDC C813/.6—dc23

This book is funded in part by the Government of Canada. *Ce livre est financé en partie par le gouvernement du Canada.* We acknowledge the support of the Canada Council for the Arts. *Nous remercions le Conseil des arts du Canada de son soutien.* We would like to acknowledge the funding support of the Ontario Arts Council (OAC) and the Government of Ontario for their support. We also acknowledge the support of the Government of Ontario through the Ontario Book Publishing Tax Credit, and through Ontario Creates.

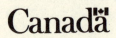

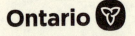

PRINTED AND BOUND IN CANADA

PRINTING: MARQUIS   5 4 3 2 1

Purchase the print edition and receive the ebook free.
For details, go to ecwpress.com/ebook.

To my family:

family of origin and family found

PROLOGUE

Somewhere, Nova Scotia
Night

The Old Woman had never seen a human being on fire before. It was mesmerizing, and messier than she'd expected.

The body did strange and wonderful things as it burned before her eyes. Twelve things, to be precise. She counted them as they happened. Collected them. Rearranged them in her mind.

Number three: The whole body screams.

At first, the fire struggled. As if it didn't want to burn this person. Or didn't like the taste. Flames crackled low in the sticks and spit puny embers into the brittle grass, igniting wildflowers into fireflies. The veil-thin flames singed the feet, but they refused to burn any further up the legs.

The Old Woman looked at the sky. The half moon overhead meant the night was half-gone. She needed more time. Or more fire.

She knew ways to get more fire.

Number nine: The black smoke that rises from inside human flesh smells like pain.

She considered the tiny box in her hand. The muffled *tock-tock* of the last match inside it. But it had already taken her too many matches to get the fire this far. It wasn't time to use the last match. Not yet.

She considered the object in her other hand. A tenpenny nail. Rusted and rough against her skin. Sharp.

The Old Woman blew on the nail. One quick breath. *Hah.*

With a single fluid motion, the Old Woman drew a hammer from her bootleg, spun it on her finger, and caught it. She tapped the nail into the trunk of the dead tree she had lashed the body to. *Tap-tap-tap.* As high as she could reach.

Number five: The eyes stay open.

She spun her old hammer with a gunslinger's grace and holstered it back down her bootleg. She waited. The wind rose from a shivery breath across the hairs on the Old Woman's skin up to a bitter gust. The fire climbed. Knee high. Fingertip high. The black sky rolled. Her braids whipped like thick rattlesnakes in the wind. A gust of salt air heaved off the water and blasted the Old Woman and her fire.

FOOM.

The fire exploded into a blinding ball that swallowed the body whole. Flames ripped through skin and bone, cracking the air like a sail. The heavy chain holding the body upright against the dead tree was so strong, it didn't let the body fall apart while it burned. It looked as if someone was standing inside the fire as they burned alive, as the body shrivelled into the horror of its final form: a ghastly silhouette of a human being.

Good, the Old Woman thought.

Her squinched eyes peered at the shadows of the forest behind her as she listened. No voices. No sirens. No one coming.

Good.

Number six: The body vomits fireballs as it burns. Not big ones, like a dragon. Small ones. Like bunches of yellow dandelion heads.

She'd chosen this place for right good reason. It was her own idea, this back-breaking haul through the woods, across the field, to the very edge of this cliff by the sea. She could've done this somewhere easier. Somewhere closer to the house. Somewhere more hidden and less deafening. She'd nearly snapped herself in half, lashing the body against the lonely tree. It had to be done. It had to be there, with the body facing west, overlooking the bay. So the eyes could see the ocean until the very end.

And they did.

Satisfied with the brutal fire, the Old Woman picked a place to sit in the tall grass. With every step she took, she jingled. Her apron was smothered with pockets, from top to bottom. Every last inch. Pockets of all sizes, made from mismatched scraps of cloth and sewn with jagged stitches. Every pocket strained, packed to the brim with strange and wonderful things. Teaspoons and keys. Bones and dead flowers. Knives and nails and vials and sticks of willow and witch hazel. Fog-grey wool and ivy-green yarn. Animal skins and bird skulls. Things to make people sleep. Things to make people dream. A collection of oddities that jingled with her wherever she went.

The Old Woman sat down in the dead grass. Skeletons of dead lupines rattled around her. Heat prickled her skin with needles and pins. Her wild eyes glittered and let off orange light. She looked a little wicked.

She had thought the fire would burn the body into a pile of ash she could sweep off the cliff with a broom. She thought she'd sit with the fire under the stars, have a hot cup of tea and a bite of bread, and then, with a few flicks of the wrist, be done with all this for good. Instead, she was left with a nightmare mass of charred meat and bone, still in the shape of a person. Still sizzling.

She wondered briefly if she should just leave it. Let the scavengers and the maggots and the hurricanes have it.

No.

Too risky. The meat could be anything, any animal on earth, but the bones spelled murder. When she unlocked the chain, the body stayed standing. It had seared to the surface of the dead tree. The Old Woman rolled up her sleeves. She drew one of her knives from one of the pockets in her strange apron, and she began the bloody work of prying the corpse from the tree, inch by inch.

Shuck-shuck-shuck.

With every cut, she reminded herself, *It's just meat now. Just bones. No one is here. You are alone.*

But she wasn't alone for long. Wild animals were coming. Lurking at the edge of the field. Watching her butcher prey on the brink of the cliff. She heard their lathers of slobber. Inhaled the sharp musk of familiar furs. She had no fear of them. She had spent her childhood making friends with wild things, after all. Spiders, mice, rats. Born in her pockets. Died in her bare hands.

She was a little bitter, and a little proud, that she had more in common with starving coyotes and weasels than with other human beings.

Except this one.

Shuck-shuck-shuck.

The coal-black shadow of a lone beast lifted itself from the tall grass. It lurched forward and stopped just shy of the Old Woman. Must be more desperate than the rest. She felt the hot breath in her hair. Drool dripped from its quivering jaw.

The Old Woman knew not to move too suddenly. She thought about the knife in her hand. How deep could she get her blade into a wild animal's throat? How deep into its brain through its eye?

The shadow and the Old Woman stared into each other: two hungry hunters with nothing to lose.

Fine then.

With the toe of her boot, the Old Woman nudged a bony slab from the pile of hacked-apart corpse. She twisted her fist deep into the broken ribs, pried out a steaming clump that had been—just hours ago—a human heart, and tossed it to the shadow. Before the heart hit the ground, it was snatched by fangs and carried into the distant trees.

Good.

After that, whenever the Old Woman pulled off a good-sized fistful of meat, she flung it to the drooling shadows and listened to the wild things gnash.

In return, they left her alone to work.

Shuck-shuck-shuck.

Slathered in soot and sweat, the Old Woman heaped the bony remains onto the wooden toboggan at her feet. Done, she leaned against the old tree. Hardwood of some kind. Limbless. Lifeless. Blackened by soot and curved by ages of ocean wind. Didn't burn, though. Didn't crack. She patted the still-smoking tree. Steam unfurled from her touch.

One last thing.

She used the claw of her hammer to pry the tenpenny nail from the tree and put the nail in a pocket of her apron. A strong tree, to withstand so much fire. Even in death. She lifted her broom and her teacup from the patch of dead thistles where she'd left them. Wrapped the links of the toboggan's chain brake around her wrist.

Seagulls wheeled in the sky. Seven crows watched from the trees. With a nod to the birds, the Old Woman escaped deep into the murmuring hemlocks and creaking black willows, pulling the toboggan and the bones behind her.

BOOK ONE

Missing

CHAPTER ONE

I wake up under a gravestone with frost in my hair and bony little fingers digging in my hoodie pocket.

Now, if a person was rifling through my pockets in the dark, I'd snap. I'd come up swinging like a grizzly and not stop till my knuckles hit bone and broke it.

But it's just a raccoon. A skinny little guy, digging like he's starving. He must be looking for my supper leftovers from last night—a half-gone bag of ketchup chips—crumpled up with me under the old tarp I sleep in.

I lie stone-still and let him dig.

Cold air curls off the black gravestone above my head like smoke. Frost crackles in dead grass. Even on the brink of winter, graveyard smells hang in the air. Oakmoss. Old earth. Crumbling stone.

This grave isn't mine, by the way. I'm not dead. Just homeless. Just needed a place to sleep. According to the words carved into the stone above my head, this grave belongs to one Mrs. Pleasant

Goose-Everlean, Beloved Mother O She Walked in Dignity and Grace, which definitely isn't me. Not even close.

Graveyards aren't the worst place in the world for the living to sleep. They're quiet and private, and the dead don't seem to mind. This whole city is built on unmarked graves, anyway. Everyone living here sleeps with the dead every night. Only some of us are willing to admit it.

My phone trills in my sleeping bag. The startled raccoon skitters away, empty-handed. *Sorry, little guy*. The busted phone screen is dim, but I see the name.

Doreen.

That can't be good. Ma hasn't called me once in two years. And I haven't answered a call from her in at least three. The picture I have in my memory of my mother is probably out of date by now, but I bet her eyes flick around behind her glasses the same way as always. Calculating value. Quick to judge. Never missing a thing. But who knows. Three years is a long time.

A bad feeling sinks my guts. That raccoon peeps its head out from behind a stone shaped like an urn. Moonlight glints from its berry-black eyes.

The ringing stops. No voicemail. Text messages pop up, glowing one by one.

Phaedra, this is your mother.

Thanks for the warning, Ma.

I need your help.

Well, that's different.

I need you to drive up to the county to your aunt Madeline's house.

That's very different.

The cops just called me at home. They had bad news.

That bad feeling in my gut turns cold.

Your aunt Madeline is missing.

Missing.

The word clangs my head like an iron bell.

Dead leaves slide off me as I sit up. I haven't always slept in graveyards. Once upon a time, I had a home. Balcony garden. Clean clothes. Sunday afternoon naps under sun-warmed blankets. Crisp, apple-scented air drifting through window screens. A teaspoon's gentle *tink* against the lip of a honeycomb mug the only sound.

But the rest of the week, I worked in the city, in dim air and grey rooms. Paid to let evil creep into my brain through a cold screen so no one else had to. I hunted monsters who hurt children. Tracked them down online so they could be brought to justice. But there's a cost to wading in that much darkness that long. One day, the mind snaps like a rope holding too much weight. It whips backwards and unravels and falls apart in the dust. It forgets how the world works. It starts to see evil everywhere.

So, I am alone. A shadow in a graveyard, hunched over and hollowed out and cut off for good reason from the rest of the world. Bruised up and useless.

It's fine. Alone is good. Alone is safe.

Missing.

If I went missing, who would look for me? Who would even notice I'm gone?

I know the answer because, in a way, I've been missing for a long time.

Nobody.

I pry my tired bones off the cold ground and stand up. Shake the frost off my tarp and out of my hair, then rummage my car keys from my backpack. I toss my leftover chips to the raccoon. Its purring, chittering, and the crinkle of the chip bag vanish into shadows.

I remember Aunt Madeline. All good memories of her, except one.

Would Aunt Madeline even want my help?

My keys quiver in my frost-scarred fingers. My car key and a door key that doesn't fit in any door anymore. I don't know why I keep a key to nothing. Just can't bring myself to throw it away.

Even if Aunt Madeline doesn't want my help, she might need it. And I don't need anything in return. Maybe she'll tell me to get lost.

Or maybe she'll ask me to stay for tea. One last cup, for old time's sake.

I'd stay for tea in a heartbeat.

I'll go.

I'll leave the dim, grey city behind and drive to the North Shore of Nova Scotia. To the countryside with high tides and hunting grounds and a tiny place in the woods I barely remember from my childhood. Willow Sound.

CHAPTER TWO

The old highway under my tires rises and falls, past copper hillsides and rose-red blueberry fields and little cemeteries with snow-white stones where half my people are.

They say every time you touch a memory, you change it. It's been a lifetime since I've thought about Willow Sound. I remember deep dark woods. No markers. No signs. Isolated and ghost-quiet.

It's easy to forget how quiet Nova Scotia can be sometimes.

I think this might be the place. It has to be close. Something about the trees and the sharp curve of the old highway tugs at my memory. Something about the weathered wooden guardrail creaking along the ditch, steep and smothered in dead wildflowers. I've passed through this place before.

I pull over and shut off the car. It only overheated twice on the way. Not bad. The car clicks as the engine cools. The pavement crumbles under the weight of my boots as I stretch the stiffness out of my legs and look around. My gut rumbles, so I grab a packet of ramen from my back seat and kick the door shut. Last one. I sit up on the hood of my car, plant my boots on the bumper, and wake up my phone. My mother's last text glows, unread.

The cops are the ones saying she's missing but they're idiots.

I flick the text aside, open GPS, and type in Willow Sound. The app flashes back a warning: *Unknown location—turn around.*

Frig.

Without GPS, I'll have to find my way through the woods by dead reckoning, or by memory. I don't remember much. I tug open one end of the ramen packet and break off chunks of the brittle noodles to munch on like chips while I think.

The sweet earthy smell of this place is familiar. And the loneliness.

The sun has risen just enough to let me see the little road I'm looking for. At least, I think it's the right road.

If it is, then it's not a road anymore. Just a couple of muddy ruts that turn off the old trunk highway, dip down into the ditch, and head straight into the woods. White mushrooms grow in the ruts, like little bones that refuse to stay buried. Looks like no one has taken the road into the woods in a long time.

You're the only one besides me who knows the way to her house, Phaedra. And you're probably the only person she would let in. Including me. Because she's that stubborn. You have to go.

In among the impressive collection of guilt trips Ma managed to cram inside her flurry of texts, there was truth. Our last visit to Aunt Madeline's hadn't ended well. I was a kid then, but even a kid knows when a bad fight between adults is the last fight.

Rows of dandelion heads quiver in cracks in the old highway's yellow line. Red and brown leaves rustle in the breeze. Some of them break off. Some of them fall.

A sharp whiff of something wicked stings my nose. A wretched smell. Burnt. Like scorched meat.

It's bad. Smells like a bad death.

Where the heck is it coming from? There's no sign of smoke in the trees or in the sky. No people. No cars. No houses for ages.

The smell fades after a few seconds. Lingered just long enough to turn my stomach, then gone. Maybe an animal died somewhere in a field and rotted and cooked in the sun.

Maybe—

RAWWWWW.

The harsh roar of an engine rips through my thoughts. Birds take off from the trees and fill the sky. Back over my shoulder, a black pickup truck splits the horizon like a chainsaw, coming this way. Ruining the quiet. Crushing the dandelions down the middle of the road. Sun glares off the windshield and jabs into my brain. It's the only other vehicle I've seen in an hour. Hopefully, it'll just drive on past, rip-roaring off to someplace else.

It grinds to a stop and idles right beside me. Of course it does. I glance back slowly, to let them know I don't care they're there and I don't need any help. I notice a few strange things. There's moss growing on it. Underneath the front fender and some on the rim. It's not an old truck. 2021, probably. Never, ever seen moss living on a vehicle like that. Not one that still runs, anyway.

There's no red dust on the truck. My car passed through long stretches of red road dust on the way here. Which means this truck didn't.

The truck's tires are instead packed with black muck. Sticky and gritty. It smells like graveyard dirt but doesn't look like it. The truck came here from the same direction I did, but there's not a bit of black muck like that on my tires.

So, where the frig did this truck come from?

The truck's windows hum and slide down. Two deep voices guffaw inside the cab. They're yapping at me before the window's even down. They smell like whole leaf tobacco and trouble.

I don't acknowledge them. Keep my head down. Crunch my ramen in silence.

"Darlin', you don't even realize where you are," a scratchy voice says. Sounds like the voice is coming from over on the driver's side.

"Hey, honey, you alone out here?" a second voice asks.

Well, that has to be the creepiest sentence someone could say to a woman all alone in the middle of the woods in the middle of nowhere.

"Just a fair warning," he says. "If you even dare walk down that little road in the woods, right there, you'll regret it till the day you die."

I guess I stand corrected.

"Hey, are you even listening to us?"

Ramen gone, I crumple the little packet into a ball, stuff it in my hoodie pocket, and stare off into the distance. Still purposely—and happily—ignoring them.

"Grand Tea is that way," the scratchy voice says. "If that's the town you're looking for."

Pfft. I spit-laugh at the idea.

I know a thing or two about the town of Grand Tea. And the people who live there. And their bizarre, collective death wish. Everyone in Nova Scotia knows about that town.

"You got a problem with our town?" the second voice asks.

Oh dear. Seems like I've offended him and his precious town.

Two truck doors creak open and slam shut. Boots scuff, purposely slow and casual-like, across pavement. Two men come toward me to confront me to my face.

I stand up.

They stop dead in their tracks.

One man's cigarette smoulders in his mouth. The other man's sunglasses slide down the sweat on his nose. They stare at me as if I'm not real. As if I'm some kind of mythical creature.

To be fair, I probably smell like some kind of mythical creature. In my sky-purple hoodie. Ratty and slashed and stained all over. Old coffee. Old paint. Old blood. New blood. Whatever life throws at me. It's my favourite hoodie.

"She looks like *her*," the man with sunglasses says. A flash of fear swipes across his face.

Oh. I get it.

They're right, I guess. I probably do look like *her*. Tall. Quiet. Long black hair. Olive skin. Green eyes. Not pretty Anne of Green Gables green. More like oakmoss frozen in ice.

"Oh man, I bet that's her niece!" the man with the cigarette says, pointing at me. "They said her niece was coming up from the city."

"Who said that?" I ask.

They don't answer me. The man's cigarette has fizzled right down to the filter. It sits between his lips like a little orange stub.

"Who said that?" I repeat, and take a step toward them.

They step back.

I didn't expect that.

The man with the cigarette finds a crumb of courage and flicks his stub on the ground by my boot. "I bet you never find her."

"What did you just say to me, pal?" I ask.

I take another step toward him. He steps back again.

Their strange fear of me is either going to be useful or a serious problem. I'm not sure which yet.

Sunglasses man gawks like a caught fish. Cigarette man keeps walking backwards, away from me. Slowly back toward the truck. Back toward the driver's side door. He opens it, but he doesn't jump inside. Instead, he ducks his head down.

I know what that means.

He's reaching for something under the seat. He's going for a weapon.

A serious problem.

For him.

Because I'm not going to scream or beg. I'm not going to panic or run or fall down or faint. I'm going to do what I always do. Stand my ground and fight.

By the time he retrieves his rather pristine baseball bat from inside his truck, I'm already jamming the tip of my switchblade against his rear tire, blade glinting and sharp.

He stops. I can practically see the math happening behind his eyes. Tow trucks aren't cheap. Truck tires aren't cheap. Rental vehicles aren't cheap.

"Drop the bat," I say. "I'll put away the blade."

His baseball bat drops and rolls under his truck toward me. I stop it under my boot.

The two men curse and slam themselves back inside the truck.

I pick the orange cigarette filter up off the pavement and flick it inside the open truck window. The truck engine fires up and roars.

I step back. My switchblade in one hand, the baseball bat resting on my shoulder.

"We were trying to help you," the sunglasses man says.

I raise my eyebrows.

"It's true," he says. "Nobody should go in there. People from around here know better than to mess with the old woman who lives at the end of that road. Those are her woods."

"So what?"

"She's insane," he says.

"She'll kill you," the cigarette man says. "Then she'll eat you."

I toss the baseball bat into the truck's cargo bed. The truck jolts into a furious U-turn. Heads right back the way it came.

As the quiet returns, and the birds return to their perches in the trees, my thoughts return to that little road in the woods.

Whoever those two guys are, they're fools. And they're wrong.

I happen to know the woman who lives at the other end of that road.

She's my aunt Madeline.

She's not insane.

Or at least she didn't used to be.

The overgrown little road in the woods is the road my mother and I used to take to visit Aunt Madeline when I was a kid. It was more than just two ruts back then. It used to be clear enough that my mother's car could drive on it, winding slow and steady all the way through the woods to Aunt Madeline's little house.

I remember the jack pine. The towering tree stands guard next to the road's entrance to the woods. Its rough grey bark is scarred by two deep, violent slashes down the trunk, impact scars from two lightning strikes long before I was born. When I was a kid, every time my mother's car turned off the old highway and took the little road in the woods, I peered up at that massive jack pine through the back-seat window. I wanted to see if it had gotten hit by lightning since the last time we passed through.

The jack pine is still alive. Still a battle-scarred warrior standing watch over all who enter here. The jack pine glints. Something small and silver jabs its trunk.

I skid down into the ditch and crouch by the trunk.

A small silver nail hammered into the bark. Hammered through two black feathers, holding them in place. Crow feathers, looks like. Weathered and broken.

I don't remember that being there.

Weird.

I guess I'll have to leave my car parked on the shoulder of the old highway and walk to Aunt Madeline's. Hopefully no one else bothers to drive past this way.

My car keys jab my palm. I shove them deep in my back jeans pocket. I zip up my backpack with a few things inside, just in case.

My mother's orders when she messaged were clear: Follow this little road to Aunt Madeline's house, check on her and see she's fine, phone the cops and tell them she's fine, send my mother a text and tell her she's fine, and then, I guess, drive myself back to the city, back to sleep with the graveyard dead.

That's later.

Right now, I have a road to take.

Even though the sun is up, the trees are thick and let in no light. My boots sink deep in the space between the two ruts. Those little white mushrooms gleam. I'm careful not to step on any. They might be destroying angel mushrooms. Or they might be harmless. Doesn't matter which kind they are if you're smart enough to leave them alone.

The jack pine creaks mournfully behind me. The way ahead is dark and deep. Cold creeps in. Evergreen needles prick my skin. Red leaves hiss in the wind and snap off. My phone light is not enough to push the shadows back.

The trees close in.

CHAPTER THREE

The forest is too quiet. A suffocating quiet that makes you wonder if you lost your hearing, or lost your mind. Nova Scotia has places this still. For now.

Somehow, Aunt Madeline loves living out here, in the middle of nowhere, in this surreal quiet. Alone. Living out of mind, she called it once. To this day, I think she means living outside the thoughts of everyone else on earth. Exquisitely forgotten.

My mother took it to mean living out of her damn mind and was quick to tell her so all those years ago. I remember how the heat prickled my cheeks as I overheard their conversation from the guest bedroom. The fierce whispers between my mother and Aunt Madeline got so hard to ignore, I abandoned my pile of books and peeked around the door frame to watch them in Aunt Madeline's kitchen.

"Give me the key, Madeline!" my mother snapped.

Aunt Madeline remained poised and calm at the kitchen table. "No."

"I know you have it!"

"No."

"If you don't want that land, it should be mine!" my mother hissed. "I deserve it, don't I? I had to live there long after you left me there with *them*!"

Aunt Madeline took a sip from her teacup and looked out the window.

"If you won't give it to me, then give it to Phaedra." A change of tactic. "If she's so special to you, let her have it."

Aunt Madeline lowered her eyes from the window. "No."

"Fine, Madeline, then we're leaving. Obviously, you don't care about me. Or Phaedra. And obviously you don't want things to get any easier for us. Well. That's. Just. Fine." My mother snapped into action. Snatched up her own suitcase and my backpack. Grabbed my arm and pulled me out of the house. Marched me through the white rose garden and into her car. Through the sun-blasted back window, over the burning-hot vinyl seat, I saw Aunt Madeline standing inside her open front door. Through my tear-bubbled eyes, Aunt Madeline looked angry. Was she angry at me? I had no idea what key they were fighting about at the time, but I knew Aunt Madeline didn't think I was special enough to have it.

I buried my face inside my crumpled-up jacket in the back seat and stayed like that the whole drive home. Angry at my mother for making us leave. Heartbroken that Aunt Madeline didn't love me anymore. Ashamed of whatever I had done to break a whole family apart. I wanted to tell them both I was sorry, but I didn't know what to be sorry for.

That was our last visit out here. I was nine. We never came back.

I could have, I guess. When I got older and had a car and no one to stop me. When loneliness sank in. Nothing kept me from coming back except a vague sense of shame, except not knowing how to mend what was broken.

Aunt Madeline exists to me only in a handful of childhood memories of summertime visits to her little house in the woods. Tea towels snapping on the clothesline. Piping-hot steam curling over forget-me-not blue tea. Dollops of apple jelly shimmering on gingersnap cookies. It hurts to do the math of how long it's been since I've seen her. And how fast twenty-four years goes by.

Chickadees swoop and *dee-dee-dee* past my head as I pry burrs from my bootlaces. My soles grind into the soft red humus of the forest floor, releasing whiffs of cedar needles.

I'm on the right track. I can tell by the willows. I haven't seen the gentle-giant willow trees yet, but I can tell they are close by the delicate whiff of wintergreen in the air, by the soft *whip-crack* of their dancing branches, by the *hiss* of their leaves.

My phone shows one bar. There will probably be even sketchier cell service past this point. Better call my mother now before I head any deeper into this dead zone.

"Phaedra?" my mother's voice says through the crackling echo of static. "Are you there yet? Where are you?"

No greeting. No formalities. That's my mother.

"Hey, Ma," I say. "I'm on the old road in the woods heading to Aunt Madeline's house."

"Yes, you'd better be," my mother says. "You have a duty to your family, Phaedra Luck. You don't want to end up a selfish and sneaky weirdo like my sister."

Here we go.

"I know, Ma."

A heavy silence hangs on the line between us. I've heard my mother's don't-end-up-like-your-aunt-Madeline lecture so many times, she doesn't have to say it out loud anymore. It lives in my head, word for word. Even though I don't want it there. The silence crackles with bitterness.

"Have you seen her yet?" she asks.

"Nope."

"Have you seen anyone?"

"No one important."

"Don't trust anyone you come across, Phaedra," she says. "There's no need for anyone to be in those woods except my sister and you. And don't expect the crackpots in that town to know anything when they don't even know how to find their own way out from under a rock."

True.

"And don't trust the police," she says.

Rural folks in Nova Scotia rarely do.

"Understood," I say.

"Do you remember where the front door key is hidden?" she asks.

"I do."

"Good."

"Are you coming out here, too, Ma?"

"I suppose I have to," she says. "If Madeline will even let me in. I'll get on the first plane I can, and you can let me in. But you listen to me, Phaedra. Get to her house before the police do. Do not let them into your aunt's house, do you hear me?"

"I accept this quest," I say.

"Don't be glib, Phaedra," my mother says. "This is serious. They'll all want to get inside Madeline's house. Especially the cops. But if you let those Grand Tea crackpots in there, you'll never get them out. The inside of her house is nobody's business. Even if you have to stand guard at her house all day until Madeline gets back. Do not let anyone set a foot inside your aunt's house. Not. A. Foot."

The connection dies before I can ask her why.

CHAPTER FOUR

Aunt Madeline's house stands on the edge of a cliff overlooking the Atlantic. A beautiful view for the fearless. Through the trees, I hear the distant crashing of waves against rocks and feel the weight of salt in the air.

Almost there.

As I step out of the woods into a clearing, worry floods the spaces between my thoughts. The closer I get to Aunt Madeline's house, the more sunlight and garden beds there should be. Not this icy gloom. Not this dank air.

Fence posts lie around me, like bodies on a battlefield. Rotting. Swarming with beetles. Garden boxes sink into black earth, growing nothing but weeds and slugs.

This is bad.

Aunt Madeline is eccentric, maybe, but she's not lazy. She worked her heart out maintaining this little place. She would never let her gardens go. Her front garden should overflow with cascades of fragrant tea roses and honeysuckle vine, not heaps of rot and death.

When the police called my mother to tell her Aunt Madeline was missing, I assumed they meant she'd been gone a few days. A week at most. But this place has been neglected for a lot longer than that.

How long has Aunt Madeline been missing?

The string of brass bells that once lined her gate—to signal someone coming—rusts in a tangle of dead leaves. I drag the string from the muck and lay the bells out. They're so corroded they can't make a sound.

How many people came through here without jingling the bells? How many walked up without her knowing? A hundred people?

Or just one?

Flashes of memory crack through the blackness of my mind. Aunt Madeline's house. Teeny-tiny, like a cottage. Tidy and bright. Outside walls painted the soft silver grey of pussy willows. The perfect grey to make her house almost invisible against the Nova Scotian sky when it rains.

Purple front door. Stained glass windows glowing violet and orange, as if it was always sunset inside her house. Always the gentlest hour. Always the right time to come home.

The house itself was almost entirely hand-built by her from the earth and forest around it. As if the little building pushed up from the soil like a native plant, no different than any plums-and-custard mushroom you'd find on your way through the quietest places in the province. A house that was *not* there as much as it *was* there.

As a kid, I was sure fairies could live in that little grey cottage as easily as the quiet-wild woman I had known a little, once upon a—

Jingling.

Not bells. Different. More like silverware jostling against glass. Behind me.

Tink-tinkle-tink. Crrk.

Quiet snap. Rustling. I don't see anything move.

"Aunt Madeline?"

Silence. No crickets. No birds. Is it good or bad when the birds go quiet? Probably bad.

"Who's there?"

My skin crawls. Cold pounds my brain.

Frig this place.

Not wanting to spend another second in this garden of rotting horrors, I hike my backpack higher and lurch in the direction of the ocean's roar. Hustling hard over the shattered remains of Aunt Madeline's front stone walk, my toe catches on something—

"Cripes!"

The word gets sucked back down my throat before it's all the way out of my mouth. I fall arse over tea kettle and land in a bush. Ferns spring over me, and the understorey swallows me up.

My backpack survives the tumble in one piece. So do I, more or less. So, I laugh. I let myself lie there under the fern blades and laugh like a brain-cracked maniac. Whatever flying monkeys were jingling and stalking me this far will probably change their minds about having anything to do with me right about now. They're hightailing it out of here, their monkey-butts flying away in the autumn breeze, haunted by the laughter of a woman who lost her mind in a bush.

I haul myself up out of the damp mulch and tree needles. My palms bleed a bit. Not enough blood to write home about, even if I had a pen. Or a home. Enough blood to make a mess, though.

I wipe my hands on my jeans. My palms leave ghoulish smears of blood on the stone path behind me. It'll be gone next time it rains.

Some of my oldest memories begin to brush against me. I remember how it felt when my mother and I got out of the car and stretched our legs from the long drive. I remember Aunt Madeline's garden as it had been: a towering maze of vivid greens and glittering pinks. I remember the smell of freshly baked molasses cookies and blueberry pie telling me Aunt Madeline was expecting us, telling me, *Welcome back, quiet little niece from away.*

But that's not what I find now. Not at all.

At the end of the stone path, Aunt Madeline's house is still there. Sort of.

The little cottage hunches in cold shadows like dark stains. No longer a fairy tale.

It's a nightmare.

CHAPTER FIVE

No one could live here.

The roof droops and oozes like rotten molasses. Rust bleeds from every hole of every nail. Right in front of me, the whole house is disintegrating beneath its overgrown veil of dead vines.

Maybe her little house is screaming, but I can't hear it. Or maybe—somewhere deep in my bones—I can.

I kick my way through knee-deep cow vetch and nightshade to get to the front door. I remember the once-solid feeling of her bright purple front door. Now, the purple paint is filthy and peeling. The warped wood is smothered by black spores and white moss. The stained glass windows on either side of the door have no colour, no light left in them—just dirty, cracked glass held together by spiderwebs riddled with dead flies and spider egg sacs.

No one could live here. Not even Aunt Madeline with her wild ways.

Even still, I knock on the door, clinging to the small hope that she's in there. Just overlooked. Taking a nap when the police stopped by, and they took one look around her depressing, neglected dooryard and walked away. They called it in. Then they called my mother and made it her problem. And then my mother called me.

I knock again.

Nothing.

Frig.

I holler at the door: "Aunt Madeline!"

I holler her name a few more times until I hear something back.

"Ma'am! Step away from the door!"

Definitely not the words I was hoping to hear.

The stern voice whips across the garden like a slingshot rock. A woman in a grey and navy Mountie uniform strides up the stone walkway toward me. She stumbles—and almost falls—right where I'd tripped and fallen into the ferns earlier. Catching herself at the last second, she recovers clumsily and mutters sailor-worthy curses to herself from the edge of the dooryard all the way up through the garden and into my face.

I look down at her.

She glares up at me from under her hat brim. Everything about her is chiselled and dense. Like a pile of dusty construction rocks got dumped into a Mountie uniform and learned to walk around and play cop. She doesn't seem intimidated by my size or my scowl. Or my silence.

I don't find people with her level of confidence standing in my shadow very often.

This cop seems confident but not cocky. Not one of those cops with stockpiled rage who seems ready to snap. Don't want to come across that kind again.

"Who are you?" she asks me.

I don't answer her. She leaves me lots of time to talk, to ramble, to say too much. But I don't. Filling silences is human instinct. It's polite. But I know from experience that silence is useful. I have the right to remain silent. So I do.

"Are you Madeline Luck's niece?"

Two seconds ago, I was yelling "Aunt Madeline" at the door. I know this cop heard me, so she's playing dumb. I don't like when people act dumb on purpose.

And I don't like messing with cops.

I love it.

"My name is Corporal Quill," she says. "I spoke with your mother on the phone last night. Do you have any identification on you?"

I stare at her.

"How do you spell your name?" she says.

I keep staring.

"Is that your blood on the stone walkway back there?" she says.

I don't budge.

"Is that your vehicle I saw parked by the side of the road?" she says.

Not an inch.

Quill blows a frustrated sigh at me. "Look, if you don't start talking about who you are and what you're doing here, I'm going to bring you into town and ask you the same questions on the record, and if you say nothing there either, I'll have to leave you there and come back here and kick down this door and I'll find my own answers to my questions. The old-fashioned way."

I don't cave in to threats. But I do have a promise to keep to my mother. Not to let anyone set a foot into Aunt Madeline's house.

Fine.

"It's my car," I say.

"Can I see your driver's licence?" she asks.

"Nope."

"Why not?"

"I forgot my handbag in my armoire."

Quill snorts. Her lip goes up on one side in contempt, just for a split second. Like a tell. This cop laid eyes on me for the first time thirty-three seconds ago, and she's already figured out that I'm not the kind of person who has ever had or ever will have a handbag. Or an armoire.

"Are you here alone, Miss Luck?"

"Do you see anybody else?" I say.

"You didn't go to charm school, did you, Miss Luck?"

"I didn't go to obedience school either."

We lock eyes and hold the stare with more intensity than I expected. Like two kingsnakes right before a fight. To hell with law and order and the old Mountie motto. I can tell this woman is a scrapper. Takes one to know one, I guess.

"How old is your aunt, Miss Luck?" Quill asks, getting her line of questioning back on track. I haven't confirmed my name with her, but she's going ahead with calling me Miss Luck. Probably hoping I'll give a hint either way.

"Don't know," I say.

"Why don't you know how old your aunt is?"

"None of my business," I say.

"Do you know her birthdate?"

"I can do basic math, so obviously no," I say.

That gets me the hateful glare from Quill I was hoping for.

"Does your aunt have any friends or family that live nearby? Does she have a social worker or a nurse? Does she have anyone in her life who cares about her at all?" Quill asks.

Point for Quill. I grumble just loud enough for her to hear it.

"Where do you live, Miss Luck?"

"Nowhere."

"Where do you live?" she asks again.

"Nowhere."

She almost asks a third time but stops herself. She seems to reconsider my answer, and maybe she even believes me. This is Nova Scotia, after all. Here, you're either homeless or on the brink of homeless or a millionaire. Nobody left in between.

"What do you do for work?" she asks.

"Code," I say.

"Computer code?"

"Sure."

Quill scribbles in her notebook, which is tilted away from me. I can't see the page, even from my height, but I can see her pen move. She's writing too much. With a telltale squiggle of the pen at the end that can only mean a question mark.

"Do you know if your aunt has a second house or hunting camp?" Quill asks.

"Don't know."

"Do you know anything about anyone?"

"Sure."

"Like who?"

"Like you," I say.

"What could you possibly know about me?" Quill asks.

"I know you spend a lot of time at the gym. Way too much for someone with a life. I also know you're dying to tell me how much you deadlift, because it's a lot. You're way past elite level. Maybe even freak level. And you want to tell me so I back down and shut up."

She fights a smile. Just for a second. Then it's gone. "And your job is in computers? Not . . . anything else?" Her words trail away, as if she's asking herself and not me. She's inside her own head. I've put her off her game a bit.

Good.

Perfect time for me to ask her a few things I want to know.

"How did police figure out Aunt Madeline is missing?" I ask Quill. "She's completely cut off from everything out here. Who even noticed?"

"Canada Post. Your aunt gets her mail in a super box up the highway. No one has been retrieving her mail for a while. They called us."

"How old was the oldest mail in there?"

"Three months," Quill says.

Three months. Seems like Aunt Madeline's house has been neglected way longer than three months to me.

"Miss Luck, your mother told me on the phone last night that she has a spare key to this house," Quill says. "Did your mother happen to give you that key before you came here?"

She didn't. But I know where it is. Or where it should be. But there's something about how quickly Quill jabs her hand out to take Aunt Madeline's key from me that sets off every internal alarm I've got.

"Nope," I say.

"Is there another key around here, then? Hidden somewhere? Under a planter or on top of the door?"

"I presume you've already looked," I say. "And didn't find one."

"Is there a key to find?"

"Nope."

Quill's mouth twitches. I can tell she thinks I'm lying. And I can tell there's nothing she can do about it.

"You expect me to believe you're out here alone in the woods to look for your missing aunt, and you don't have a key to her house."

"You saw me knocking on the door when you got here," I say. "Would I knock on the door if I had a key?"

Quill grumbles at the logic. Even if it is false logic.

"My mother will get here eventually," I say. "I'll hang out here on the front step and wait for her till she does. Let the cold air blow the stink off me."

Quill looks me over. Scanning me like an X-ray. My hoodie. My jeans. Zeroes in on my front pockets and decides there's nothing in them. I know she's itching to spin me around and pat me down. She wants to get Madeline Luck's house key off me and never give it back. But she has no right to lay a hand on me as long as I keep my hands to myself.

So I do.

She flips her notebook shut and turns her attention to the house. I watch her step backwards a few steps. Calculating something. She bows down to look low, then pops back up to standing. Her jaw grinds back and forth while she thinks.

Without a word, she shoves past me and heads around the back of the house.

CHAPTER SIX

I find Quill out back, ripping fistfuls of dead grass from the back corner of Aunt Madeline's house. She probably works in that that town. Grand Tea. That town of certifiable psychos.

"What the frig!" I snap at her.

Quill falls to her knees on the ripped-out grass and sticks her head under the house. "Daylight!"

"Quill, are we going to have a problem?"

"No. Look. You can see daylight right through, under the house. Clear through to the yard on the other side. The whole house is just propped up on old cinder blocks in the corners."

Sure enough, there is a one-foot gap between the bottom of the house and the ground underneath.

"So it's on blocks," I say. "So what?"

"There's no cellar!" Quill grins and claps the dirt off her hands. Almost congratulating herself on a pretty unremarkable bit of police work. Then she jams her fists on her hips and surveys Aunt

Madeline's back garden. The raised vegetable beds; the chaotic hedge of spiky brambles planted along the back, overgrown and fierce; the outhouse; the shed. Quill mumbles to herself, "If there's no cellar, then there can't be a . . ."

"Be a what?"

"You know, the . . ." Quill's hands churn through the air as if I should know what she's taking about.

"The what?"

"Never mind."

It was a good call, not letting this cop inside Aunt Madeline's house.

"Does your mother have a key for the shed?" Quill rattles the shed door. The padlock thuds against the hollow wood. Quill doesn't knock or call Aunt Madeline's name at the shed, so she clearly isn't concerned about a missing woman being locked in there.

What is Quill really looking for here?

Her police radio crackles on her shoulder. A pair of brown garter snakes dart out from beneath the ripped-up dead grass. They slither past Quill's black boot as she returns to stand next to me.

"I have to go, Miss Luck. For now. I'll put out a missing person alert for your aunt. Do you have a recent photo of her that I can have?"

A normal person probably would. But I don't. I shake my head.

"You don't really know much about her, do you?"

"Guess not," I say.

"When you get the keys and go inside the house, take a look around. Look for any unusual damage or things out of place. Don't touch anything your instincts tell you is not right. And call me. Immediately."

No chance. But I take her proffered card anyway.

"Are you planning to remain in your aunt's house overnight, Miss Luck? There's no electricity here. No running water. Next nearest town is Grand Tea, and it's a fair drive from here."

"Don't know."

"I've seen a lot of poverty in my lifetime," Quill says, "but this place is worse than anything I've ever seen. An old woman living out here alone with nothing and no one. It must be like living in hell."

A clang of hard reality hits me. I've always thought of Aunt Madeline as happy here. In my mind, my aunt is a tough nut who has never needed anything from anyone. Thriving out here, living her dream with everything she needs.

My chest tightens as I look at the house again. The fragile wooden box propped on cinder blocks. The falling-down outhouse. The garden of rot. Suddenly, I can see what it must look like to Quill. The tragic story of an inconvenient old woman abandoned in the middle of nowhere.

Quill watches me. She's either reading my mind, or acting like she can. "Do you need a lift into town, Miss Luck?"

"Nope."

She nods and turns to leave but stops herself. "Oh, one more thing. The forecast is predicting a significant storm here in the next couple of days. A tropical storm named Lettie is making its way up from Bermuda. It could make landfall anywhere along the coastline here. Good chance Lettie might upgrade to a serious hurricane when it hits, and you don't want to be caught out here on this cliff in this tiny house in a hurricane, Miss Luck. Trust me. I'll come by tomorrow, anyway. Whether you're here or not. Around one."

"Sure," I say.

Good to know about Lettie. Good to know Quill will be back to snoop.

"There are no signs of struggle or break-in," Quill says. "No busted locks, no busted-out windows, nothing out of place. No blood, except yours on the path. It looks like everything was normal when she left. It's as if Madeline Luck stepped out the door and locked it behind her, walked away, and never came back."

With those words hanging on hooks between us, Quill finally walks away. I return to where I was when she interrupted me: at Aunt Madeline's front door. Quill leaves the same way she arrived.

I don't move. Don't run for the spare key. I just wait. Wait enough time, I think, for Quill to spy on me through the trees for a few minutes. Enough time for her to give up on spying and slog all the way through the rotted dooryard garden.

I wait until all I can hear is ocean crashing on rocks.

I wait for the birds to sing again.

Conk-la-ree. Red-winged blackbird. Somewhere in the trees to the east. Telling me I'm alone.

I'm better off alone.

Time to see if the key to Aunt Madeline's house is still hidden in the same spot.

When I was four or five, Aunt Madeline made up a rhyme to help me remember where to find the key. She hid it in the garden in a special place.

If you make it home before me
Don't wait outside alone
Find the labrador tea
With the forget-me-not bones
Find the forget-me-not tree
With the labrador stone
Turn the forget-me-not key
And make yourself at home

Right there. The Labrador tea shrub at the far side of her back garden. Bigger than it used to be, and its white flowers are gone, but I recognize the droopy leaves, dangling like brown gloves. In spring, forget-me-nots froth around its skinny trunk. We used to visit here in summertime, when the few flowerheads left teetered on bare-bone stems. *Forget-me-not bones.* Brittle now and nearly dead against my frost-scarred fingers. The key is close.

Find the forget-me-not tree
With the labrador stone

Of course, there's no such thing as a forget-me-not tree. That's what I called my favourite tree in Aunt Madeline's garden. The towering height. The swooping branches. The fog-grey bark still looks forget-me-not blue in the shade of its own leaves. I used to climb this tree so high my aunt and mother were dolls way down on the ground. I'd brace myself in the branches and shake the whole tree as hard as I could without falling. I'd shake enough green fruit down it fell like rain and filled every last berry basket. I'd climb down, quietly proud I'd done something to help Aunt Madeline have food for winter. I know what the tree is supposed to be called. But I don't call it that. Never have.

I look up. The rough blue-grey bark, ridged with criss-cross lashes, calls me up. But I'm too big and too old to climb now. I look down.

There. The Labrador stone. Labradorite. At the base of the tree. Smothered by weeds. Only visible to someone who knows the rhyme. Heavy and smooth. Glittering like northern lights in the night sky. I drop on one knee, pry up the stone, and set it aside.

Turn the forget-me-not key
And make yourself at home

The key is here. Hidden right where Aunt Madeline showed me. Hidden inside a rhyme.

I turn the brass key over in my palm. Forget-me-not flowers hand-painted on both sides of the key shimmer at me.

And make yourself at home

Aunt Madeline left this key here. For all these years.

This means I was wrong. This means I had been welcome all along.

With three grindy clicks of the forget-me-not key, the lock on Aunt Madeline's front door lets go.

I pause outside. Let my eyes adjust to the heartbreaking darkness inside the house.

Bugs skitter away from the sunlight flooding inside. The house groans without the front door to help hold it up. The walls *tick-tick-tick-tick* as they settle into place all around me. The floor planks are steeped in shadows and seem to dissolve into ink-black corners.

Herbs, tied into bundles, dried out and brittle, hang from the vaulted ceiling. A necropolis of little hanged bodies, swinging by their necks.

The house sighs with rot and worms and desolation.

Sirens go off in my skull. My stomach churns.

It's wrong in here. All wrong.

Every cell in my body begs me to turn back. But I force myself forward and step inside the house.

CHAPTER SEVEN

A thick cloak of dust covers every surface in Aunt Madeline's tiny house. Old memories lurk beneath the dust, shivering under the cobwebs, as if they're trying to rise from the dead.

"Aunt Madeline? It's Fade. Are you in here?"

She's not. No one is here. It's too still. Everything is clammy and seedy. Ducking my head carefully under the hanging herbs and ceiling beams, I close the front door behind me, lock it, and look around.

Memories I didn't even know I had flick at me from everywhere, like sparks. I take a step and the squeak of the wooden floor under my foot instantly transports me back through time. Back to my childhood in a snap. I remember the feeling of my muddy little bare feet pitter-pattering across the floor, from the back of the kitchen to the front door and out into the clover.

Out there, I ate carrots with dirt on them and let blueberry guts tumble down the front of whatever three-dollar Frenchys bathing suit I had on.

Out there, I used to squeal with the freedom of a child who is wild. Used to.

Now everything in the house seems comically small to me. As if someone made perfect miniature versions of all the furniture in Aunt Madeline's house and replaced the normal-sized pieces while I was gone, as a joke.

This must be how Alice felt after she fell down the rabbit hole and ate the *EAT ME* cake and grew into a giant. That giant is me.

One piece of furniture still towers: Aunt Madeline's purple cabinet.

Deep and imposing in full gothic splendour, handmade from oak, it looms to the ceiling, and I love it. Aunt Madeline painted the whole thing unapologetically purple—the rich blue purple of wild Nova Scotian pansies—and packed every shelf to bursting with all her best treasures and most amazing things.

The bottom third of the cabinet is row on row of neat apothecary drawers. Each one small and square and perfect. Each drawer handle made of black ash wood carved into the shape of a different flowerhead. This one, the star shape of a bittersweet nightshade flower. That one, the round pompom face of a chrysanthemum.

Reminds me of that children's rhyme Aunt Madeline taught me when I was little. How did it go? *Chrysanthemum and nightshade something-something tea.* I remember the tune, but I guess I've forgotten the words. Too bad.

Each drawer of the purple cabinet has a handwritten label:

Fire	*Water*	*Feather*	*Stone*
Oil	*Ink*	*Needle*	*Pin*
Tobacco	*Wax*	*String*	*Glass*
Blade	*Mirror*	*Coal*	*Salt*

No miscellaneous junk drawers in Aunt Madeline's house. Everything thoughtfully set in its place. Nothing extra. Nothing just in case. Everything with a purpose.

The Fire drawer is open. I push it shut.

The middle third of the cabinet is crowded with pigeonhole shelves in a spiderweb shape. Locked behind glass doors, the top third of the cabinet holds her collection of old-fashioned apothecary bottles brimming with liquids to heal and clean and preserve.

But that's not the best part.

Every spare nook and cranny in the cabinet overflows with unusual and wonderful curiosities. Sticks and shells. Candles and photographs. Paper scrolls. Strange stones and stranger dolls. Tiny hand-carved creatures tucked among jars of flowerheads and buttons and seeds.

Even now as an adult with zero attention span, I could stare at Aunt Madeline's cabinet of curiosities forever. Like a favourite page in an *I Spy* or a Kit Williams book. I find it hard to look away. But I have to. I wipe dust off the kitchen table where Aunt Madeline used to serve me wild berry tea for breakfast. Bird's eye maple wood. The beady black eyes gleam up at me from the wood. Her dainty teacups are there in their proper place, next to her blue betty teapot. Empty and cold. Covered in dust. Waiting for company that didn't come.

Waiting, maybe, for me.

Wait.

The teapot's in the right place, and there are two cups beside it. There should be three.

I remember three. One for my mother. One for my aunt. One for me.

One of the teacups is missing.

CHAPTER EIGHT

There are only three rooms in Aunt Madeline's tiny cottage: the kitchen, her bedroom, and the guest bedroom where my mother and I slept during our visits here. Both bedroom doors are closed.

The door to Aunt Madeline's bedroom opens at my touch without a sound.

"Hello?" I say.

No one answers. No one in the room. No one in the bed.

There is something different in here, though.

The walls.

They're beautiful.

With thick paint strokes and a folksy, child-like style, Aunt Madeline has turned her once-plain bedroom walls into a black, purple, and yellow starry night masterpiece. The night sky swoops and curls around a high, bright moon above a field of light grey dandelions in their fluffy make-a-wish state. It's as if the restless spirits of Maud Lewis and Van Gogh reached out through Aunt Madeline's hands and painted this mural together.

Hundreds of hand-painted dandelion seeds swirl and float across the walls, as if carried on the wind. It must have taken her ages to paint it.

I have no memories of this beautiful mural. It wasn't here before. Can't wait to see what she's done with the guest room walls.

The guest room door is locked.

I rattle the handle and lean my shoulder carefully against the old wood. Careful not to lean too hard and accidentally launch my shoulder through it.

Oh, frig.

As I lean on the door, air seeps out of the cracks around it.

That smell. That deathly smell of burnt, greasy, rotten meat.

Same smell from the woods.

This time, it's coming from inside Aunt Madeline's guest room.

With one strong, well-placed kick, the guest room door flies open, slams against the wall, and flies back at me.

I brace for a full blast of that nightmarish stench to knock me back, but it doesn't come. It's bad for a second, then not so bad.

Thank frig.

Aunt Madeline's guest room is also her library. Three walls of the room are packed, floor to ceiling, with her collection of books. On rainy days, I used to stretch out for hours on the guest room floor, surrounded by these books. Sometimes to build forts. Sometimes to read.

There's something wrong inside the room.

The air wafting out is cold. Colder than the rest of the house.

But that's not it.

The bad smell is in there. Faint, but there.

But that's not it, either.

I ease inside the guest room.

The bed is empty. No mattress. No guests, so it makes sense.

Two library walls are impeccably lined with built-in shelves proudly displaying a thousand well-ordered, well-loved books.

The third wall is a horror. On the far-left wall, the middle shelves have been hacked apart and ripped away. Where bookshelves should be, holding their rows of books, there is something else. Something I know for damn sure wasn't there before.

A door.

BOOK TWO

The Door

CHAPTER NINE

That door doesn't belong here.
Aunt Madeline's home is rundown and dusty, maybe, but it's still tidy. Everything is still just so and neatly in its proper place.

Not this door.

Everything about this door is sickening, botched, and wrong. It is a horror hacked into what was once a beautiful and cherished library wall.

It could be a patch-up job. A board covering a hole in the wall. A hasty repair. This I could understand. Some damage in the wall, caused by wild weather or a wild animal, patched over with an old board before winter comes.

But it's not a patch of old wood nailed up over a crack in the wall. It's definitely a door. About four feet tall and pretty narrow. Crooked and mangled. Rough with splinters and slashed with violent hatchet marks on every edge. The door itself is made of scraps of rotted wood strapped together. The hinges are mismatched, as if scavenged. The door's handle is nothing but a dirty bent nail.

How can it be a door, though? On the other side of this wall is Aunt Madeline's bedroom, and her walls are intact. All mural. No holes. Definitely no other side to this hideous door.

Is this a door that opens into nothing, then?

Am I going to have to open it?

Focus, Fade.

It's insane to think Aunt Madeline would slash up her own books and suture this nightmare door right into the heart of her beloved library.

And that smell. That smell of burnt nightmares.

It's coming from behind the door.

And a sound. Not behind the door. Behind me.

Is that—jingling?

Seagulls screech. My eyes snap open. The floor is cold against my forehead. A sweet taste clings to my teeth. Everything is darker than it was before. Time has passed. How much?

What happened?

Must've blacked out. That never happens. Not for a long time, anyway. It's been a while since I've eaten anything half decent, really. It's probably just that.

I'm on Aunt Madeline's kitchen floor. Somehow, at some point, I left the guest room and opened the back kitchen door. To leave? To get air? I can't remember.

The guest room door gapes open. Its insides seem too dark and too full of shadows compared to the rest of the house. My head feels like a sack of rocks. I swipe dirt and dust off my cheeks. If I'd known I'd end up face down on the floor at some point during my visit, I would've picked up a frigging broom.

Outside, seagulls fill the sky—and my brain—with their relentless piercing, honking shrieks. I stand and step outside from the kitchen into the back garden.

Aunt Madeline's back garden has no back fence. Doesn't need one. This stretch of garden ends in a cliff. Her little piece of land is one sliver along a vast cliff above the ocean. The cliff is a killer. Massive black boulders coated in slime and littered with pieces of smashed fishing boats.

Gulls circle above the cliff. Is the storm pushing them inland? Is there something out there along the cliff or down on the rocks?

Or someone.

Rain falls, ice cold. It hits me and shivers down my face. My heart thrashes because I know what I have to do. I have to find out what the gulls are circling. I have to look.

A familiar feeling blasts against the inside of my skull like trapped steam. It's not fear. It's this drive I have to protect vulnerable people, even if it puts me at risk. It starts in my scalp. Tingles my skin. Makes every hair on my body stand up. Makes every muscle in my body lock in for a fight.

I can't wait and let anyone else find Aunt Madeline. Especially if she's hurt.

I don't want to find her hurt. I want to find her perfectly fine. Waiting for me with cookies and tea. I want to sit with her and tell her all the things she should have heard me say, all these years. The things everyone should hear from someone, sometime. How much I love her. How much I admire her. How much I miss her. How much I am like her. How sorry I am it's been so long, and I shouldn't have let old fights come between us.

Why didn't I come sooner?

My brain spirals. *Calm down. Come back. Focus.*

Somehow, I'm already past the wild roses. Past the purple beach peas. I stand on a slippery patch of moss that spreads over the rocks of the cliff. The ocean is all I hear, all I smell. The roar of Aunt

Madeline's only neighbour. I wonder if the ocean knows what happened to her.

From here, I can't see all the way over the cliff without climbing down it. If I don't check down the cliff, I'll never rest. For the rest of my life, every time I hear a crash of waves, every time I smell salt air, I will imagine her down there, clutching against the rocks. Waiting for me.

It's a bad idea.

I have to do it.

The rain will make my climb deadlier. When will the rain stop? Maybe never.

I have to do it.

Soaked to the bone, I cling to the clammy boulders like I'm scaling a pile of dead giants. Easing from one rock to the next, the scrapes in my palms open again, leaving smears of blood behind me.

I see something.

Maybe ten feet away from me, jammed between rocks. A suitcase. Small, like a child's suitcase maybe. Seems old. Could be nothing. Could be important.

I have to get it.

Hugging the cliffside, I grind my fingers and boot tips into the slightest crags. My cheek scrapes against sharp rocks. *Ignore it.* Salt water stings my eyes. I got it. I grab the leather handle and pull. Coated in salt water and sea slime, the suitcase whips out of the rocks more easily than I expected it to, yanking me off balance, nearly sending me backwards into a watery grave.

Cripes.

The suitcase has something inside it. Something big, tipping back and forth. And something small, rattling around.

I sink my teeth into the handle, carrying the suitcase in my mouth, so I can use both hands free to drag myself back. I collapse next to the wild roses at the edge of the back garden. My body vibrates. My hands sting.

Aunt Madeline wasn't down there. At least there's that.

I slog my soggy carcass back to my aunt's house and peel off my soaked boots. The smell of salt water off my clothes is strong. The ocean has come back with me.

The rain has stopped, for now. I kneel on the kitchen floor and lay the suitcase in front of me. It is engraved: M.L.L.

Only one person I know of with those initials.

Madeline Lee Luck.

CHAPTER TEN

This is Aunt Madeline's suitcase.

Why was it down there? She must have stood on the edge of the cliff and thrown it off. She must have intended for this suitcase and its contents to disappear into the ocean forever.

Maybe I shouldn't open it, then. Maybe I should honour Aunt Madeline and her secrets. Maybe I should go back to the cliff and throw this suitcase all the way into the sea. As she intended.

If she wasn't missing, I would do that for her.

But there could be something inside the case that helps me find her. And better for me to open her suitcase than Quill.

The latches are thick with grit, but they open. With a low creak, the lid comes up. The inside lining is satiny. Maybe once a pretty peach colour, now faded and stained with dirt and sea water.

The heavy object knocking back and forth inside is a bedpan, of all things. Stainless steel. Heavy. Clean, thank frig.

Sitting loose in the bottom of the bedpan is a handful of blue jay feathers and a dandelion stem with those puffy seed things all gone.

And a key. Not in the bedpan, but loose in the suitcase. Definitely not a mailbox key. Or a house key. This key is thin and looks like something from a medieval castle.

Underneath the bedpan is a folded cloth. White, but grimy. It looks delicate but feels starchy and rough. I hold the cloth up, letting it unfold itself.

It's a hospital gown, tattered and worn thin. And covered in blood.

I drop the gown back into the suitcase and close the lid with shaky hands. I shut my eyes, trying to unsee the gruesome, dried bloodstains.

Through the escalating chaos of questions pounding inside my brain—

Tappity-tap-tap.

Knocking.

Tap. Tap.

On the front door.

I stash the suitcase under Aunt Madeline's bed.

There's someone here.

Through the cracked, dingy glass of a front window, I see what I think is a man in a suit. A well-tailored peanut-beige business suit—appropriate, because his whole head is shaped like a peanut. A greasy one. One you'd throw back in the bag.

Tap-tap-tap-tap-tap.

"Madeline?"

His head bops all around, nosing and snooping. He almost sees me watching him, but his eyes flit past me like I'm a bit of dust or a dead bug. The filthy stained glass must hide me well.

"Madeline Luck?" he says.

Calling her by her first and last name.

Not a friend, then.

Even if he was Aunt Madeline's friend, I have no intention of answering the door. Anyone who shows up to somebody else's house uninvited is automatically labelled a sociopath in my book. Frig this guy and his peanut-shaped head, wandering out in the middle of the woods in a suit. Snooping around Aunt Madeline's property where he doesn't belong.

He doesn't hide the truth of himself for long, even through the filthy glass. His whole face twists into a nasty scowl. There he is. That's what he looks like when he thinks he's alone. When the mask comes off.

He gives up and trudges away from the house. His carefully ironed business pants jut, crumpled and stuffed into stiff and shiny rubber boots that look like they've never been worn before. Still have the gleaming white price tag on the bottom. Not a hiker, this guy.

As he walks off into the woods again, I find I can't watch him long, because my eyes keep straying back to the forest floor.

Looking for a hand. A foot. A familiar braid of long white hair.

Stop.

Stop picturing Aunt Madeline fallen in the forest.

Clutching after my ankles.

Calling out to me.

Unheard.

Stop.

I have to focus on what I can do to help right now. What the hell can I do to help?

A picture. Right. Maybe I can find a photo of Aunt Madeline around here somewhere. For Quill to use. So she can get her name and face out across Nova Scotia. Aunt Madeline will hate that. But it's something we have to do. So someone out there will recognize Aunt Madeline's sweet face and take her by the arm and bring her home. Safe and alive.

One last glance out the stained glass. I don't see Mr. Peanut out there anymore. Good.

If nothing else, I can make myself useful and find a picture. Maybe there's one tucked among the treasures in her cabinet.

I walk past the guest room door. It's closed.

I guess I must've closed it.

CHAPTER ELEVEN

Aunt Madeline's purple cabinet holds quite a few old photographs, tucked here and there among its curiosities. I pick up the first one I see. So old. So delicate and small. A woman with stoic dark eyes sits primly. Her eyes pierce into mine from who knows how many years ago.

I flip the photograph over. *Clare. Tulips. Ployes. 1846.*

I look at the woman again. There are no tulips in the picture. No ploye flatbread either. Just the woman with a white scarf covering her shoulders and a white bonnet on her head. What does the note mean, then?

The next photograph I pick up feels even more delicate. A young woman wearing a peaked cap decorated with beads in geometric patterns. She looks at the camera with slightly amused and curious eyes. There's a note on the back of this photo too: *Annie. Red clover. Maple ice. 1899.*

Curiouser and curiouser. I pick up two more photographs. In one, two adults sit stiffly. They wear matching plain tunics. A temple looms behind them, but it's just a studio backdrop image. Not a real temple. Written on the back: *Peg. Wild strawberries. Lawrence. Mian pian. 1924.*

In the other photograph, two little girls stand, side by side, against damask wallpaper. One is taller than the other. The shorter one has messy hair. Probably sisters. They hold matching funeral urns. Pretty grim. On the back of the photo: nothing.

The photograph of the girls goes back into the cabinet, but I hold on to the ones with the notes on the back, shoving them in my jeans pocket.

No closer to a photo of Aunt Madeline, and my data limit is almost maxed out. I can't research anything myself without setting up an antenna. Maybe my mother has a picture. Maybe I can find a coffee shop with half-decent internet. Maybe a local archive has a picture of Aunt Madeline in their files, somewhere.

Maybe I just want to get the hell out of this house.

No aunt here. No picture here. Nothing here, except that smell.

Frig that smell. And that door.

Might as well head into town for a minute. But not much longer than a minute. I don't have a death wish, like those Grand Tea townies do.

Hopefully, they're all preoccupied with preparing for the coming storm. Hopefully, I can completely avoid interacting with any weird people from Grand Tea.

BOOK THREE

Weird People from Grand Tea

CHAPTER TWELVE

The Nova Scotian community known to locals as "the town of Grand Tea" is not a town at all. It's a hamlet, at most, located in Colchester County, and it exists under the constant threat of doom.

The town gets its name from the colossal rock—shaped vaguely like a teacup—that sits above the town on the edge of a cliff. Geologists say the teacup-shaped rock was once the top of a mountain range—older than the Appalachians—that broke off three hundred million years ago and toppled partway down the mountainside. The broken-off top of the mountain landed, upside down, on the edge of a very strong, very tall cliff. The cliff is called Harrow Mountain.

Narrower at the bottom of the teacup shape, and a kilometre across at the teacup's brim, the Grand Tea rock looms over the tiny town below it, casting a cold shadow over the people who live there. No one told those people to live there. They could've lived anywhere. But this insistent little cluster of human beings settled in the shadow of the rock, and they have lived there by the ticking hands of their own doomsday clock for generations.

Why? Probably some weird reason only they know.

The rock is so massive, it has permanently detached the town from the reality the rest of us know. Days and nights in Grand Tea don't line up. From ten to two every day, the people under the rock have no sun. While sun beats down on top of the rock, people under the rock mill around in the shadows like coal miners on a day shift. Their street lights turn back on in the middle of the day.

Every storm, every snow, stories go around: *The Grand Tea rock is tipping. It's finally falling. The whole town is done for sure this time.*

But it's never done. Storms come and go, and the Grand Tea rock withstands them all.

I don't know these things because I know Grand Tea. I've never set foot in Grand Tea. Everyone who lives in Nova Scotia just knows it. Stories go around.

I pull into the tourist parking lot just outside the perimeter of town. Can't imagine what would bring tourists here. They must stop by here to gawk at the Grand Tea rock. To *tch-tch* at the town below it. To take selfies in the shadow of death.

Through my windshield, I look up at the Grand Tea rock. It's orders of magnitude more massive than I had imagined. And like the legend says, it vaguely resembles a teacup. And there is the handful of little houses way down below. Huddled underneath the looming rock. The buildings are painted bright colours, but it doesn't help. Everything about that strange, shadowy-grey existence under their sky of solid rock is dull.

My car is the only one in the tourist parking lot. Everyone else is probably at home, tying down their deck chairs and gassing up generators. People who live near the ocean know the drill.

I step to the edge of the shadow of the Grand Tea rock, the shadow touching the toes of my boots.

I hesitate.

Not much makes me hesitate. It's a flaw that will get me killed someday, I'm sure.

My brain tries to calculate how many seconds' warning the rock would give me before it fell. Probably not many. My ears grasp at every tiny sound. Listening for cracks or creaks. It's quiet. It's still. It's going to be fine.

I force myself to leave the warm afternoon sky and step in. One step. Two steps.

Ten steps inside the dull shadow underneath the doomsday rock.

Every step feels like a bad idea. All my survival instincts scream at me to *get out*. But I push myself further and further into this surreal underworld of mossy buildings, spindly trees, and grey air. It's not that cold, but my teeth chatter as the darkness oozes over me.

Psychopaths don't feel fear. They don't feel much of anything. A dark truth I learned at my old job. They have an insatiable desire for danger, even if it puts themselves in harm's way. That rush of adrenaline is the closest they have to feeling something.

How many psychopaths live in Grand Tea?

A dark question to ask myself as I walk down the main road right into the middle of town.

CHAPTER THIRTEEN

Not everything in Grand Tea exists directly under the rock. An apple-red convenience store, a few sheds, and the back end of a motel all stand outside the rock's shadow. There aren't any people around, which is a little creepy, but I guess it makes sense with the big storm on the way.

That black pickup truck is here. Parked in a gravel driveway next to a black-painted house. No wonder the truck has moss growing on it. Moss grows over everything here, a faint green haze slithering over every surface.

That sticky black muck I saw embedded in the black pickup's tire treads is everywhere too. It pools along the edges of buildings and at the bottoms of ditches. There are no lawns or gardens here. Not enough sunlight to grow them. Just black muck and moss and musty air.

And still no people. No one walking along the main road or sitting on benches or loitering on steps. No children playing. It feels like a ghost town.

The motel's hanging vacancy sign creaks. The motel looks empty, and the signs in the window indicate its rooms have fresh towels and plumbing. Not a single car in the lot. Maybe there's a half-decent vacant room at the far end of the motel. The far, far end way outside the shadow of the rock, sitting in the sun. I wonder how much one night costs.

A path of white-painted cobblestones leads me to the motel office. The screen door bounces three times before settling in place behind me.

Someone must've bought salmon-pink paint on sale in the eighties and given every surface in the lobby ten coats of the stuff. Even the ceiling. Smells like warm toothpaste and plastic flowers in here. A display of decorative spoons takes up half the front desk. Some of the spoons have pictures of flags engraved on the handles. Some say World's Best Mom. A sheaf of flyers curls next to the spoons: Spend All Hallows Eve at Harrow Park. Not many takers, I guess.

The elderly clerk of this fine two-star motel hobbles out of his office and squints up at me through the longest eyebrow hairs I have ever seen. They corkscrew out of his forehead like white wires. "You're a tall one, aren't ya? How tall are ya?"

Neither question deserves a response.

"Quite the storm coming our way, that," he says. "Hurricane Lettie, she's called, wha?" His accent is old Colchester County and thick. "Lettie, that's a good old name, that."

"How much for one night?" I ask.

"How's forty-five sound?"

I consider the crinkled-up cash stuffed way down in the bottom of my backpack. Forty-five is too much. Gas to get here cost a small fortune. And I haven't eaten in a while. Comes down to the same choice every time. Food or roof. Never get both.

"No, thanks," I say.

"Wait now, wait now," he says. "Haven't had a single customer in two weeks. Tourist season ended, and hurricane season came up. Twenty-five if you give me good stars on the internet hotel review page. Nice towels. Nice old feller at the desk. Five stars. Stay as long as you like. I really do need the business, you know."

Twenty-five I can do.

"Deal," I say.

He manoeuvres his reading glasses into the grooves in his nose. I slide my driver's licence across the desk at him.

"Luck," he says, reading my last name aloud. "Where you from?"

I squint at him.

"Originally," he says. "Where you from?"

I keep squinting.

"Who's your mother?" he asks me.

"Who's *your* mother?"

"What is your mother's name?"

I don't have any intention of answering him. His eyes peer up at me through the gap between his glasses and those monstrous eyebrow hairs. "Your mother."

"One night," I say.

He shoves my licence back at me. "You can't stay here. Get out."

I place my knuckles on his desk, my elbows up like a gorilla posing before a fight. "What?"

He shrinks. "I-I've got no rooms."

"All of a sudden?"

"No rooms for the likes of anyone with that last name." He points at my driver's licence with his knobby fingers.

I lean in closer to him, making him lean back. "My mother's name is none of your damn business!"

He scuttles away like a cockroach.

Frig him. Creepy weirdo.

I grab my licence back. The motel office screen door bounces three times behind me when I go.

CHAPTER FOURTEEN

The apple-red convenience store gleams in the sunlight, outside the shadow of the Grand Tea rock. The sign reads Rita's Trading Post and Convenience. The door jingles when I open it. If I'm going to sleep in my car tonight, I'll need snacks.

Inside, the store is bright and clean. Tidy shelves packed with road-trip supplies for people on their way to somewhere else. Chips and bars. Seeds and nuts. Coffee and tea machines bubble softly. An ice cream machine hums.

The warm, comforting aroma of chai fills the store. It comes from the cup cradled in the hands of a friendly faced woman in a red sweater sitting behind the counter. She is the only person in the store at the moment, besides me. She smiles a warm, comforting smile. "Can I help you find something?"

"Half Moons and storm chips," I say.

The woman points with her chin toward an aisle to the right. I grab a box of Half Moon cakes off the shelf and pause to study the chip selection. Picking the right storm chips is an important decision.

"Are you Madeline Luck's niece?" the woman asks gently. "I heard them say her niece is here."

Them.

"Do you know Madeline Luck?" I say.

"A bit, sure. She's been coming here for years and years for flour. Longer than I've been alive. Going back to when my grandmother owned this store. Madeline never buys boughten bread. Only flour to bake her own. Every three months like clockwork. She walks all the way from her home in Willow Sound to here to buy a bag of flour."

"That's a long walk."

"Not if you walk through the woods. But it's dangerous. Easy to get lost in there. You have to know the way, and she does." She smiles. "Sometimes, she brings a few things for me to sell for her in the store. Your auntie is not much for conversations, but that's her way."

"What does she sell?"

"Tea. Bags of homemade wild tea. The tourists love her tea. They buy me out every summer. Most popular thing the tourists buy in this whole town is Madeline Luck's wild berry tea."

"What colour is the tea?" I ask.

"Forget-me-not blue. Never seen blue tea like that anywhere else."

I smile. I know that blue tea very well.

"I'm sorry to hear your auntie is missing," she says. "We organized some searches for her."

"This town did?"

"No. My people, from my community out home. We walked for her. Don't expect this town here to walk for her. And don't expect the police to help much either. It's sad to say, but I'll say it."

She and I share meaningful silence for a second.

"When was the last time you saw my aunt Madeline?" I ask.

"Six months back. It was March. She asked me for a bag of rye flour. I remember it very well because that was the first time she ever asked me for rye flour, and I felt bad because I didn't have any. After that day, though, I decided I'll keep both kinds of flour in stock. Just for her." The woman lifts two paper bundles of flour from behind the counter. She must have set the flour aside for Aunt Madeline. A thoughtful thing to do. "I never got to give Madeline the rye flour, because she hasn't been back in yet. Here." She slides both bundles into a cloth shopping bag. "Give these to your auntie when she gets home. Tell her it's from Rita. I'm Rita."

"I'm Fade."

"Fade, sure. Here you go, Fade."

"Thanks, Rita," I say. "I'll give it to her when she gets home."

Rita smiles softly and sadly as she hands me the bag. She returns to the steam of her chai, and I return to my storm chip selection. The store door jingles behind me. I glance over my shoulder to get a look at who has come in. There is no one there.

"That's weird," I say. "I thought I heard someone come in."

"I think they changed their mind," Rita says. "They turned right back around and left."

I don't wonder who. Or why.

Rita sips her tea. "They're going to talk about you."

"Who is?"

She nods toward the door. "The town. They like to talk. They're bad for it."

I bet.

"Does the town have an archive or museum of some kind?" I ask.

"Yes. Grand Tea Archives. Old building. Brown brick. Very easy to find, sure. The town is all one road, really. Follow it all the way to the end. Right through the middle of town, from the tourist parking lot, past the shops, past the diner, past Harrow Park. Just past where the sidewalk ends. Very last building on your right is the archives."

"Would it be open today?"

"Doubt it," Rita says. "They don't get a lot of visitors so they don't have a lot of open hours."

The disappointment must register on my face.

"Were you looking for something specific from the archives?" Rita asks.

"I need a picture of Aunt Madeline," I say. "For the police. To help them identify her. I was hoping the archives might have one. Kind of a last resort."

"Listen." Rita puts her tea down. "Go around to the back of the archives building. The very back. There's a little green door back there. You knock on that door. There's a man who lives there, sure. He'll be there if you knock. Maybe he can help you."

"What kind of person lives in an archive?"

"A dusty one," Rita says.

Her cheeky look and tea sip get a laugh out of me.

CHAPTER FIFTEEN

I see them now. I see the people who live in Grand Tea. I thought they were nowhere, but they're everywhere. They stand inside the windows of all the houses and shops and stare out through the glass.

Their stares are spooky and sharp. There's no way these Grand Tea townies stare down their precious tourists this way. This creepy fixation must be something special reserved for the niece of Madeline Luck.

No wonder my mother doesn't trust these people.

People stare at me everywhere I go. Not just here. *Too big*, their eyes say. *Too much*. So I'm used to people staring at me, but the people in the town of Grand Tea . . . their stares are different.

I lumber down the gravel road through the middle of town, past a handful of touristy boutique shops and a little diner called Odes. Past the stares.

Behind the diner, a depressing public park struggles to exist right next to the base of the mountain. It must be Harrow Park. There's no one in it. Looks less like a park and more like a lake of gravel, scattered with rust-gnawed playground equipment, a metal pole stuck straight up with no flag, and anemic trees. Poor spindly things.

There are a lot of touristy boutiques for a town this tiny. An occult-themed shop with skeletons in the window. "Charge your wand at Harrow Mountain $20." No thanks. A horror-themed T-shirt store dangles its wares on metal racks outside, with classic monsters gawking from their polycotton blends. The new-age store beside it boasts an assortment of pieces of the Grand Tea rock for sale. "Great selection. Freshly fallen."

The boutiques all have glass bottles hanging next to their door. There's something inside those bottles, but I don't care what. Must be a weird local thing. One of many.

The whole town of Grand Tea must be Halloween-crazy. Not just the shops, but the houses too. Store-bought witch-themed Halloween decorations clutter every building, strew every window, and drape every fence. Garish green-skinned witch heads with black triangle hats hang everywhere. Legs in striped socks stick shamelessly out of woodpiles and car trunks, the tops of shop doors and the bottoms of windows. There are so many jutting out of everything, it feels like walking through the site of an Oz witch massacre.

Metal springs squawk somewhere to my right, followed by the *shoof-shoof* of pointy shoes walking over gravel.

A familiar peanut-beige business suit slides into my peripheral vision. The person who came knocking on Aunt Madeline's door. The one who is not her friend.

He strides toward me, arms pumping like a power walker.

I face him abruptly. He skids to a stop. He teeters on his toes ever so slightly, to give himself a bit more height next to me. Doesn't work.

"Welcome!" he says. "To the town of Grand Tea!"

I stare at him. My silence sends him hurtling into his next set of scripted sentences.

"I am the mayor. Mr. Mayor Dinwald H. Davish at your service. Here's my card." He offers me a shiny golden business card with his knobby-knuckled, manicured hand and waits for me to take it.

I don't.

"Have you stopped into any of our delightful shops? Serving all your metaphysical and occult needs. Open all year."

I raise my eyebrows.

"Yes, all year! However, you, I surmise, are not a tourist, are you? Another pause.

He pockets his golden card. "You, I surmise, are extended family to this town. Yes? Possibly related to our very own, very wonderful Miss Madeline Luck. Very shocking what we've heard, that she is not to be found in her sweet little house, where she should be, safe and sound. You know . . ." He pretends to come up with the thought just now. "What we should consider for the wellness of our own Miss Madeline Luck is an access road. Right to her house. A beautiful lane. A lifeline, you could say, to allow all the amenities a venerable senior citizen might need. Deliveries. Ambulances. Right to her front door. What do you think? Why, the town"—he stretches his arms wide in a Willy Wonka way—"the town would even plow it for her come winter, for free! It's the least we can do for our longest-living citizen."

His arms still outstretched and his sales-pitch smile working hard, he awaits my approval. But I'm not interested in anything this peanut is selling. Not what he claims he's offering, or whatever he's really selling. He's been talking for less than five minutes, and I'm already sick of him.

"What is your name?" he says.

I start walking again. He keeps pace with me.

"Go into a shop. Any shop! Right now. Off-season discounts in store. Today only. Fantastic deals."

I keep walking.

"Is there some reason you won't go inside our shops?" He says this as if he's proving some point to someone other than me. Too bad I don't care what. "Are you intentionally rude, or did you inherit the trait from your family?"

He's clearly trying to bait me into an argument as a last resort to keep my attention. Since his perky, polite mayor schtick didn't work. But I don't take the bait.

He stops walking beside me and drifts into the background. "If you don't find her," he says, louder than he needs to. "I'll take her house off your hands. Market value. As is. No inspection. No conditions. No questions asked."

I just keep walking. I don't owe him a damn thing.

"Where are you going?" There is a glint of fear in his voice. "Are you going to the archives?" Even with some distance between us, I hear him mutter to himself, "She's going to the archives."

With the *shoof-shoof* sound of him and his shiny shoes retreating, I am alone again. I keep my sights on the end of the road. I can see a brick building from here. Must be the archives.

Just have to get a picture of Aunt Madeline and get the hell out of this forsaken town.

CHAPTER SIXTEEN

The Grand Tea Archives is a two-storey brown-brick cube. No decorations. No windows. No nonsense.

Rita was right. It's closed. Nothing left to do but walk to the back of the building.

Around back, I find a small shed-like shelter tacked on to the back of the archives. Compared to the sombre, proper building, this little add-on shelter looks wonky and cheap. As if the main building was made by a sensible architect, and the little shelter was added on later by the architect's drunk cousin who skipped shop class to hang out at a garbage dump. It's no bigger than a dorm room. Or a jail cell.

I knock on the ivy-green door.

A minute later it opens, and a floofy puff of curly hair pops out the door. Within the puff is a man's happy face with eyes the colour of a tornado. "Good day!" he says, and he means it. He has a British accent of some kind.

This floofy-haired man steps out the door and looks up at me. Way up. I look down at him. Way down. Our heights are so vastly different, it's as if we're two characters from two different mythologies brought together by mistake.

We both smile about it. Friendly-like. It's nice, for a change.

"Are you the archivist?" I ask.

"Yes!" he says. "I am the historian-in-residence, literally and figuratively! I am Dr. Nishant Chaudry, at your service. How may I help you?"

"I don't need anybody's help, really," I say. "I just want to look up a few things in your archives, there."

"No, I'm afraid we're closed today," he says. "Autumn hours are Mondays only. We'll be open next week."

Frig.

"What if it can't wait?" I ask.

"Urgent archival business?" he says. "I have never heard such a thing!"

"Can I just go in and look around for myself for a few minutes?"

"I'm afraid not, I'm sorry to say." He shrugs his apology at me. "But I would be very happy to research on your behalf."

I'm not really sure what to make of this person. He seems all right. But he also chooses to work here under the big rock for some reason. Maybe this is where they banish the archivists who aren't very good at archiving.

"I found a bunch of old photographs," I say as I scrounge three of Aunt Madeline's photographs from my pants pocket, making the archivist cringe. I hand them to him.

"Wonderful!" he says.

"They have notes written on the back," I say.

He handles the photos with great care as he examines each in turn, front and back. "Superb historical portrait photographs with atypical notation."

"Sure, okay."

"I have never seen notes like these before," he says. "Not exactly. Dates and names, of course. But flower and colours and foods? I can honestly say I have never seen notes like these on any photographs I have ever come across. On either side of the Atlantic."

"Huh."

"The dates appear reasonable," he says. "I suppose we may sensibly assume the names belong to the subjects of the photographs. So. Perhaps it is as simple and as elegant as a note recording the subject's favourite flower and food. It's lovely, really. Where did you find these photos, may I ask? Here in Grand Tea?"

"No. In my aunt's house. They're hers."

"Ah." He places the photos back in my hand with deliberate care, subtly demonstrating how they should be handled. "Aunties are often good for such things. Where does she live?"

"She lives in Willow Sound," I say. "Her name is Madeline Luck."

The archivist freezes and stares off into space. Then he springs back to life with a jolt and points at me. "Amazing!" He presses his hands to his chest as if trying to keep his heart from exploding out of it. "I am deeply humbled to meet you!"

"Wait," I say. "Why? What is happening?"

"Madeline Luck of Willow Sound is a legend!"

"She's a what-now?"

"A legend! It would be my sincerest privilege to help you document and preserve *the* Madeline Luck Historical Photograph Collection," he says.

Before I say "What?" again or walk away from this man who is speaking with an alarming amount of exclamation points, I turn his offer over in my mind. There's something about him. His over-the-top enthusiasm. His curly hair waving around his head in excitement. His kind face.

"Dr. Chaudry—" I say.

"Please, call me Nish," he says.

"Nish."

"Sorry, I interrupted the niece of Madeline Luck. Please, do go on." He looks like he's on the verge of exploding into confetti.

"Have you heard that my aunt Madeline has gone missing?"

"No," he says. The way he says it, I think I believe him.

"This morning, a cop asked me very basic questions about my aunt Madeline, and I couldn't answer any of them. I don't really know her that well." My throat betrays me for a second, tightening around my words as I speak them. "I'm not the kind of person who knows much about people. Or old stories or old days."

"I see," he says.

"I don't even have a picture of her to give to the cops, to help them find her. That's what I came here for. Do you think you might be able to find a picture of her, maybe? Somewhere in the archives?"

He smiles. "I accept this quest!"

I can't help but smile at that. Something tells me Nish and I are going to get along fine.

"There's a hurricane coming," he says.

"I heard."

"It might be a big storm, and it might cause a power outage. So I'd better look in the archives right away. Where can I reach you to give you what I find? Are you staying in town?"

"Nope," I say. "I'll probably sleep in my car."

Nish's eyebrows pop up. "You wouldn't stay in your aunt's house? I bet her house is amazing. Is it true she built the whole house herself out of wood and rocks from the forest around her?"

The memory of that deathly smell seeping out from underneath the door in the guest room makes me flinch. I clear my throat. "Sure. Maybe. I guess. There's no internet out there, but I can hijack internet from a satellite up there somewhere. I have the gear in my car."

"You keep satellite gear in your car?" he says. "That's impressive!"

"Once I get set up, I'll email the archives," I say.

"Well, I don't have a satellite. Just a pen or two. Or ten. But I shall get my best pens to work right away! And here is my card. It has my email address on it."

"Thank you. My name is Fade, by the way. Fade Luck."

"Fade Luck," Nish says my name with a nod.

"And listen, Dr. Chaudry. Nish. If any cops come around asking about me, don't tell them anything. Not my name, not this conversation, not anything."

His head tilts to the side, his eyes shiny with curiosity. "I wouldn't dream of it."

BOOK FOUR

Nightmare

CHAPTER SEVENTEEN

I decide to stay the night in Aunt Madeline's house. Even with the sinister door. Even with the smell. Just in case she comes home. Just in case she needs me here.

I grab my backpack and two duffle bags of gear from my car and carry it all through the woods to the house in one trip. Computer hardware in one bag. Basic-needs survival stuff in the other. It's all I really own.

And the flour. I remember to bring the cloth bag of flour from Rita. To put it on the kitchen table, so it's waiting for Aunt Madeline when she gets home.

By the time I get back to Aunt Madeline's house, it's dark out. The beam of my phone flashlight sweeps across the rundown gardens. The house looks hollow and deathly dark with no warm orange glow in the windows. No lanterns inside to read by. No fire in the little stove. No waiting pot of tea.

There could be people or wild animals lurking anywhere, and I'd never see them.

But I remind myself there's nothing here.

Just darkness and shadows and me.

Bugs drone past the kitchen door. Owls shriek at each other somewhere in the black woods. The darkness is brutal without Aunt Madeline here to light her candles one by one. To warm up the corners and push the shadows away.

I don't have any matches. Just my phone, a flashlight, and some LED screens.

On my drive here this morning, I'd pictured myself sleeping in the guest room. Like old times. Now, my bones turn cold at the thought.

I will have to face that awful door eventually. Not right now, though. It's too dark. Whatever is behind that door will have to stay there till I'm good and ready.

Not tonight.

Better set up my satellite gear before I get too tired to think. My hands fumble through the contents of my backpack; I grab my LED flashlight and flick it on.

Icy grey-blue light floods the house, casting freakish shadows. So different from candlelight, which warms and glows. The harsh beam drains the life out of everything I see. The house looks like a crime scene. Or a morgue. But at least I can see.

The guest room door gapes open.

Armed with cold light, I march through the open door right into the middle of the room. The scabby door festering in the middle of Aunt Madeline's library wall seems to twitch in the light. It's even more nightmarish than I remember.

Frig that thing.

The bed frame in here is a rickety cage of metal and old springs. It used to be comfy. It used to be piled up with straw-filled mattresses and crocheted blankets. Now, it's an empty beast. I grab it with one hand and shove it against the nightmare door, glad for the ear-splitting racket it makes. If anything moves that door even a millimetre, the bed frame is going to screech about it.

And I'll be ready.

I pull the guest room door shut tight behind me. Good enough.

I shine my light around Aunt Madeline's room. Should I crash in her room? Pretty quilts rest neatly across her bed, folded and tucked and cloaked in dust.

No. Wouldn't feel right to sleep in her bedroom while she's away. This bed has been hers and only hers forever. She chose to live out here alone, away from the world, so she didn't have to share her bed with anyone. I respect that.

A small detail catches my eye just before I leave the room.

Two pillows. There are two pillows on her bed. Side by side.

That is definitely different.

Aunt Madeline never had two pillows in this bed. She had one, dead centre. She took up the whole bed, spread like a starfish when she slept. I am sure of it, because when I moved out on my own and got my own place, the first thing I did was buy one pillow and put it dead centre at the head of my bed. Even though it was a mattress on the floor. To this day, the only way I ever want to sleep is like a starfish. Like Aunt Madeline.

So, it matters that there are two pillows on her bed, side by side.

It matters, but I don't know why.

CHAPTER EIGHTEEN

Aunt Madeline's broom hangs next to her back door. Long and light. The handle is a jagged willow stick. The bristles are birch twigs, held together by whips of ribbon-thin willow twigs and trimmed into a tidy pointed shape.

As I sweep dust and dead bugs from the kitchen floor, the smell of rosemary drifts up from the broom. She must keep rosemary sprigs inside the bristles or something. The drowsy *sh-sh-sh* swishing against the floor makes me yawn.

Clean enough now. Although I wish I'd brought chemical cleaners. Strong ones. To scrub the whole place down and drive the mould and bugs away. Make it gleam for Aunt Madeline when she gets home.

Another yawn creeps up on me. Maybe tomorrow.

I unroll my sleeping bag in the middle of the kitchen floor. Every Nova Scotian who lives under a landlord keeps a sleeping bag and tent on hand, just in case. It's that heartless here. It wasn't always, but

I'd say the good old days are gone. Don't think this little province will ever get its heart back.

I dump out my snacks to get to the real reason I lugged these bags all the way out here: my nerdy survival gear. Portable battery-powered supplies and an antenna made from pipes and trash I found in a work site dumpster. With this antenna made from literal garbage and enough knowledge to locate and crack into satellites with weak encryption, I can reach up into Earth's orbit and hijack free internet anytime I want.

Cramming down handfuls of ketchup chips, I tote my junky antenna outside to set it up. I can't imagine a clearer view of the sky than right here in Aunt Madeline's back garden. The antenna fires up and connects my laptop and phones on the kitchen floor directly to the stars.

Even though I know there's no one near Aunt Madeline's house, in any direction, I lock the doors and keep the key where I can grab it. Until she gets back, her house is my responsibility, and she took the time to lock it before she left.

An email from my mother vibrates my phone. *Any news about where Madeline is? I called the hospital and she's not in there. She's probably off being stubborn somewhere. Don't let her make you feel bad.*

Only four sentences, yet so loaded.

I email my mother back. *Hey, Ma. No sign of Aunt Madeline yet. No news. She hasn't picked up her mail in three months, but her house looks like it's been neglected for a lot longer than that. Do you have a picture of her? The cops need one. When did you hear from her last, anyway?*

My LED screens light the kitchen too well. Their cold light beams from the floor up, casting eerie shapes. The bunches of dried herbs that dangle from the ceiling like little hangmen swing and rustle whenever I move or breathe. It sounds like they're whispering behind me wherever I go. I feel surrounded.

Tired and with who knows what fresh hell awaiting me tomorrow, I power my devices down, one by one. Let the darkness back in. Let the heavy quiet take over.

How does Aunt Madeline handle the complete darkness and suffocating quiet of this place? There is no relief from the nothingness. Just the hiss of distant waves. The occasional *crr-crr-kih* of katydids. My heartbeat. My breath.

I wonder if, some nights, Aunt Madeline wishes for company. Someone to bring a new sound, a new smell, a new idea. Someone to laugh at a joke or compliment her cleverness. Someone to break up the silence. Someone to lay their head on the pillow next to hers.

So dark. So tired. Can't tell if my eyes are closed or open. There's no difference. Until the unexpectedly lovely moment when the moon moves to where its light trickles in the window.

No wonder Aunt Madeline celebrated the moon in her mural. The moonlight comes in politely, in delicate touches, grazing one thing at a time until everything lost to the darkness is slowly returned.

In the ratty nylon cocoon of my sleeping bag, I shift from my back to my side.

Just before my eyes close, they lock on the darkest corner in the room. Just as the moonlight falls on something strange.

There's an old woman standing there.

I freeze. My eyes are so wide they burn, but I don't dare blink and lose sight of what I think I see. What I know I see.

A woman. A woman in the corner.

She stands, stooped. Hair wild. Face in shadows, but I know she's looking at me.

I try to speak but can only gasp. I'm like a fish sucking on air.

The moonlight moves, and she moves with it. Staying in shadows. I can't see her, except for two pinhole dots of moonlight reflected in the sockets in her skull. The pinhole eyes see me.

I try to move. I think my sleeping bag is pinning me down. Why can't I move?

She is unreal. She is awful. Staring at me with those pinprick eyes.

I find a terrified version of my voice. "Aunt Madeline?"

She stands too still. I hear a soft *huff, huff, huff, huff* of her breathing hard, and I realize it's a word: "No, no, no, no, no—" A whisper, a rhythm. She whips around, facing the corner. Her hair tangles in knots on the back of her head. She trembles and jerks as if possessed. This sight is worse than her pinprick eyes.

Into the empty corner, she speaks in an ancient-sounding voice that crackles like fire: "Ahhhh-puullllls."

What the hell—

I break my arm free from my sleeping bag and grope for my flashlight. "What the hell are you doing in this house?"

In a disturbingly perfect mimic of my voice, crackling with static like a record player recording, she echoes back: "What the hell are you doing in this house?"

She whips her head back around to face me. Her pinprick eyes snap.

I tear my way out of my sleeping bag, scramble to my feet, and, in the chaos of cloth and darkness, accidentally drop the flashlight and kick it across the floor.

Its beam whips lightning-white across her gaunt face. She looks startled. And mad. She rushes at me, face first, her cries forcing hot air into every hole in my head until I black out.

CHAPTER NINETEEN

I wake up in the morning with no air in my lungs, and my eyes dart to that corner. But the old woman is not there. There's just a small stool with a basket on top, stuffed with dusty balls of yarn. Like there should be.

Sunrise warms the floor. The lazy *zz-zz-zz* of cicadas rises with the sun. I wish I could lie here and enjoy it, but I can't.

Instead, I grab my aunt's broom as a weapon and investigate every corner and cranny in the house. The broom vibrates in my trembling grip. I leap into the guest bedroom.

It's still awful but mercifully empty and undisturbed.

There is no one else in the house. No old woman. But I don't dream. I don't have nightmares.

In sock feet, I creep around the yard, wielding my broomstick, jumping at every sound, scrutinizing every leaf flicker, every smell. Nothing. No one.

"HEY!" I holler at the top of my lungs. Partly to startle someone out of hiding. Partly to shake the steel ball of fear from my gut. "HEEEY!"

Starlings flee the treetops, and that's it. By the time my holler echoes off, I catch my breath. I feel calmer. Laugh at myself, relief sinking in.

It was a dream.

She was a nightmare.

Or I'm just losing my mind.

I need coffee.

Remembering only to walk east, I hope to stumble across a familiar landmark or two to help me find Aunt Madeline's stream. The pressure of bright yellow morning sunlight against my eyelids feels right. Feels like following Aunt Madeline to the stream as a kid. I can almost hear the *hooo* of air passing by the top of the copper jug on her shoulder as she walked.

I hear the stream before I see it. It's smaller than I remember—the stream must be drying up, exposing more of the rock. But still there is enough water running through here to use. I kneel on the rock and dip my hand in. The ripples flow against my fingers like cold silk. I steady the jug's mouth at the water's surface, as Aunt Madeline used to do, and the water trickles inside.

No rushing this part. Water takes its time. Willow trees sway gently over me. A towering audience of elegant skeletons draped in delicate yellowing veils. The soothing *hiss* of their leaves shivers the spine. The earth creaks beneath them.

I feel grateful to this little stream. For caring for Aunt Madeline all these years. For being here for her. For giving her clean clothes, clean cuts, warm soup, and hot tea.

I only take enough water to make coffee and wash up and sling the big jug on my shoulder.

When I get back to the house, I'll look for matches so I can boil water.

Maybe there's some in Aunt Madeline's purple cabinet.

Maybe in the drawer labeled Fire.

The drawer has lots of matches in it. I only need one.

I'm too paranoid to make a fire inside the kitchen stove, in case I screw up and burn the house down. So, I take my one match outside and coax a half-decent fire in the fire pit out back.

I stand in the morning sun, sipping coffee, listening to the ocean roar.

Corporal Quill will be here at one. That gives me four hours. I wonder if that archivist has found anything yet.

Madeline Luck of Willow Sound is a legend!

What does that even mean? I was raised to believe Aunt Madeline barely exists. Her life is invisible. Out of mind. On purpose. This archivist evidently knows things about my aunt that I don't.

He could be useful. Could be trouble. Easy enough to figure out which one he is. Ten minutes online is all the time I need to dig up all Dr. Nishant Chaudry's shadiest secrets.

There's not much on him. Born and raised in London, England. Master's from Oxford. Ph.D. in history from University of York. Researched in thirteen different locations around the globe. Latest on the list: Nova Scotia. Arrived eight months ago. Has written five books, all with brain-numbing titles. All about history.

His headshot is buried on the Grand Tea Archives website. I can't help but chuckle at the goofy enthusiasm radiating from his face. Unlike the humdrum headshots of his fellow historians, Nish is all big eyes, big grin, big curls. He looks like he probably puts his heart into things.

That's what Aunt Madeline needs, and deserves, right now.

There's no way the people of Grand Tea want him around. This odd man from away poking through the Grand Tea historical records for some reason. There's no sign of big money in it. Whatever his reasons are, they're not on the web. I wonder if he has no choice but to live in that ramshackle pile of bricks if he wants to live in Nova Scotia.

I know how that feels.

And he said nice things about Aunt Madeline.

And he didn't seem to mind me, for some reason.

I have an idea. It's either a great idea, or a terrible one.

It's probably terrible. I'll probably regret it. But I can handle it.

I email Nish and ask him how long it would take him to get here. And I send him directions to Aunt Madeline's house.

CHAPTER TWENTY

An email from my mother dings as I rinse out my coffee cup, and it gives me some hope.

Remember, Phaedra, your aunt Madeline isn't young anymore, so let's cut her some slack for not dusting. Madeline sent me a card for my birthday last month. And she has never, ever sent me a birthday card in all the years before. Not one. So she's getting soppy and sentimental in her old age. Maybe she finally realizes she was wrong. I'd say she probably has some kind of dementia, now, or shaky hands. Either way, she's probably just acting out and looking for attention. No pictures of Madeline at my house or probably anywhere. She's as hell-bent as you are about avoiding having her picture taken. More so, maybe. I'll call the hospital again.

Aunt Madeline sent my mother a birthday card one month ago; that must be a good sign. Maybe the assumptions Quill and Canada Post made about her mailbox and the three months were wrong.

Duly caffeinated and sugar-high from scarfing down my entire collection of random snacks, I grab my boots and face the woods.

The thick trees. The smothering leaves. The understorey. Hiding things. Swallowing things up.

I have three hours before Corporal Quill shows up here. Three hours to pace a methodical search grid through the woods around Aunt Madeline's house. Hunting for clues.

The thing I have been most wanting—and most dreading—to do.

~

I untangle my bootlace from a hedge of unforgiving thorns and tell myself stories. It's possible Aunt Madeline lost her mail key and didn't care to replace it. Nothing good ever comes by mail, anyway. It's possible she goes away on extended foraging trips, little adventures to get out of the house for a while. Maybe she's away on one now. There is no one to leave a note for when she goes, so she just goes.

Even if Aunt Madeline got lost in some woods, she'd not only survive, she'd thrive. She'd set up a second home without a second thought and wait there for me to come find her and join her for berries and tea.

I cling desperately to that picture in my mind, but other thoughts creep around it.

For two hours, I walk non-stop, eyes trained on the ground, hunting for clues. A mail key. A handwritten note. A ribbon.

I know in my heart I am also looking for . . . her.

After three months, what would be left of someone who died out here? Would she be bones? Would the earth have grown over her all summer, blanketing her body with the forest floor forever? Or would wild animals find her first? If wild animals pulled her apart and carried her away, is she everywhere and nowhere now?

"HELLO-O!" a voice echoes through the woods. The voice is friendly and distinctly British.

~

Beaming and tilting like a sunflower, Nish stands at the far end of the path to the house. It looks as if he's politely waiting for permission before setting foot in the dooryard. Seeing me step out of the woods, he waves his whole arm over his head. "Fade!" He points at his own head. "It's Nish, from the archives!"

"Come on up! Oh, Nish, watch out for the—"

Too late. He catches his toe on that same bumpy bit of ground that tripped Quill and me yesterday. He topples into the bushes with a very British "Gack!"

He is laughing when I reach him.

"Sorry about that, Nish. I should have warned you sooner," I say.

"Please, Fade, don't apologize."

"Same thing happened to me yesterday. Fell right on my face."

"Mine was a lucky fall. I think there's something buried here."

"Something buried?"

He pokes at a smooth rounded glimmer embedded in the ground. "May I?"

I shrug. Nish scrapes at the hard ground and unearths a glass jar with a metal lid. He holds it up and dusts it off with genuine awe. As he turns the jar in the light, we can see an odd collection of objects inside.

I tap on the glass. "What the frig is it?"

"I believe it is a spell."

"Nish," I say.

"What?"

"Did you just say the word *spell* with a straight face?"

"I did," he says.

"Nish," I say.

"No, really. Historically speaking, magic spells are memory devices. They're used to pass down information from one generation to the next."

"This jar is a memory device?"

"If there is an incantation associated with this jar, then that incantation would be the memory device." He hands me the jar.

"But the jar itself is a spell jar. It holds traditional objects with ancient meanings."

"Cool," I say. "Hold out your hands."

"Wait, what—" Nish scrambles as I twist off the rusted lid and dump the jar's contents into his hands: a black candle, a white candle, a clove of garlic, a wild rose stem smothered with thorns, a sprig of elderberries, and a snip of a rosemary. Everything is flecked with some kind of sparkly black spice.

"What is that stuff?" I say. "Pepper?"

"That would be black salt," Nish says.

"So . . . it's pepper."

"Not pepper. Traditionally, black salt is made of sea salt, ash, and charcoal."

"I bet it tastes like pepper," I say.

"Well, I'm not going to taste it."

"Not even for science?"

"I'm a historian," Nish says. "You taste it for science."

"No thanks," I say, but I have to smile.

"You know, black salt is used in protection magic. I study folklore from all over the world. I know a spell when I see one. And given the objects I hold in my hands and their long-standing traditional meanings, I can confidently state this jar contains a protection spell."

"Go 'way."

"And I would speculate this spell was buried in the earth right here, to protect"—he indicates with his overfull cupped hands—"that house."

"Protect the house from what?"

"From anything and everything bad, I suppose."

I stare at the odd collection of items in Nish's hands until he gasps dramatically. All the moving parts that make up his face spread as wide apart as they can get, as if he's just been struck with some horrifying realization.

I give him side eye and wait.

"Fade, if I may ask, and I'm so sorry to be this bold, but . . . how well do you know your aunt Madeline Luck?"

"Not well. Like I said before. Last time I saw her, I was nine."

"So, you don't know about the jar."

"No," I say.

"You don't know why this jar is here."

"No."

"Now, myself, I have not yet had the pleasure of meeting Madeline Luck," Nish says. "But I do happen to know a few things about her from my research. I know she lives alone, but still she is very well-known. Not just to people in Grand Tea, but to people across the whole county. Possibly further."

"How is that possible?"

"Mostly because she lives *very* alone, which people find strange. And she keeps to these bygone, very old-fashioned ways that have been lost to the rest of us for a hundred years, which people also find strange."

"I thought she was invisible."

"Quite the opposite! When I moved here from England, in the dead of winter eight months ago, I came specifically to help document and record the cultural memory and folkways of the diverse people of Colchester County. For my work, I speak to people, and almost every person I have spoken to in this part of the province has told me stories and legends about Madeline Luck."

"Go 'way."

"I shall not!" he says. "Stories are passed down through families, and whispered throughout the county, about the reclusive and mysterious Madeline Luck."

"What are the stories about?"

"Well . . . many are . . . unkind."

"Are they true?"

"I don't know."

"So, they make up lies about her."

"I don't know."

"That's a weird answer."
"I know."
"Let me guess. These stories are probably sexist."
"Yes."
"Racist."
"Yes."
"They cast my aunt as an old crone."
"Yes."
"A useless burden on society."
"No."
"No?"
"In their stories, your aunt is powerful," he says. "And dangerous."
"Really?"
"Really. People are afraid of her."
"Why are people afraid of her?"
"Because she is the Witch of Willow Sound."

BOOK FIVE

The Witch of Willow Sound

CHAPTER TWENTY-ONE

I have a memory from my childhood that never made sense to me until now, and for some reason I decide to share it with Nish.

That trip, I was five or six. I can't remember exactly where we stopped or why. I can only recall it was a farmers' market. Grey concrete floors. Crates everywhere. No walls. Gentle summer breezes rushing through, carrying smells of fresh basil and recently unearthed potatoes. Wooden produce display tables piled with fresh vegetables and fruit.

I strutted around the market, holding an apple. I was full of butterflies because I was convinced I'd found the best apple in the whole world. It was beautiful: big, heavy, jewel red. Not a single dent or scuff. Smooth and flawless, like a crystal ball in my hands. I could even see myself in the shiny skin of it. The skin smelled of summer mornings.

At some point, I showed my apple to another kid about my age, who also happened to be at the market that day. An impromptu show-and-tell opportunity. I held it up and proudly declared my find a dream apple.

He recoiled and looked at me as if I was some kind of monster. "It's probably a witch apple!" He flinched, as if expecting me to hit him for saying so. But I was too confounded by his odd reaction. In a split second, his face contorted from fearful to near tears. He grunted and shoved me so hard I fell back. The apple flew right out of my hand and through the air and bounced across the hard market floor.

"Hey!" I scrambled after it and scooped it up like a shortstop. Always quicker to anger than tears, I biffed my apple, with every bit of fury I had, right in that kid's face. He exploded into a blubbery wreck and ran off to rat me out.

Let him. I was too busy chasing after my apple a second time. I crawled under the vegetable stands to find it busted, dented, skin split. My dream apple was a mess in my little hands. Bruised up and useless.

My little heart broke apart. When my mother found me and yanked me out from under the vegetable stand, I was crying.

"Look what the stupid kid did to my apple for no reason," I said. "It was perfect and now it's wrecked. It's not fair."

I don't think my mother looked at me. She was too busy looking around us. A crowd had gathered to gawk at me. No one seemed upset by what that boy had done to me. Boys will be boys. But I'm a girl and I needed to know my place. So, I stood there. Head low. Snide comments drilled into my mother from all sides.

"You're the Old Witch's sister!"

"Your kind aren't welcome here!"

"Your daughter probably threatened the poor boy with a poisoned apple!"

The anger started winding up inside me, and I raised my apple behind my head to biff it again. At an adult this time. At all of them, if I had to. But before I could, my mother brought the whole spectacle to an end. She dropped the basket of grapes she was going to buy, clutched my forearm, and marched us out of the market and straight into her car. Gravel kicked up as we sped out of the parking lot and skidded back onto the highway to Aunt Madeline's house.

After a physical fight, pain is helpful. It keeps the mind too busy to feel pointless feelings like remorse or regret. It tells you you're still alive, whatever state you're in. The back of my head hurt from hitting the floor when he shoved me. No blood, though. My jaw ached from clenching it so tightly. I looked down and realized I still had the apple in my hand. We had left the market without paying for it.

Genuine terror gripped me. The police would drive up behind us and put us in jail for stealing it. They'd put my mother in grown-up jail and put me in kid jail. I hadn't meant to steal it. I just forgot to let it go.

My eyes strained out the dusty back window, afraid with every blink I'd open my lids to see the blue lights spinning. Coming for me. Guns blazing. Hunting us down.

I hatched a plan. I wouldn't let them arrest my mother. I'd tell them it was me, that I was the bad one. Instead of sirens, I heard a soft sound. Sobbing. My breath caught.

My mother was crying.

I'd never seen her cry before. It scared me. My mother has always been very together, very composed, very private. I had seen her angry. I had seen her exasperated. And tired. But I had never seen her cry. Before that moment, I didn't know she could cry.

I didn't know what to do. It felt like walking in on someone in the bathroom. A violation but by accident. So, I pretended I didn't notice. I pretended to look out the window, but really, my eyes were closed, as if closing them would block out the sound of her choked sobs. As if she'd think I was asleep and didn't hear a thing.

Before long, the sobbing stopped. Her breathing was quiet and even again. We drove the rest of the way to Aunt Madeline's house in silence.

I stashed my apple way down deep in the bottom of my backpack. Just in case it was the apple that had made her cry. Hid it from two crows watching us turn off the highway and into the woods. Just in case they would see it and fly off and tell Aunt Madeline what I'd done. Last thing I wanted was another person mad at me.

True to her own way of silence, my mother never spoke to me about what happened that day.

※

"Do you remember what happened to the apple?" Nish asks me, his hands still cradling the objects from the jar. Protecting them.

I remember.

"My mother must have told Aunt Madeline what happened at the farmers' market, because I definitely didn't. That night, after supper, Aunt Madeline found me playing outside and asked me to bring her the apple. So I did. She looked it over and said I was right. Even with the bruises and everything else that had happened to it, it was still a dream apple. I thought, *Aunt Madeline would know. She knows everything about plants. More than anyone else in the world.* Even with the bruises, she could see it too.

"Aunt Madeline always keeps this knife in her apron. A Pictou Canadian belt knife. Small one. She washed the apple and cut a piece off it. She told me it was okay for me to eat it. The inside of the apple smelled like raspberries. It tasted like an apple, but also, somehow, it tasted like honey. I followed Aunt Madeline to a spot outside, and she showed me how to plant the rest of the apple in the ground. Seeds, flesh, skin, and all. She said the apple would always be part of me, because I ate it, and part of the earth, when I plant it. So, I'll always be linked to the apple two ways. Which meant I didn't have to be sad about my apple. And I know it all sounds strange, but it helped me feel better at the time. I really wasn't sad, or scared, anymore."

"Did it grow into a tree?" Nish asks.

"I have no idea," I say. "I doubt it. I don't even know what an apple tree looks like."

Nish scans all the way around the dooryard and points. "Looks like that."

In a far corner is a grey tree with silver-green leaves. Between the leaves: apples. Dark and past ripe and low. Ready to drop. The tree isn't tall, but it reaches quite wide. It struggles for attention and light against the overshadowing forest behind it, but it's there.

The memory of the taste of that apple snaps back to me in a flash, honey-sweet and a just little bit sour, as if the apple bit me back.

I turn away from the apple tree to look at Nish, this kind man who has clung to every word of my apple story. He nods and smiles at my story, just like Aunt Madeline had nodded and smiled at my apple a lifetime ago.

It's the first and last time I will ever tell this story out loud.

―

I hold the jar while Nish eases the candles and plants and black salt back inside it.

"Given the state of the house," I say, "I don't think this so-called protection spell thing worked."

"I suppose that's true, but there is so much to protect here, I can certainly understand the motivation to try," Nish says. "The house, the gardens. The trees alone are worth a fortune."

"What trees?"

"At the far edges of the gardens, and all around." He points. "The lumber value of the trees is staggering. Bird's eye maple. White oak. Black cherry. Black walnut is the most valuable species of timber in North America, and she has a whole bank of them right there."

I look where he's pointing. All I see are trees. Nish spins the lid back on the jar and hands it to me.

"Aunt Madeline's place didn't always look like a dystopian wasteland. It used to be amazing. Like something out of a fairy tale."

"Believe me," Nish says. "The bones of the fairy tale are still here. The variety of plants. The marvellous layout. So much heart and hard work in every square inch of this place. What Madeline Luck has accomplished during her lifetime cannot be diminished by anyone. And when you find her and she comes home, I can already imagine her pushing up her sleeves and working more miracles before she is done here."

He's so sincere. No sales pitch. No hidden agenda.

I think I like this particular human being.

We walk to the front door, and Nish gasps dramatically again. He holds his hands open beneath one of the odder decorations outside Aunt Madeline's house, as if he's discovered a religious relic. Which it isn't. It's a sieve. A hoop of wood and iron with a mesh screen pulled across.

"She hung a sieve!" Nish says. "By the front door! That is stunning!"

"You're a weird dude," I say. "No offence."

"None taken."

"So tell me. What makes this crusty old sieve stunning?"

"Sieves have an obscure but ancient history of magical use."

"Go 'way."

"I shall not!" He leans toward the sieve but doesn't touch it. "Tradition says you hang one by your front door to stop bad spirits in their tracks."

"Because spirits are lumpy and can't get through it?"

"Because spirits have to count every hole in the sieve before they can come in."

"That would take awhile."

"Indeed," he says. "I've only read about this belief in very old, very arcane books."

"It sounds like you have a fun life, Nish. No offence."

"None taken. I never dreamed I'd see one hanging by a door, for real, in my lifetime. Next to a witch's front door no less, with my own eyes."

I didn't know the tradition behind the sieve. It's always been there, but I've never paid any attention to it.

"I can't help but notice Madeline Luck has put a lot of mechanisms in place to keep bad things away from her home," Nish says.

"You're right. Like she was scared of something."

"Or . . . someone."

"Nish?"

"Yes, Fade?"

"Has anyone ever told you you are very dramatic?" I say.

"Only every human person I have ever met," he says.

"That tracks."

The front door opens a little easier this time. Nish pauses before stepping over the threshold into Madeline Luck's house.

When he steps inside, he is speechless. Motionless. Except his eyes. "Time travel," he says softly after a long while.

"That's how I felt too," I say. "I stepped in the door and travelled back twenty-four years in a second."

"For me, this is way back." Nish stands hand on heart. "Before either of us existed. Before the Great Depression. Before the Second Industrial Revolution. Before Canada. The past is present tense in Madeline Luck's world. Not for show. For real. As if time stopped here."

"I'd say Aunt Madeline stopped it exactly where she wanted it."

Nish nods and laughs softly. He takes a step, and the floor creaks under his dusty, worn Oxford shoe. The sound seems to shake off the shock of the moment, and the excitable Nish I have come to recognize returns with two words at top volume: "Holy Hekate!" He lays his eyes on Aunt Madeline's purple cabinet and nearly loses his educated mind. "Look at all of this! This is a real-life witch's cabinet! I'm sorry I'm yelling right now, but I am freaking out! The Witch of Willow Sound has a genuine witch's cabinet and it is beautiful and real and I am standing in front of it, looking right at it. Oh, Fade, this. This. This is a dream come true for me."

He takes a moment to take it all in, then leans in to begin the work of gasping dramatically over individual items in the cabinet one by one, touching none. I stand behind him, stifling my laughter at this extremely excitable nerd.

"Nish, man, do you need a paper bag? You're gonna pass out."

"Dried flowers and herbs! Preserved insects and woodland animal skulls and bones! Oh the sky above and the dirt below, give me strength. All the hallmarks of real and true traditional Green Witchcraft. Kill me now, right here, in this perfect moment! Don't kill me. But if you have to kill me, Fade, just do it here. Right in front of the cabinet. Right in the middle of the Witch of Willow Sound's home."

"What are you going on about? Traditional green what?"

"I am *so* glad you asked."

"Oh, lord."

"There are different kinds of traditional witches, each defined by how they practise their craft. Look! A raven skull! Sorry. That's why it's called witch*craft*. It is highly skilled work. Is that a hand-carved blackwood cat? So, Kitchen Witches' sacred place is their kitchen. They express their magics using food and cooking. A rough amber dagger moth, are you kidding me right now! Water Witches use water. Green Witches use plants and other elements found in nature. Usually for healing work. Madeline Luck speaks for herself, of course, but, Fade, there are signs of very traditional Green Witchcraft in every inch of this cabinet, and look at that hand-carved purpleheart wood mallard duck in flight that is giving me life right now!"

"So, all these things in her cabinet, they're not random," I say. "They're from old books and stuff."

"They are! These curiosities represent the oldest traditions from a very old world. And her scrolls! She has scrolls, I cannot believe it, she has scrolls. I'm not asking to touch those scrolls with my mere mortal hands, but I would bet you a Canadian toonie they contain her grimoire."

"What the hell is a"—I purposely pronounce it like it's not a real word because I can't help myself—"greem-wire?"

"Thank you *so* much for asking."

"Oh, lord."

"A grimoire is a written record of her craft. The recipes and the rituals that she uses. A grimoire is usually a book, but scrolls are the forerunners to books. Madeline Luck is possibly, hand on my heart, the coolest human being alive today."

I place the spell jar on the floor next to the wood stove and wipe dust off the kitchen table with my hand. Nish drags himself away from the cabinet and opens a disappointingly thin paper file on the kitchen table and sifts through it.

"I only had time to locate a few government records and directories that include Madeline Luck's name. Most records count her as living here, in her house in Willow Sound, of course. She has lived here for a very, very long time. However, I did manage to find a county directory from when she was a child, living in her parents' house in the village of Blueberry Brook. There are two parents and two daughters. I presume your mother is Madeline's sister?"

"Yes, she is."

"Perfect. I couldn't find Madeline Luck listed in any phone directories but"—he looks around—"I don't see a phone anywhere so . . ."

"No phone. No electricity. No running water."

"Be still my historian's heart. Fade Luck, your aunt is phenomenal."

"Did you find a picture of her?"

"Madeline Luck is masterfully elusive. There is not one image of her in the Grand Tea Archives collection. According to the locals, even in summer, she wears a cloak with a hood to hide her face from cameras."

"What cameras?"

"The townspeople and tourists of Grand Tea are obsessed with getting a picture of her. So, there are many photos in the archives and elsewhere claiming to be pictures of Madeline Luck, but none of them have her face showing, and I would guess most are fake. You can put anyone in a cloak and claim to have photographic proof of the elusive and near-mythical Witch of Willow Sound. So I had to go back in time and think outside the town, so to speak. There is no hint of her on highway cams, street view cams, or satellite shots. She has never been caught on camera walking along the road through Willow Sound. Except maybe once."

Nish hands me a printed scan of a newspaper article from 2003. National paper. The article is about a big wildfire in Nova Scotia. The journalist clearly meant to take a photo of the roadblock and firetrucks only, but accidentally captured the image of a person too.

Photo of an unidentified local woman walking along the old highway in Willow Sound. She had no comment about the fire.

There she is.

Aunt Madeline. Pulling her cloak hood up over her white hair a few seconds too late. Staring right at the camera lens. Right into me. She doesn't look scared at all. More amused, maybe. Knowing. *You have no idea who I am, and I love that.* In the newsprint, her green eyes look grey, but they are still lit up with that clever spark of hers that I remember so well.

"The second I saw this picture, I saw a resemblance to you," Nish says. "Is it her?"

"It's her. This is my aunt Madeline."

"Do you think this picture might be helpful to the police?"

"Yeah, I do. This is a big deal, finding this. This took otherworldly patience and back-breaking dedication to help a stranger. You are clearly brilliant at this work, Dr. Chaudry. Thank you for finding this."

Nish waves my thanks away. I can tell he's quietly pleased, but he tries to hide it by squinting more closely at the newspaper photo.

"You know a lot about witches, Nish," I say. "Is that what you write about?"

"I do know some things and collect some historical facts, but I am reluctant and unworthy to write about witches. The history of those who have been accused of being witches, in any culture, is often a story of hatred, oppression, and fear of strong women."

"All the witch trials and witch-burning stuff, you mean?" I say.

"Yes and no," he says. "The image of burning witches is locked into popular culture, but most witches—at least in England and the colonies—were hanged. Early modern era witch trials treated witchcraft as a crime of treason, not heresy, so witches weren't burned as heretics but hanged as traitors. Though in many places in continental Europe, they were burned, and that seems to be what the public has glommed onto."

"Weren't some crushed by boulders and drowned in rivers?" I say.

"Ah. Now you bring us to the fascinating topic of torture versus execution."

"Oh, lord."

"Witch trials needed accused witches to confess to deals with the devil, to harmful magic, to any number of bizarre things. The trials used torture to extract those confessions, including pricking needles, ducking stools, and the rack."

I shake my head. "Those poor women."

"Some men too," Nish says. "But yes, women were most often targeted."

"You know your stuff."

"I appreciate that. The stories should be remembered. Wait, wait, wait—" Nish returns to the purple cabinet—the middle part with the open shelves—and points at the old photos nestled here and there among the curiosities, put right back where I'd found them. "Those are the same pictures you showed me yesterday. With the notes on the back."

"Yep."

"Madeline Luck keeps them in this cabinet?"

"Yep."

"Oh, then, Fade, they must be very important to her to be kept in her cabinet."

We carefully pluck every photograph out of the cabinet and lay them out on the kitchen table, spread like playing cards face up. There are twenty-two. All photographs of people. Most are very old black-and-white portraits. A few time-faded Polaroids. None of them are framed, and most of them have names, plants, a year, and sometimes something else—like a food or a colour—written on the back. All written in the same careful, tidy handwriting.

Except one.

One photograph has very different handwriting on the back: jagged, deranged, deep.

The picture itself is a black-and-white snapshot of a young girl with dark eyes and long black hair, standing as stiff as the wooden toboggan propped upright next to her. She wears a peacoat and buckle shoes. She stands outside in what had to have been bitterly cold air and painful snow. The photo itself is furrowed with creases, its edges stained brown. It looks as if it's been carried around in a back pocket for a hundred years. Taken out in hard times. It wants to fall apart, so we handle it carefully.

On the back of the photo in that unhinged, jagged handwriting: *iZi pasi Wollo wuNDrs 187x.*

Nish mutters aloud precisely what I am thinking. "Yikes."

I lay this photo among the other overturned photos arranged on the table. This slashing, hideous scribble overshadows all the others with its madness.

It reminds me of another, more recent horror with the same chilling effect.

The door. Jagged, deranged, and deep.

"Dr. Chaudry, do you scare easy?"

CHAPTER TWENTY-TWO

Nish and I stare down the ugly door marring Aunt Madeline's library. The door seems to take jagged breaths with the movement of air in the house.

Nish shivers.

"I feel like I have to open it, but I also really don't want to open it," I say.

"That I understand. What is that smell?"

"I don't know."

"What is on the other side of this wall?"

"Aunt Madeline's bedroom."

"And this door doesn't lead into her bedroom?"

"No."

"Where does it lead, then?"

"It can't really lead anywhere," I say. "It either opens to nowhere. Or to hell."

"Who's being dramatic now?"

I smirk. Nish shivers again.

"Bad feeling?" I say.

"Bad feeling," he says.

"I'm going to open it."

"Okay."

The bent nail is the door's only handle. I hook my finger into it and pull slowly. The filthy planks open with a hollow groan, shedding splinters and rust.

It opens to nothing.

Nothing behind the door but a one-foot-deep gap in the plaster wall. Horizontal scars show where the bookshelves used to be, before they were torn off the wall. The left-side hinges holding the door up are nailed into the splintery ends of the busted shelves, right into the books. Some nails are hammered deeply; some stick out like cactus spikes.

From the bottom of the door comes cold air. I nudge the floorboards with my foot and they shift, so I pull up the loose floorboards and toss them aside, exposing the subfloor underneath. Or what's left of it.

Cold air hits us from a hole in the subfloor about the size of a manhole. Hacked right through the bottom of the house.

"It looks like that hole was made with an axe," Nish says. "And some serious rage."

I agree. I shine my phone's flashlight down the hole and see earth. Beetles and millipedes scuttle away from my light.

"Nish, this house is propped up on bricks, about a foot above the ground. A person could crawl down through this hole, under the house, and right out to the yard. Their elbows and everything else would be shredded to hell, but they'd be outside the house."

"A questionable escape hatch, then." He bends over to peer at the blackness. "And a hole goes two ways. And I apologize for how that sounds. I just mean if a person could crawl out this way, then a person could crawl in. Theoretically."

"Theoretically."

"I have to think it would be dangerous to have a hole this big in the floor even if theoretical persons were not inclined to crawl about the place. It would compromise the integrity of the house come winter. Cold air would come through it, and cold animals. The house would freeze inside out."

"Aunt Madeline is too smart to do this to her own house. Even if she needs a way to get out of her house fast, why would she hack a hole in the subfloor and hide it with an uninsulated, useless, hideous door?"

I reach down into the hole in the subfloor, avoiding the vicious splinters gnarling on all sides, and touch the ground below. I expect to feel cold solid ground. Instead, it feels wobbly. Hollow.

"Nish, I'm wrong," I say. "I don't think that's the ground at all right there. That feels like a board."

Nish holds my phone so I can reach both hands down into the hole. I try to find the edges of the board. My knuckle jabs on another dirty, bent nail.

It's another handle, maybe. Another door? A trap door?

Before my brain can stop me, I hook my finger into the bent nail. It's heavy and hurts to lift, but I have to do it. Loose soil scatters. I pry the board up a few centimetres. I force my fingers underneath one edge of it, get a grip, and really pull.

The board lifts up. With a grunt of effort, I shove the board off to the side, underneath the house.

Nish steadies the light for me. "What do you see?"

"Another hole."

"What in the name of Lewis Carroll is going on around here?"

Nish gives me back my phone so I can get a better look.

It's a hole in the earth. The dirt along the hole's edge feels crumbly and loose. It's a good-sized hole for two people to drop through. Or one, if you're me. Bits of soil break off the edges of the hole and fall in. They disappear, devoured by blackness.

That terrible smell curls up and claws our faces, then disperses, leaving behind the acrid sweetness of rotting wood and damp earth. This is what Corporal Quill had been looking for yesterday.

It's a cellar.

CHAPTER TWENTY-THREE

I slash my phone light over the hole in the earth, trying to catch a glimpse of something down there. All I see are cobwebs, drifting and hazy.

"The cop on Aunt Madeline's case came here looking for a cellar. Corporal Quill." I sit back from the hole and turn my phone light off. "She was acting weird about it too."

"Uh, Fade, I may be able to offer some insight as to why Corporal Quill was asking about a cellar."

"Oh yeah?"

"You won't like it."

"I bet I won't, but keep talking."

"One of the local stories passed down through generations is that Madeline Luck has . . . a magical portal. In her cellar."

"She has a what now?"

"They're just folk stories," Nish says. "Tall tales. Part of the myth. Some people claim she goes into the portal in her cellar and astral projects herself into people's homes at night, and—"

"And?"

"And she sits on their chest to suffocate them in their sleep."

"Oh for frig's sake."

"It's bizarre, Fade, but it's also not bizarre at all."

"Keep talking."

"It's a local variation on a very old, very common superstition that tries to explain sleep paralysis. That a witch or an old woman sits on your chest and makes it so you can't move."

"Oh, sure. Perfectly normal."

"It's not normal but quite universal. It's where the English word *nightmare* comes from, when the word was coined in the thirteenth century."

"So, let me get this straight," I say. "People around here believe Aunt Madeline teleports through a mystical, magical hole in her cellar, because she has nothing better to do, and then she suffocates them in their sleep. And they have the gall to call her the weird one."

"For a long time, the people in this area have blamed your aunt for the bad things that happen to them. Sometimes they're serious, but sometimes they're just saying what people say here."

"And what do people say here?"

"They say, 'That's the Old Witch done that.' They all say it. Even the young people. It's a unique idiom here. Even folks who don't have the old Colchester County accent say it that way."

"Oh, I have several idioms I can use to describe all of them really well."

"In some ways, their fear has worked in her favour," Nish says. "People are afraid of her, so they leave her alone. They have deeply ingrained beliefs about not provoking the wrath of the Old Witch, or else she'll curse them. They attribute enormous mystical powers to her. Otherwise, as a woman of limited means living alone, she would really have no power."

"I get how that might work."

"By the same token, though, they've cast her as the enemy," Nish says. "As evil. Some people blame her for every last bit of bad luck: a flat tire, a lost boot, a hole in a bucket. Some believe she's responsible for diseases, and even deaths."

"They scapegoat her for diseases and deaths?"

"And bad weather. The increase in recent years of hurricanes and extreme snowfall and extreme temperatures and floods in Nova Scotia. They attribute that increase to her."

"That's not good," I say.

"I have never heard them utter the words *climate change*, but they do not hesitate to say the words *Old Witch*. They openly state it, and none of them seem to question it. They say the Old Witch is getting madder and madder as she gets older. Mad as in angry at them, and mad as in insane."

"That's not good," I say again.

"They're already blaming this next storm on her. 'The Old Witch is going to punish the town with the wrath of Hurricane Lettie.' They think she's using the storm to bring the rock down. I think they're genuinely afraid."

"Do you think that cop Quill who came here actually believes that portal crap? Is that why she was looking for the cellar?"

"I sincerely hope not," Nish says. "When law enforcement joins in with that kind of conspiracy thinking, innocent people die."

That makes me think dark thoughts. "Do you think some Grand Tea townie is so deranged by conspiracy paranoia that they might want to hurt Aunt Madeline? To get revenge? Or to try to stop the storm?"

Nish doesn't answer me. Which is answer enough.

"I'm going down there," I say, feeling around the edges of the hole. "How deep do you think it is?"

Nish digs a handful of change from his pocket. He picks out a dime and drops it in the hole. We hear the gentle *thud* of it landing somewhere, way down there.

"I guess I'll to have to Indiana Jones it," I say.

"I'm the historian," Nish says. "I should be the one Indiana Jonesing it."

"Good point. I'm the computer scientist, so I guess I'll have to Tony Stark it."

Our chuckles fall into the hole. The hole echoes back a hollow *ha, ha, ha*.

"Does your aunt have a ladder?"

Good question. "Let's check the shed."

I know exactly where Aunt Madeline keeps the shed key: in a teeny wooden bucket in her kitchen cupboard, along with a few spare pennies.

The small shed at the edge of Aunt Madeline's back garden was always off limits to me. It feels brazen to march up to it with the key she kept out of my reach as a child and open it now.

The shed door is locked with a big padlock. Medieval looking. The keyhole is protected by a brass cover, to keep ice and snow out. It has an eight-point star and the words *Tumble Lock* engraved in the brass.

"This lock is more than an antique, you know," Nish says. "It's a treasure. In anyone else's possession, this lock would be at auction or in a museum and no longer functional. However, Madeline Luck clearly takes good care of everything she owns. Museums wouldn't exist if we all cared for our things the way she does."

"You'd be out of a job, then, Dr. Chaudry."

"I have other skills."

"Such as?"

"Such as . . ."

"Dig deep."

"PowerPoint presentations?"

"Too deep."

The padlock releases as easily as if it had been forged yesterday. The shed door creaks open by itself.

It takes the eyes time to adjust. The shed is windowless and packed to the rafters with typical shed things, but antique versions. Each item looks sturdy and well mended and hung precisely in its place. Gardening and woodworking tools. Old jars of paint with telltale drips: pansy purple, moonlight yellow, soft grey, pitch black.

A wooden ladder hangs on the wall. It's painted in plain beige, but it isn't plain at all. The whole thing is stippled and dotted all over with many different paint colours.

"Old ladders are fascinating pieces of history," Nish says. "Especially a ladder passed down through a family line. They're always covered in paint drops of different colours. All the colours of the walls and windows of a family's home through time. The wear and tear on the rungs from people stepping up and down, over and over, because they have pride in their home and work hard to keep it shipshape. It tells a story."

I can see what he means. I can also see, for the first time, the reason Aunt Madeline's shed was off limits to me as a kid. About a dozen reasons strapped to the back wall of the shed in neat rows: axes, saws, knives, and an old hunting rifle. The rifle is a compact little armful of steel, brass, and wood.

"I never thought about Aunt Madeline needing a rifle," I say. "Never saw her use it."

"Maybe it serves the same purpose as the spell in the jar and the sieve by the door," Nish says.

"Protection."

"The rifle, I understand, but what is that for?" Nish points to a rusty iron chain hanging just inside the door. The chain folds over itself and ends with a heavy metal shackle. The C-shaped shackle is hinged with an iron peg.

"No idea," I say. "Is it a dog chain? I don't recall ever hearing anything about Aunt Madeline owning dogs, though."

Maybe she should have a dog. Maybe I should get her one. Soot smudges my fingers when I grab the chain.

"It resembles a medieval dungeon shackle," Nish says.

"Like a leg iron?"

"Not exactly. Leg irons had to be cut off. This shackle has a lock and hinge, so it was designed to come off and go back on the leg."

"What the frig is it doing in my aunt's shed?"

"An important question," Nish says. "Everything in this shed is perfect. Clean and tidy and purposeful. But this chain is quite the opposite."

"You're right. It's cruddy and messed up. Looks like it's been left outside for countless Canadian winters and is about ready to fall apart. Unlike the lock on the outside of this shed, which has been exposed to countless Canadian winters and still works perfectly."

"My thoughts exactly," Nish says. "The lock on this chain would probably no longer work, it's so, as you say, cruddy and messed up. Even if you did have the skeleton key for it."

Skeleton key.

"Nish, I saw a skeleton key. Yesterday."

"Among your aunt's keys?"

"No. In a cruddy and messed-up suitcase intended for the bottom of the ocean."

CHAPTER TWENTY-FOUR

Nish rests the ladder against the kitchen wall, while I grab the suitcase from under Aunt Madeline's bed. In the back of my mind, I know all this can wait. I know I'm showing this suitcase to Nish to delay my drop into the dark hole underneath Aunt Madeline's house.

The suitcase is too filthy to put on the kitchen table, so kitchen floor it is. Nish kneels to the side at a respectful distance. My fingers shake as I pop the latches.

Outside, the wind picks up. It presses against the cracked stained glass windows and pulls at the roof. I turn the suitcase so Nish can see.

He peers at the blue jay feathers and the dandelion stem. "These items must mean something, but I . . . I don't know what."

"They're not witch things?"

"Is that a bedpan?"

"There's nothing in your fancy old books about ancient bedpan magic?"

"There is not."

As soon as I see the skeleton key again, I feel pretty confident it must belong to the lock on that awful chain in the shed. I hand the key to Nish.

"There's something else in there," Nish says.

"Where?"

"In the lining, there." He points to something the shape of a pen, maybe, resting at the bottom of the lid, behind the satin.

There's a tear in the lining. Too small for my hand to fit inside without tearing everything, so Nish offers to reach in and retrieve whatever it is.

Another key.

This one is much larger than the other. This one is black iron and heavy. The bow of the key is a circle with a cursive letter *L* inside. It's too big to be a house key or fit a regular lock. This key unlocks something really big.

"Good eye, Dr. Chaudry."

"Two mystery keys! Fade, this whole thing is so exciting!"

"There's also this." The horror of the bloodstained hospital gown unfolds itself when I hold it up. Nish's eyes flash from the blood to the two keys in his hand and back to the blood. The excitement drains from face. No dramatic gasp for this discovery. No breath at all.

"What happened here?" he says.

The wind seems to answer with an ear-splitting whistle forced up through the hole in the guest room floor. Dead leaves and debris whip out of the guest room on the wind.

"Looks like Hurricane Lettie is on her way," I say.

"Fade, maybe we should wait for the police." Nish backs away from me just a little. "You have bloodstained clothing and a chain with shackles and . . . something very bad happened here."

"I don't trust that cop or her weird obsession with Aunt Madeline's cellar," I say.

Nish watches in silence as I put everything back into the suitcase, close it with two clicks. Everything except the skeleton key, which I pocket.

Nish's furrowed brow tells me he is unsettled by this.

Doesn't matter. I shove the suitcase way back under Aunt Madeline's bed, grab the ladder, and drag it to the guest room, crushing the dead leaves under my boots. I'm doing this, with or without Nish's help.

He decides to help, joining me in the guest room. I'm secretly grateful as I realize it will take the two of us to lower the ladder down inside the cellar and open it in the hole without dropping it. It works, though. The old ladder stands on its own down there, on the cellar floor. In the dark.

"I'm going down," I say, more to convince myself than to inform Nish. I dangle my flashlight by its strap on my wrist. Nish keeps glancing back toward Aunt Madeline's room. Probably thinking about the bloodstained gown in the suitcase.

The icy-blue light from my dangling flashlight casts wild shadows down the hole.

"Hello?" I call down into the hole, into the cellar.

Frig knows why I did that. Or why I pause for an answer back.

I can't see much. Just cobwebs and darkness and nothing. I half hope Nish will say something brilliant to talk me out of going down there. But he doesn't. Silence seems to be an uncomfortable state for my excitable new associate, but he maintains it. He looks at me with doubt.

Maybe he doesn't trust me.

Maybe he's afraid of me.

To him, after all, I am the niece of the Witch of Willow Sound. He's not going to try talking me out of anything. Seems it's a double-edged sword being the niece of a witch. On one hand, he's not disagreeing with me about going down there. On the other hand, he's not disagreeing with me going down there.

My boots feel around mid-air until they tap against the ladder. I stand on it. It's steady. One step at a time, I go down. In the hole, it's freezing cold. Lowering into it feels like sinking into a pool of ice water.

Once my feet are firmly placed on the cellar floor, I look up. Nish closes an eye against the glare of my flashlight.

"Are you all right?"

"So far, so good." My words echo and slither around me.

I exhale to steady my nerves. My breath is an icy cloud. I try to orient myself. Is this place narrow and deep, like a pit, or wide like a room?

I cast my light left and right to find the walls. It's wide like a room. Almost as wide as the kitchen, therefore almost as wide as the house itself.

"What do you see?" Nish asks.

"I see zero magical portals," I say. "What a shock. There's not much down here. A pinewood shelf that's mostly empty. Just a few jars on it."

"Are they spell jars?"

Six jars. The jar labels are handwritten and faded and caked with dust. A few random items rest on the shelves here and there. Ordinary things. A penny. A matchbox. A cracked glass thermometer with no mercury in it. Cobwebs sweep across my face like sea jelly tendrils. I shudder and bat them aside to take a closer look at the jars.

"No spells," I say. "Just normal food jars. Green tomato chow chow. Blueberry jam. Lavender jelly. That kind of thing. Way past their expiry dates."

"I wonder why she abandoned the cellar."

"If I had to guess, the cellar was flooding. It's soggy underfoot and smells of mould. Probably black mould in corners I can't see with this cheap light. Probably not safe for people or food down here."

"That's too bad."

"These jar labels have the same neat handwriting that's on the backs of the pictures. It must be Aunt Madeline's handwriting."

"Do you see any labels or anything with that other, messed-up handwriting on them?" Nish asks.

Good question. I glance my light across the labels of every jar I can see, scanning quickly for a stand-out, ugly exception.

"None." My shoulders drop in relief.

Over my head, the plank ceiling sags and leaks dirty water. Doesn't look sound. The cobwebs jerk and drift, disturbed by the nervous vibration in my breath.

"The ceiling is shot," I say. "I think it's only held up by a wish."

Behind me stands what must have been the original cellar door. Narrow and short. The old door's edges smothered in plant roots like the snarled legs of giant spiders.

Three hard yanks on the old cellar door and it falls off its hinges, and I drop it at my feet. Behind the door stands a solid wall of hard-packed earth. If there were stairs at one time, leading from the cellar up to the yard, the whole stairwell has been backfilled and blocked off completely a long time ago. Like heavy earth packed into a grave.

"Found the old cellar door," I say. "But it's definitely not useful as a door anymore. She blocked it off with earth, maybe to keep the cellar from fully flooding."

"So, this rather frantically shovelled hole from the guest room floor into the cellar makes some sense, then," Nish says. "If one were desperate to access the cellar, but they could not use the original cellar door. A faint semblance of logic to the madness."

"If my sense of direction is right," I say, "I think Aunt Madeline blocked off the other end of this old cellar door by planting brambles over it. Back left-hand corner of the house, in her back garden. No one would know a cellar door was under that mass of tangled thorns."

"Even though it's reasonable to assume Madeline Luck chose to block the cellar off due to flooding," Nish says, "the fact she planted a bramble of razor-sharp thorns makes me wonder if she chose to block the cellar off due to the rumours about her cellar portal believed by people in the town. To protect herself."

"I was thinking the same thing," I say.

"Is there anything else down there?"

There is one thing. Resting in shadows against the shelf.

"A toboggan." I knock on it. Wood. The chain brake clanks.

"That's an unusual item to keep in a root cellar."

I agree. I should be satisfied with the cellar and hightailing it out of here, but something nips at the edges of my brain. I sweep my light back over the jars.

"Still," I say. "It doesn't explain why she hammered that ugly door up there in her library wall, of all places. Why did she have to shovel her way back down to an abandoned cellar through her guest room floor? Was she trapped inside her house and afraid? And why did she have to do it all with such . . . violence?"

Ready to leave, I shine my light to find the ladder. There is something behind the ladder.

A nightmarish pile of charred bones in the shape of a human being.

CHAPTER TWENTY-FIVE

Aunt Madeline's house is infested with police and medical examiners. Corporal Quill barks orders and her people listen. Outside the windows, yellow Do Not Cross tape is strung around the house like a vibrating spiderweb being strummed by the wind. Inside the house, blue latex gloves pass the first of the blackened bones up through the hole in the guest room floor.

Chills rattle me as I watch the bones come up. Passed from gloved hand to gloved hand and placed in a paper bag. Little bones. Fingers and toes, maybe. That scorched death smell clings to the air. Clings to my skin.

Nish stands against the wall. An outsider not included in the commotion. Hands folded in front of him as if he's at a funeral.

He is.

Focus, Fade.

A human skull rises from the hole in the floor. A singed snarl of white hair clings off the back of the skull. Not the whole skeleton. Just the head. The jawbone gapes, stuck in a scream.

Aunt Madeline has long white hair she wears in a braid. Every bone in my body aches, like it's my bones that are burning.

I lurch out of the guest room and into the kitchen, hoping to get out of the house before Quill can corner me. But she's too quick. She darts in front of me, blocking my path.

"Can I get you anything, Miss Luck?" Quill asks. "Some water? A blanket?"

"No."

"I need to ask you a few questions."

"Yes."

"We will need some way to identify the remains. We need a sample of your aunt's DNA, from a hairbrush maybe. Something we can use to compare your aunt's DNA to the DNA of the remains. Do you know where your aunt kept her hairbrush or toothbrush?"

"Yes." Glad to have a reason to step away from Quill, I walk to Aunt Madeline's bedroom. Everyone in the place backs away from me as I walk by them, as if they're scared of me. Good. I duck into Aunt Madeline's bedroom.

It's easier to breathe in here. That burnt smell is fainter. Aunt Madeline's grooming kit is tucked exactly where it should be, in her top dresser drawer. The brown case is soft leather. Old but not brittle or cracked, giving off a scent that's earthy and sharp. The smell reminds me of the early morning, because Aunt Madeline gets up so early. Always in the dark. Always up before the sun.

One morning, I happened to see Aunt Madeline get up. I was still burrowed under blankets in the guest room bed, next to my mother who was still asleep. Through the quiet, Aunt Madeline's dresser drawer scraped open and shut. She materialized from the shadows. She looked like a ghost. Her long white nightgown and her long white hair shimmered around her as she walked, like a soft veil. She didn't notice me tiptoe out of bed to peek around the door frame.

Still in her nightgown, still in bare feet, Aunt Madeline didn't make a sound as she unlatched the kitchen door and took this leather grooming kit outside. She sat in the back garden and brushed her hair. Patient strokes. No hurry. The back of her brush was silver and reflected the sunrise in flashes as she brushed. Ribbons unfurled from the leather kit like a slither of snakes asleep at her feet. Her fingers were nimble as she wove her hair into the long tight braid that would stay tidy all day while she worked.

My memory of Aunt Madeline's brush pulled through her hair in the sunrise is replaced by the memory of the mangled fright of hair handed up by blue latex gloves through the busted hole in the floor.

Mangled. Like the hair of the old woman in the corner. In my nightmare. The deranged mess of hair snarled with the moonlight. The cries.

I shake my head as if I can shake the nightmare from my own brain that way. Quill is in the room with me now, watching me with iron nails for eyes. I don't know when she got there.

"Her grooming kit." I hand it over.

Quill opens the kit with gloved hands. Somehow, I know this kit was given to Aunt Madeline by her parents when she was little. The silver grooming pieces inside are still held in place by their original green ribbons. The silver of every item inside still shines.

"Don't consider it a quasi-known," I say to Quill. "I'll go on record. It's definitely hers."

"Quasi-known," Quill says. "That's a pretty obscure law enforcement term for a civilian to use."

I don't answer. Quill stares at me for a long moment.

The wind picks up, and rain pelts the little bedroom window. Raindrops run down the bedroom wall, down the mural. This storm is going to be hard on this house.

"Corporal Quill!" A voice from the kitchen shouts over the clatter of the people and the rain. A voice intended to be serious, but it's tinged with a hint of glee that I immediately hate.

"Corporal Quill, you need to see this!"

"See what?" Quill asks.

"We found something else down there, with the body."

CHAPTER TWENTY-SIX

The second I see Nish's face, I can tell he already knows what the police have found. He stands in the kitchen, bursting with unspoken information. The guy really needs to work on his poker face.

A Mountie with his beard stuffed inside a gauzy beard net brings Quill an evidence bag. "We found this," he says, "inside the bones."

Inside the bones.

The bearded Mountie lifts a teacup out of the evidence bag for Quill to see.

Quill pulls on new latex gloves before taking the teacup. She looks in it. "What are those two things in it?"

"The yellow thing is a crocus flower," the bearded Mountie explains to Quill. "It's hard to tell because it's dried up. It has the bulb and the roots still attached. And the brown thing is a desiccated wood frog."

Someone in the group speaks up. "My mom's neighbour once said the Old Witch can turn people into frogs." Other people nod.

"My uncle said the Old Witch can turn herself into a frog," someone else chimes in.

"I heard it's a rabbit."

"She can turn into any land animal."

"Frogs are water animals."

"What about toads?"

"What's the difference?"

Holy frig. Are these people for real? I glare over all their heads right at Quill. Her crack team is sounding pretty cracked right now.

"Enough!" Quill barks the word, silencing them all. "How do we know this frog is, specifically, a wood frog?"

The bearded Mountie slowly points at Nish. Nish responds to the sudden attention by taking a slow step back, as if he wants to sink inside the wall. Head down, eyes up. He doesn't seem to trust these people either.

"That temporary foreign worker guy that lives in the archives," someone pipes up.

"And talks to everybody's grandmothers."

Nish purses his lips tight.

Corporal Quill turns her steely eyes on Nish. "Dr. Chaudry," Quill says to Nish. "You're the historian from overseas who knows a whole lot about witches."

"I specialize in folk stories—"

"About witches," Quill says.

"Yes, I do."

"You go around asking people lots of questions." Quill tilts her head. "About witches."

"Yes, I do."

"You know exactly whose house this is, then. Don't you, Dr. Chaudry?"

"Yes, I do."

Quill saunters over to Nish, like a sheriff in a cowboy movie. Somehow, she has enough swagger to pull it off. "Tell me, Dr. Chaudry, do you know why there would be a crocus and a dead frog in a teacup set down next to human remains? Is there some old . . . tradition, maybe? Some old superstitious belief you can tell me about?"

Quill is smart. She knows what Nish might know about whatever the frig is going on, and she wants it.

Everyone in the room waits for Nish to answer. He takes a long breath before he speaks. "No, I'm sorry. Honestly, Corporal Quill, those three items do not belong together in any folk tradition I know. And I know many."

Quill squints at Nish, deciding if she believes him or not.

"If it will help, I can do some more research," Nish says.

"Yes," Quill says. "You will do that, Dr. Chaudry. You will tell me everything you find. And you will report your findings to me directly." She shoves her card into his personal space and holds it there until he takes it. "Thank you for your cooperation in this investigation, Dr. Chaudry," she says, hitting him with her most official tone.

Quill turns to me and holds the teacup in my face. "Does this teacup look familiar to you, Miss Luck?"

"Looks like one of Aunt Madeline's," I say.

"Do the contents of the teacup mean anything to you?" Quill asks.

The macabre contents of the teacup tip back and forth. A dried-up wood frog with eyes long gone gapes up at me.

Everyone in this room is probably thinking *witch* except me.

I'm thinking, *Idiots*.

"A dead frog means a frog died," I say. "End of frog, end of story."

The teacup, the frog, and the crocus are yanked away from my face and passed back to the bearded Mountie. They'll be bagged and analyzed and turned into ridiculous bedtime stories to scare children into behaving lest the Old Witch get them. Idiots.

A zipped-up body bag is passed from the guest room and carried out the front door. That must be the rest of the human remains. Placed inside the bag. Except for those stray finger and toe bones. And the head.

Two men huddle together at Aunt Madeline's purple cabinet, poking through the contents, like kids in a candy store working up the nerve to steal a couple bags of chips.

I lean my head down between theirs and look at the cabinet with them. "What do you think you're doing?"

I clamp my big hands on their shoulders. They shrivel right out of my grip.

Quill steps in before I do anything worse to them. "Miss Luck, you need to listen—"

"No, you listen," I say. "You're all acting like a mob of drooling groupie weirdos freaking out because you believe these asinine stories that Madeline Luck is a witch. Well, grow up and get the hell over it. Because she's not a witch. There is no such thing, and I can't believe I have to say that out loud to a bunch of grown adults with jobs that require solemn oaths and criminal background checks."

The storm shakes the house, as if the wind has my back. A sweet coincidence that seems to make them even more scared of me.

Good.

I get the irony of the moment. I understand the only reason I'm allowed to get away with a rant at a room full of cops is because they all believe my aunt is the Old Witch.

"We'll go through whatever we need to go through, Miss Luck," Quill says calmly. "But only if and when we need to." Quill eyes her people accusingly. I admit, I appreciate the gesture. "Under normal circumstances, we would remain here, on site, day and night until I say we're done. But the storm has been upgraded to a hurricane. They're predicting Hurricane Lettie will make landfall along here as a category four. Or worse. So, it's not safe for anyone to stay here."

"Good," I say. "There's the door."

"Before I leave here, Miss Luck, I'm going to get a DNA sample from you. Even if I have to stand here all through the hurricane to get it."

I have to hand it to Quill for not backing down from a seething half giant. Anyone else would have.

Quill waves a forensics tech over and directs him to me. The tech hesitates. He doesn't want to come near me, but he reluctantly steps into my shadow. His little spit kit vibrates in his shaky hands.

"And Miss Luck," Quill adds, "don't leave town."

"I'm not going anywhere," I say. "I'm staying here tonight. In my aunt's house."

"No, you're not," Quill says. "Lean down and open your mouth, please."

The dry swab probes inside my cheeks. I see Nish out of the corner of my eye. He's acting strange. Lurking behind everyone as they pack up. Sneaking. No one else seems to notice him drift backwards into the dark quiet of Aunt Madeline's bedroom with the ease of a ghost.

I don't let on that I've seen anything.

"This is my crime scene, Miss Luck," Quill says. "In a few minutes, I will escort you across my police line, and you are not coming back in across my line until I say so. You can close your mouth."

I close my mouth and stand tall again.

"It's unfortunate, but the storm is going to hit this old house hard," Quill says. "You won't want to be here when it does."

Nish eases out of Aunt Madeline's bedroom. His jacket rests over his arm, definitely hiding something. He must have taken something from her bedroom, and he's trying to sneak it out.

The suitcase.

Surrounded by cops and cornered by Quill, I can't do anything. Quill would be all over the suitcase and I'll never see it again. Or figure out what it means. Or find out why it was stuck on a cliff next to the ocean.

If that history nerd turns the suitcase over to the police, I will frag him.

Nish's eyes glance my way. He jolts when our eyes meet, and he snaps his eyes away from mine. Quill catches my glare. Follows it. She clocks Nish but questions me.

"Miss Luck, why did you call a folklore historian out here?" Quill says. "What did you want him for, exactly?"

"Dr. Chaudry brought me a photo of Aunt Madeline from the archives," I say. "There's no pictures of her here, so I figured there might be some there. There wasn't, but he kept looking till he found one. The only photograph of Aunt Madeline I've ever seen."

Quill follows me to the kitchen table, where all the photographs from the purple cabinet are laid out. It's obvious people have touched them. Moved them around and shoved them aside. Nish's manila file isn't there anymore. He must have grabbed it too. The photocopy of the 2003 newspaper article with the picture of Aunt Madeline is still there on the table.

Quill picks it up. "May I have this?"

"It's for you. To use. To find her. Hopefully, you find her before this storm hits."

Quill raises her eyebrows at me with a question she doesn't ask out loud.

If there is any chance that the burned bones in the basement do not belong to Aunt Madeline, if there is even a microscopic chance that Aunt Madeline is still alive, then I'm going to cling to that chance with every cell in my body.

"Right." Quill holds onto the article. "I'll use this to keep looking, as long as you get yourself checked in to the Grand Tea motel before the hurricane hits."

"Sure thing," I say.

I look over the swarm of people. Nish is gone.

"Okay, folks, I want everyone out of here in ten," Quill says. "Miss Luck, you have ten minutes to grab your own personal effects, then you and I are going to walk out of here together. Ten."

I cram all my tech into duffle bags. Quill watches every item I pack, like a raven on a rooftop. When I reach for Aunt Madeline's teapot on the kitchen table, Quill swoops in.

"Does that belong to you?" Quill asks.

"No."

"Leave it here, then."

"It's going to get destroyed by the storm."

"That is unfortunate, and it is unavoidable," Quill says. "But this is no longer your aunt's house. This is my crime scene now. You will leave it."

What Quill says makes sense. But I don't want to leave the teapot here to be destroyed.

I glare down at Quill, bristling with my most brutal black bear energy. But she doesn't back down. My head brushes against the dried herbs hanging from the ceiling as I crack my neck and pop the bones in my fingers, reminding her my hands are bigger than her skull. But she stares up at me. Unmoved. Hard and cold as stone. I'm impressed. Unless I am willing to smash into stone, I just won't win this one.

Wind shakes the kitchen walls hard enough to hide my impatient growl as I resign the teapot back to its place in the dust. I take a moment to look around the inside of Aunt Madeline's little house. Windows rattle. Rain pounds. Darkness falls. I wish Aunt Madeline was here. To give me permission to stay. To let me help protect the house.

I step outside the house and turn back to face Quill. "My aunt Madeline is not a witch." My hair whips like snakes in the wind. "And being labelled a witch doesn't give anybody the right to rummage through her personal things."

Quill holds the door. "Being labelled a witch doesn't give Madeline Luck the right to set someone on fire and hide their body in her basement."

The wind whips Quill and snatches the front door from her hand. It slams shut.

CHAPTER TWENTY-SEVEN

True to her word, Corporal Quill rides my bumper from Willow Sound all the way back to town. I trudge into the Grand Tea motel with a fake wave back at her. Let her think this is where I'll be staying during the storm.

"I got no rooms for you, I told you," the old hotel clerk says from behind his counter. He grumbles at the back of my head as Quill's car drives away.

Once her taillights are out of sight, I swivel my unsmiling mug toward the old clerk and lean in. "Boo."

He scrambles back into his office, slams the door, and locks the lock.

Bip-bip. A car horn taps outside.

Through the relentless grey rain, a set of headlights pulls in. Hard to see inside the windows, through the rain, but I can tell it's not a cop car. The driver's side door opens, and Nish pops out. He holds that old suitcase up like a trophy and waves at me. Not even driving rain can dim that man's sunny grin.

⌁

Rain doesn't fall like normal rain in Grand Tea. There's no *pitter-patter* rain shower from the clouds overhead, hitting the ground. Instead, the rain spills in grimy, chaotic splatters. It's more like runoff from a roof than rain hitting Nish and me as we walk to Odes, the only diner in Grand Tea.

"It doesn't rain from the sky here," Nish says. "It can't."

"Because there's no sky here?" I say.

"Exactly. The rain falls from the sky on top of the Grand Tea rock, and then the rain runs off the rock into town. It gets pretty messy."

I hold out my palm. "I've never seen black rain before."

"It's rain mixed with Cenozoic Era rock dust," Nish says. "Occasionally, the rain catches remnants of whatever is living on top of the rock before it runs off. Earthworms. Empty crow eggs. Wild thorns. Sometimes flowers. Dog rose and harebells grow up there, they say. The evening I arrived, it rained buttercups."

The Grand Tea rock looms over us, over the town, with the cold indifference of a permanent eclipse.

"How do people live here, day in and day out, under the constant threat of annihilation?" I swipe gritty rain from my forehead. "I would go crazy."

"The Grand Tea rock has not moved in three hundred million years." Nish looks up at it. "It won't move in our lifetime."

"You seem pretty sure."

"Mountains are unmoved by the piddly existence of humans."

"Unless there's coal inside it."

"Quite right."

"So, the tourists come here to stand under a rock that won't move?" I ask.

"Many tourists come here to stand in a liminal space," he says. "An eerie, forlorn place that gives off an unnerving feeling. Halfway between being alive and being dead. Some people compare it to the Old World folk tales of the otherworld or underworld, a place where the dead are among us. Some say it's a secret portal to Stonehenge. Some believe there's pirate treasure buried inside the rock. Of course, if there is treasure inside it, only the people who live in Grand Tea can claim it."

"Well, that last belief is a very Nova Scotian one," I say. "But then there's all the witch decorations . . ."

Nish cringes.

"I have a really bad feeling about the reason behind the witch decorations."

"You should," Nish says.

"Miss Luck, please accept my sincerest condolences!" The rain must have muffled the sound of Davish coming.

"Well, speak of the mayor and he doth appear," I grumble to Nish. He sidles right into our path. I frown down at him.

"Mayor Davish," Nish says.

"Mr. Chowder."

"Chaudry," Nish politely corrects him.

"Have you been telling Madeline Luck's niece about the wonderful idea we have?" Davish asks Nish.

I look at Nish. *We?*

Nish shrugs.

"We the town of Grand Tea, of course," Davish says. "We wish to honour Madeline Luck. Honour her for all time, with a respectful and tasteful and educational shrine."

"A shrine?" Nish tilts his head, as if that's new to him.

"Well, a museum dedicated to her life and her legend." Davish stares into the middle distance, putting on a half-decent show. "It would be at no cost to the Luck family, of course. The town will raise the funds with government grants, and we can hire Mr. Chowder to create the exhibits."

Enough.

"All right, Dillweed H. Deathwish or whatever your name is?" I glare at him. "How much?"

"How much what?" Davish asks.

I yank a cardboard witch head off the nearest boutique door and shove it in Davish's face. "How much money does this town figure it can make from occult tourism? Salem, Massachusetts, hauls in, what, hundreds of millions of dollars a year? You want witch-themed stores and witch-themed souvenirs. So, how many millions do you figure it would bring in for Grand Tea to exploit the legend of a real-life witch?"

"Well . . ." Davish says.

"Frig her life and her legend. This is all about money, isn't it?" I say.

"What's wrong with money?" Davish asks. "Who do you think you are? Standing in the way of this town's right to make a living."

"A living or a killing?"

"We can make Madeline Luck famous," he says.

"Nope."

"The legends about the witch belong to the townspeople, anyway."

"Nope."

"This town has a right to make a killing if it wants to," Davish says. "You can, too, if you'd just think about it."

"Some people don't want to be rich or famous," I say. "Some people just want to be left the hell alone."

I'm done with this idiot. Done with this conversation. So I walk away.

Nish jogs to catch up with me. Davish doesn't bother.

CHAPTER TWENTY-EIGHT

Odes Diner is open but empty, which is a relief. Nish and I shake as much black rain off our clothes as we can and step inside. The diner looks like it was decorated the same day melamine was invented and never updated. A muted TV hangs on the wall, tuned to a weather channel. Satellite images of Hurricane Lettie glow on the screen. The diner smells of burnt grilled cheese and coffee that's been sitting too long, and I don't mind it a bit.

We grab a window booth and order some of that coffee. The waitress slides two cups of the dark stuff on our table and swears she'll be right back. Nish floods his mug with so much sugar my teeth hurt just watching him.

"Thanks for grabbing the suitcase for me, Nish," I say. "For a minute there, I thought you were ratting me out."

"Understandable thought, but no." Nish stirs his coffee. "It didn't take me long to figure out Madeline Luck has no friends on that police force. Most of those people were only there to gawk."

"I'm glad you saw that too."

"Their behaviour was genuinely disturbing," he says. "So, I decided to Indiana Jones it."

He almost gets a laugh out of me, in spite of everything. We flap our plastic menus and squint at them in the dim light.

"Oh no!" Nish slaps his menu down on the table and slaps his hands on his cheeks. "I forgot about the menu here. Fade, I'm so sorry." Nish is cringing so hard I can see all his teeth. He shrinks down a little as I take a closer look at the menu.

"Witch Hair Pasta," I read aloud from the menu. "Hocus Pocus Potatoes."

Nish grimaces.

"The Old Witch's Tea. Not currently in stock."

"Now, that would be Madeline Luck's wild tea." Nish sits back up. "A tourist favourite."

"You ever try it?"

"Once."

"And?"

Nish gasps dramatically. Right on time. I have to chuckle at him.

"Her tea is the most startling vivid blue!" he says. "I have never seen blue tea before. That's the first thing that amazes people. Then the tea itself. Nothing else like it. It smells of mayflowers and oranges, but it tastes of berries and red clover and wildflower honey and something else I can't figure out. Something buttery soft. People have tried to recreate it, but no one can."

No one will. I know that tea very well.

"I do recommend the all-you-can-eat pancakes," Nish says. "They're theme-free."

My stomach growls at the idea. I am really hungry. And there's no such thing as a bad pancake.

"My treat, Fade," he says. "Please. You need to eat. It's the least I can do. And, perhaps, you can have a vegetable with it. Or a piece of fruit. Something that had leaves at one time. Just to keep you alive."

"Infinite pancakes might hold me over for a minute," I say.

We set our menus aside. Nish folds his hands on the table and leans in. "Fade, everything is so overwhelming, I can't begin to imagine what you are going through. Anyone else would be curled up in a ball and weeping uncontrollably by now. But you are a rock. How do you keep going? How are you, really?"

I take Nish's kind and well-meaning words and put them in a little black box in my brain and close the box and throw gasoline on it and set it on fire. That's how I keep going.

"I'm good." I shrug. "When this storm is over, I'll get back to looking for Aunt Madeline and bring her home."

Nish nods and returns his attention to his coffee. I wilfully ignore any sadness he might be hiding in this gesture.

The waitress wends her way to us, weaving through the maze of empty tables, shoving chairs into place along the way. Her sneakers squish out mud on the carpet, like she just came in from outside, and she smells of butterscotch vape.

"All set to order?" she says, pen ready.

"All-you-can-eat pancakes, please," Nish says.

"Same," I say.

The waitress jots in her order pad. "You guys hear about the Old Witch?"

What.

"I bet you heard about it." She points at Nish.

What.

Nish wobbles like a startled baby bird.

"The Old Witch is dead!" the waitress tells us. "Finally. She burned up in her own basement."

I press my lips together.

"I know, right? When my dad was a kid, twelve or whatever, this deer was getting into his parents' garden at night, eating their trees. Not eating entire trees, but the parts of trees deer eat. Leaves. Whatever. Anyway, one night, my dad stayed up late, waiting for the deer. When it showed up, he shot his BB gun at it. He didn't kill the deer, but he hit it in the back right leg and it ran off. Next day, guess what? The Old Witch walks into town. And she's limping. On her right leg."

The waitress pauses for awe, but she's lucky not to get a punch in the teeth.

"That's the Old Witch done that," she says. "And that deer never bothered my dad's family's trees ever again."

Nish stares at the waitress like a codfish.

"You can write that one in your book if you want," she tells Nish. "True story."

This woman obviously doesn't know she's blabbing her story to the Old Witch's niece. I stare into my coffee and bite my lip to keep from saying a word. Waiting for her to walk away. Why is she still here? Why is she still talking?

"Everybody's wondering if you killed the Old Witch," she says to Nish.

Nish sputters his coffee.

"I overheard from lots of people, in the diner and everywhere, that you're not really here to write a history book for the government or whatever," she says. "Nobody believed that lame cover story anyway. They say the mayor brought you here on a top-secret mission. They say you're not really a historian but a witch killer from the Old World—from England or wherever you're from—and you came here to kill the Old Witch."

Nish opens his mouth but says nothing.

"My grandmother told him stories about the witch bottles," the waitress says to me. "They used to use these witch bottle things to break the Old Witch's spells. They'd carry it with them, or hang it by their front door to keep the Old Witch out. Good protection idea for a witch killer, right? Some people around here still use them. Local tradition. But not the restaurant, because health and safety or whatever."

Words just keep coming right out of her mouth.

"Witch bottles," she says in a hushed tone, "are pee in a bottle of nails."

Wow. I can't imagine why Aunt Madeline would avoid someone who would put urine in a bottle of nails and carry it around with them.

"Hey, there's my grandmother going by now." The waitress jabs her pen at the window. An old woman stomps by in gum rubber boots two sizes too big, carrying a red gas can. The way the plastic can bonks against her thigh with every step, it must be empty. Her stiff olive-green raincoat flaps open, not protecting her much.

"Anyway, a witch bottle is like—oh, shoot, what did you call it again?" The waitress snaps her fingers at Nish until we turn our attention back to her again.

Nish shakes his head at the waitress.

"No, really," she says. "You called it something. What did you call it?"

"Countermagic," Nish says in a muted, reluctant voice.

"Countermagic!" she says, quite pleased with the whole thing. "So. I've got to ask. Did you do it?"

Nish is frozen.

"Did you kill the Old Witch?" She leans on the table, eyes glittering. "I won't tell the cops, although they won't care. The mayor would never let them arrest you for it. And if you did kill her, I bet the town would give you a parade." She nudges Nish's shoulder with her elbow and clicks her tongue in her cheek.

I can't believe any of this conversation is real.

Once the waitress finally leaves us alone, Nish and I sit in silence.

"Fade, I am so sorry about that." Nish presses his hands to his forehead. "What even was that vile nonsense?"

"It was . . . not your fault." I down my whole coffee in one scorching swallow. "If you lean into the witch killer thing, maybe you can get your pancakes for free."

It's a joke, but neither of us can manage a laugh.

Cold rain spits Cenezoic rock dust down the dirty window.

Weakened by six stacks of pancakes, Nish and I waddle from Odes Diner to the tourist parking lot.

"Why are you here?" I ask Nish. It's an honest question.

"Research." He says the word as if even he doesn't believe it anymore.

"Do you like it here?"

Nish's face tries to lift itself into his default sunny smile, but it falls away. "The people of Grand Tea don't like me, Fade. You saw that back at your aunt's. Apart from this new witch killer conspiracy theory, they do not want me here. They don't trust me. They allow me to stay in my tacked-on shelter as long as I work hard and don't complain, but they take every chance they get to make it abundantly clear I am hired help and nothing more."

Nish and I step out from under the rock, and at the same time, we look up at the sky. It's still there. The rain from the sky feels cold and silky and real.

"Do you feel safe here, Nish? Do they ever threaten you?"

"No, no," Nish says. "It's fine."

"Because if those townies lay a finger on you, I will rip their heads off."

He laughs at the thought, his hands up. "No, no. But thank you for your kind offer of violence."

"You're welcome."

"Do you have any family, Fade? Besides your aunt Madeline?"

"My mother. She's supposedly on her way. But we don't get along."

"I'm sorry about that," he says.

"Do you have family here?"

"No. My family is an ocean away. But they wish it was much further."

Oh.

"I don't belong anywhere," he says in a whisper I barely hear.

My heart hurts. Nish barely looks like himself. The spring-loaded, excitable man has gone way inside himself. I know what that feels like. Never knew what it looked like—skin and bones with nobody inside.

I'm not a touchy-feely person, but I put my hand on Nish's shoulder. Just to spark a bit of movement from him, to make sure he's still in there. Maybe just to remind him he's not alone. "I'm sorry, buddy."

"I'm sorry too."

"And my promise still stands," I say. "Anyone that hurts you: I will rip them apart with my bare hands and biff their severed heads right up on top of that frigging rock. Right up there on top of that old-ass Cenezoic teacup."

Nish chuckles and wipes the rain from his eyes. It's nice to see him smile again.

"I'm glad we met," he says.

"I'm glad too," I say, and I mean it.

BOOK SIX

Ghost

CHAPTER TWENTY-NINE

Alone, I drive down the highway until it starts to get dark. I pull into the parking lot of a five-storey chain hotel. Upscale and clean looking inside. Well-lit. I bet scented candles give a delicate air. Jasmine or green tea. Comfortable-looking leather armchairs and real plants in the lobby. I bet the beds are crisp, white, and king-size. I bet no one in that hotel would look twice at my last name or ask if I have relatives that fly around on brooms.

Too bad I can't afford it.

It's fine. The parking lot is nice enough. Nobody will bother me out here. I park close enough to access hotel wifi, in a quiet corner of the lot without too much light. I can use the lobby bathroom if I have to, and if the night clerk falls asleep later, I can sneak into the gym for a shower.

I recline my car seat and get as comfortable as I can. Can't really stretch out when I sleep in my car. I can stretch out much better in a graveyard, but I don't know the graveyards out here that well, and the rain is relentless.

Time to call my mother. Tell her what's happening. Before someone else does. I thumb through my contacts and tap my mother's name.

"Any news?" she says, skipping all warm-and-fuzzy formalities and getting right to business.

"Yeah. Uh. There is something. Uh—" I didn't think it would be so hard to find the words to tell her.

"Focus, Phaedra," my mother says sharply. "What are you trying to say?"

"I found human bones in Aunt Madeline's cellar."

"That's ridiculous."

"I didn't even know she had a cellar—"

"Of course you knew, Phaedra. You fell down into it when you were three."

What?

"You tumbled right in that silly bulkhead door, right down the cellar stairs. You hit your head pretty hard."

"I don't remember that."

"Well, good. I didn't want you to remember it, because knowing you, you would just head right back out there and fall into it again."

I have no memory of any cellar or any fall.

"What do you mean by human bones?" she says. "Why did you say it like that?"

"Well, I guess because they don't know whose bones they are yet—"

"Just bones? Not a—a whole—person or—"

"Just bones," I say. "Burned bones."

"Burned."

"Yeah."

Through the phone, I hear snatches of nearby conversations and a voice announcing a change of gate. She must be at the airport. "Ridiculous," she says. "How did a human being catch fire in

Madeline's cellar without burning the whole house down? Everything in the place is made of wood. It doesn't make a lick of sense."

"I'm sorry, Ma."

"No, don't be sorry, just—" *Wham!* My mother must've slammed something. A door, maybe. "She sent me a birthday card. Tell those idiotic police that bones don't send people birthday cards!"

Any other day, I would snap at my mother for snapping at me like that, but I hear the scratch of fear in her voice. I know how she feels. Her heart feels frozen. The back of her throat aches. Her stomach is a cold dark pit. Like a cellar. I feel it too.

"Are they even looking for Madeline? Bones are one thing, but they need to go out and find my sister. You need to find her, Phaedra, all right? I'm counting on you to handle this."

"I know, Ma, I will. Once this Hurricane Lettie passes through, I'll go back to the house and wherever else I have to go, and I'll find her."

"Good. Fine. Good. Don't trust the people in that awful town, Phaedra. They never liked Madeline. They never understood her. Nobody really does, but they're—"

"They're the worst. Yeah. I figured that out real fast."

"Good." Her voice trails off. "Good."

"I'm staying the night in Carmel."

My mother is quiet. I don't know if she heard me.

"I'll call you tomorrow," I say.

"Call tomorrow," she echoes absently.

I recline my car seat all the way down. Stare at the windshield. Listen to the wind howl.

My mother's full name is Doreen Leta Luck. She is younger than her sister by sixteen years. The age gap meant they didn't grow up together or really know each other as kids. By the time Doreen was born, Madeline was hardly ever home. Madeline moved out of the family home at twenty-one, when Doreen was only five.

They were sisters who were strangers, really. They rarely spoke. Before she moved out, Madeline used to lock herself in her bedroom all day and night. She never joined the family, not even for meals. On the rare occasion when little Doreen caught a glimpse of her older sister, Madeline always seemed busy or distracted. Her face in a book or her mind in another place. No time for her little sister.

More than once, Doreen overheard her parents whisper about Madeline. How she was intelligent and stubborn and disobedient and wild. Madeline used to climb out her bedroom window, up onto the roof of the house. Sometimes she would climb to the tops of the trees. Sometimes she would vanish for days at a time. They didn't seem to suspect Madeline of doing anything scandalous while she was gone, but she always returned with strange things in her pockets. Small animals. Live and dead. Insects. Injured birds. Wildflowers and cuttings from other people's gardens. Jars of dirt.

Madeline and Doreen's parents were Silas Luck and Jia Wu. They died a long time ago, and I never met them. Jia emigrated from Si County in Anhui Province in East China, arriving in Canada one day before the 1923 Chinese Exclusion Act passed, which would have prevented her immigrating to Canada for another twenty-four years. Silas's father emigrated from Birnam in Scotland, and his mother came from Caerfyrddin in South Wales. They owned a bakery in Blueberry Brook, a rural farming community not far from Grand Tea.

Silas Luck was a surgeon by profession who was rich enough to keep his foreign wife in Nova Scotian high society. They did quite well for themselves. They were so well off, they could afford two houses. One for winter. One for summer. The summer house was a big, fancy deal. A three-storey manor house with a two-acre formal garden with symmetrical clipped hedges and stone statues and fountains. Imagine.

The little I know about Luck family history I gleaned by eavesdropping at the door of Aunt Madeline's guest bedroom. Whispers crackled between my aunt and my mother on those summertime visits. Secrets seemed hidden in every word they spoke to each other.

Silas Luck was, apparently, not a very good surgeon, and not good at managing money.

Jia Luck, apparently, deeply resented not giving birth to any sons. Having daughters was a source of embarrassment. *I'd rather have a goose than a girl*, she used to say. She lied in her letters to her relatives back in China. Even to her own parents, who were led to believe they had two handsome Canadian-born grandsons. Not a daughter in sight in those letters. I know my mother tells her own lies in her letters to our distant relatives in China. I can only imagine what lies she writes to them about me.

In 1968, their big, fancy summer house caught fire. Fortunately, nobody was there at the time. So, they settled full-time into the winter house and abandoned the other one. After the summer house burned down, they didn't rebuild it. It was a scorched shell, barely any house left. Not worth the effort to fix it up or tear it down.

So, Silas and Jia paid someone a few bucks to put a No Trespassing sign on the front gate, lock the gate, and throw the key back inside the property, as far in as they could throw it. The two-acre garden was mostly overgrown by then. The key likely landed in some random tangle of weeds or neglected shrub, never to be found again. Whatever is left of the burnt-down summer house sits on a vast, untended estate property. It rots back into the earth, year after year.

Silas lived twenty-four more years after the fire. Jia passed away two weeks after him. They left both properties to Madeline in their will: the winter house they died in, and the summer house that burned down. As far as I know, Madeline never had any interest in either property. But I know my mother definitely did. Silas, according to the eavesdropped stories, overspent. There was no Luck family wealth left to hand down. Just the houses. To this day, my mother resents not owning those properties. I don't think she wanted the mansions or the Victorian gardens so much; I think she wanted the stability of a place to settle down. That's what I would have used it for, anyway. My mother and I had it rough when I was growing up, always moving from rental to rental. Always shoving our lives into boxes and dragging them to the next place, until money ran out and the power was shut off and it was time to pack up and move again. By grade five, I didn't bother unpacking the boxes anymore. There was no point.

The remains of the once elite Luck estate just sit there, empty and unused, to this day. If there is anything left, it is crumbling and sinking into its own private oblivion.

The house that burned down was the house Doreen spent the most time in growing up. Although she gripes about wanting the land, I know she hated that house. She says the only thing her sister ever really gave her in life was a deeply ingrained hatred of that house.

I've never seen either house, of course, but I know the stories.

As far as I know, Madeline never said out loud why she hated that house, but I know why Doreen hated it. She said it was haunted.

Growing up in the big, fancy summer house, Doreen heard things. Spooky things. Banging and moaning. Scratching inside the walls. Whispering at night. Voices. Muffled screams.

The few times Doreen said anything to her parents about it, Silas and Jia scolded her for being ridiculous and having an overactive imagination.

Little Doreen believed her parents. At first. Adults don't lie, she thought. Adults know better than a kid. She accepted their explanations and their warnings and quietly believed that she was crazy. She stopped telling them about what she heard. She learned to doubt her own ears and distrust her own mind. She was careful to always act as sane and proper and boring and steady as a child could possibly be.

But one night when Doreen was five, she found out she was right. The house was haunted.

She saw it with her own eyes. She saw Madeline talking to a ghost.

CHAPTER THIRTY

In the middle of the night, little Doreen Luck woke up. She had to go to the bathroom. It was scary to leave the safety of her bedroom and walk down the hall in the dark. At five, she was too tiny to reach any light switches. But she really had to go.

So, with every step she stopped to give her eyes a few seconds to adjust before taking another step. To make sure there was nothing in front of her. Or behind her.

Halfway down the hall, Doreen took a step and stopped beside Madeline's bedroom door. The door was open—which was strange—and it was dark inside the room. Curious to get a rare peek inside her big sister's bedroom, Doreen took her next step toward the open bedroom door and looked in. She let her eyes adjust to the dark.

Madeline was in there. Not sleeping, but standing up. Right in the middle of the room. She stood very still and faced the wall. Not facing a window or a picture. Just the plain, empty wall.

It was quiet in there. A bad kind of quiet.

Doreen's heart hammered against the buttons of her nightgown. She wanted to shout her sister's name, to break the silence and break the moment and make Madeline move like a normal person again. She tried, but little Doreen didn't have enough breath left in her whole body for a single squeak.

Madeline was whispering. Doreen couldn't make out the words.

Who was Madeline whispering to?

Before Doreen could take a step closer, Madeline stopped talking to the wall. She snapped her head around and saw her little sister standing there.

"It's Doreen," Madeline said in a voice that crackled and rasped. "Come here, Doreen. Come here."

Doreen's teeth chattered. That didn't sound like Madeline's voice. And Madeline had never invited Doreen into her room before. All Doreen had ever wanted was to be invited into her big sister's room. But there was something wrong in there. She was so terrified, pee trickled down her leg, down her nightgown, and onto the hardwood floor.

Madeline then said, "It's my sister, and she's going to die soon."

Doreen's survival instincts kicked in. She balled up her little fists and screeched at the top of her lungs, "I DON'T WANT TO DIE SOON!"

Silas and Jia flew into the hallway as Doreen ran toward their bedroom and crashed into them. She cracked her screaming mouth into Silas's kneecap and knocked four front teeth right out of her own head. Her baby teeth clattered across the floor like bloody dice.

Somewhere in the chaos of screams and blood and broken teeth in the hallway outside her bedroom, Madeline opened her bedroom window. She climbed out the window and up to the roof of her parents' house for the last time.

Madeline left. She left little Doreen there with broken teeth and a ghost.

Madeline left and never returned.

I don't remember falling asleep. After talking to my mother on the phone, I must've passed out. Those piles of pancakes kept me full and let me sleep like the dead all night and halfway through the morning. My legs are seriously cramped. My clothes squish against the car seat, still heavy with grimy Grand Tea rain.

Through the big glass doors of the hotel, I see there's no one at the front desk.

Yes.

I stride through the empty lobby like I belong there, step into the elevator, and see Gym listed. Follow the chlorine pool smell all the way down a basement corridor.

I lose track of time and space in the shower. Hot water drills away the dust and the darkness. The damp chill of Aunt Madeline's cellar. The death smell of burned bones.

First thing I see when I get out of the shower are three missed calls and a voicemail from Corporal Quill. Everything the hot water washed away rushes back. Wound up in fresh hotel towels, I skip the option to listen to the voicemail and press Quill's number to call her back. Get this over with.

She picks up. "This is Corporal Quill."

"You called me."

"Miss Luck, yes. I have an update for you on your aunt's case. It might be better if I can give you the update in person. Where are you currently?"

"Nope," I say. "By phone is fine."

"We have the DNA results," Quill says.

"Okay."

"I have difficult news."

"Okay."

"We have confirmed the burned human remains found in the cellar are the remains of Madeline Luck," Quill says. Her voice softens, just a little. "I am very sorry for your loss."

My heart sinks. I sit on a wooden bench. "You are one hundred percent sure."

"Yes."

"Okay."

"Miss Luck, is there someone you can stay with—"

"What happened to her?"

"We're still investigating the—"

"Was she murdered?"

"We don't know cause of—"

"Did she burn to death? Did someone set her on fire and burn her to death?"

"Miss Luck, I can't—"

"Did some conspiracy-theory nut from Grand Tea burn my aunt Madeline to death because they think she's a witch?"

I wait for Quill to tell me I'm wrong. That I'm a fool to even think that. That it's impossible. That it's not what happened at all.

But she doesn't say anything.

That's all the answer I need.

BOOK SEVEN

Lettie

CHAPTER THIRTY-ONE

Hurricane Lettie increased in intensity overnight. In three hours, she'll make landfall over the cliffs in Willow Sound. The weather forecast arrow that shows Hurricane Lettie's predicted path runs right through Aunt Madeline's little house. It's three thirty-three now. I close the local news on my phone and click on the satellite view.

Lettie churns over the Atlantic Ocean and glares up at the constellation of weather satellites with her one eye, putting on a ferocious show. Two hundred kilometres of rain and clouds whip around her eye in a white death cloak. Hurricane Lettie is a powerhouse, and she's on her way here.

A matter of hours until Aunt Madeline's house and gardens are wiped out forever.

Frig the police tape. Frig Quill.

I'm going back to the house.

One last time.

The rainfall picks up on my drive back to the abandoned road in the woods that leads to Aunt Madeline's house. There's not enough time for me to walk all the way through the woods, so I cross my fingers and drive my car through the gleaming white mushrooms and into the ruts.

It revs over piles of rotted leaves and slams on twisted roots and grinds pretty far into the woods before I decide to stop. Pull off the path and park it next to a sturdy-looking cluster of hardwoods. Hopefully the woods will keep my car sheltered until I get back.

I trek through the trees toward Aunt Madeline's front garden on foot. The storm is brutally strong already, just ahead of Hurricane Lettie's arrival. I lean in and lock horns with the wind. It's a brutal march straight into the punishing gale, but I don't care.

I'm returning to Aunt Madeline's house for three things.

Shielding my eyes from the rain, I can see her house. Still standing. So far. The police tape is mangled by the wind. The plastic yellow strands whip the house, like threatened snakes lashing Medusa's skull.

Trees creak and sway in violent circles. Their leaves hiss. Tree needles hurtle at me like darts. I keep my hands raised like I'm in a fist fight, and I keep one eye on the house.

My apple tree billows and bends. A branch snaps off it and flips end over end past Aunt Madeline's house. I watch it fly past, and my eye catches on the front window. There is a shape moving behind the glass. I nearly fall over with shock. I pound my legs faster through the cold mud, because there is someone inside Aunt Madeline's house.

CHAPTER THIRTY-TWO

Before I kick down the front door to Aunt Madeline's house, I stop myself. Every bone in my body wants to rush in and beat the tar out of whoever is in there. But there is a monster on the loose. A monster that burns people alive.

The monster could be inside the house.

I head for her shed. I still have the key for it on me. The whole shed rattles and struggles to hold itself together against the whipping wind. Inside the vibrating shed walls, I wipe rain and debris from my face.

The chain with the shackle shakes off its hook and slams to the floor.

I have the skeleton key that was hidden in the suitcase. I don't have much time. But this might be my last chance to try the key.

Frig it.

Even my big hands strain to lift it. Soot stains my hands. This is no dog chain. Any dog would tire to death at the end of this thing.

I scrounge the skeleton key from my pocket. It grinds against the shackle lock, but the keyhole is so caked with grime, the key won't go in. I spit on the keyhole, dig a slug of black grime out with my nail, and try again.

The shackle opens with a heartless snap. The metal inside the shackle hoop is engraved. I rub the faded lettering until I can read it.

HH-040

I repeat the code a few times to myself, memorizing it. I stash the skeleton key back down deep in my pocket, leave the chain where it is, and turn my attention to the other reason I came into the shed.

The rifle.

The wind pulls at the rifle as I lock the shed behind me. Brambles and broken thickets whip past. Dead and alive, every plant, every tree in Aunt Madeline's garden roils and heaves. As if her garden is angry about her death.

I rush back to her house and look in the kitchen window. Don't see anyone inside. Rifle raised and ready, I slip inside the back door.

No one.

Check the bedrooms. Every corner. Every shadow. Under the beds. No one. Only one more place someone could be.

The cellar.

Sweat and rain slide down my face. Impossible to tell if there's someone down there. But there has to be; there's nowhere else for them to hide.

"Who's there?" I shout down into the hole in the floor.

Nothing.

"I have a rifle and serious mental problems!" I shout.

WHAM.

That sound came from the kitchen. I head toward it, finger on the trigger.

Not a soul. Just the kitchen door slamming open and shut in the wind. I pull the door shut and lock it. Behind me, wind whistles over the hole in the floor. That hollow moan.

No part of me is going down that hole. Not my hand with a light. Not my head, hard as my skull may be. Only one thing I'm willing to send down there: a brass bullet.

I cock the rifle and aim down at the darkness.

BANG.

The dust and echoes—and the ringing in my ears—all take a few seconds to settle.

I listen.

Nothing.

If anyone is in the cellar right now, they'd scramble, or scream, or shoot back. I reload while I reconsider.

Maybe they went out the front while I was out back. Or, maybe no one was in the house. Maybe I just saw a reflection of a moving tree in the window glass. Either way, I have one cartridge left. Hurricane Lettie is close. Time for me to get what I came for and get the frig out.

The photographs. All Aunt Madeline's old photographs are coming with me. Like Nish said, if they are kept in her cabinet, they are important to her.

Were. They were important to her. When she was alive.

Focus, Fade.

The scrolls. All the scrolls she stored in her cabinet are coming with me. If they are instructions to remember, a record of the things she knew for sure in her lifetime, then I can't let a single scroll be lost.

The teapot. Aunt Madeline spent every sunrise of her long life in Willow Sound making tea in this sweet little teapot. I wrap it like a baby in a hotel towel and shove it deep in my backpack.

One last thing.

The spell jar.

It's not coming with me. I know Aunt Madeline isn't a witch. I know spells aren't real. But if it meant something to her to assemble these things in this jar and bury them together, as some kind of wish of protection for her house, I will honour that wish and put it back in the ground. My last act for this house.

The jar is where I left it, on the floor by the wood stove. I don't intend to bury the jar in its original place, at the front gate. I'm going to bury the jar behind the house, at the edge of the cliff next to the ocean. Right where the weather satellites predict Hurricane Lettie will make landfall. Right where Lettie will come to rip everything Aunt Madeline built off the face of the earth and fling it into oblivion. Now when Lettie comes to destroy the house, she will first have to do battle with Madeline Luck's old-fashioned magic.

Screwing the lid onto the jar as hard as my hands can manage in the cold, my neck prickles. Like someone is watching me.

I don't see anyone around me. The wind howls, hurrying me.

Probably Lettie, breathing down my neck.

I zip my backpack shut and hoist it onto my soaked back. Take a last look around Aunt Madeline's house. Thunder rolls overhead, like cannon fire. The walls and floors shudder. Every object in the house vibrates as if possessed by the storm. The dried herbs that hang from the ceiling rafters swing wildly. A few of the curiosities have fallen from the purple cabinet to the floor. I didn't disturb a single item in the purple cabinet when I gathered the scrolls. I was so careful. Too careful. Must be the violence of the wind against the house, knocking things down.

Time to go. I reach for the jar and my aunt's rifle—

The rifle is gone.

It was there. It was beside my boot. I laid it there. Seconds ago.

It's gone.

WHAM.

Behind me, the kitchen door bangs open. I see a flash of a red rubber boot and the butt of the rifle fly out the kitchen door.

Before I can run out after the boot, wind explodes in the open door like a bomb. Throws me back. My elbows screech with pain. I gape in horror as objects inside Aunt Madeline's house—things that survived for decades—are smashed to the walls and floor all around me.

Hurricane Lettie is here.

I clutch the spell jar against my chest and throw my body out the kitchen door, headfirst into the hurricane. Rain batters my eyes, but I force them open to watch for red rubber boots. Running away, or running at me, or planting themselves for a steady shot at my head. But there is no soul in sight.

The shed is gone. The outhouse has collapsed. I battle the wind to the cliffs at the back edge of Aunt Madeline's property. The rose bushes strain to keep their roots in the earth. The ocean roars and crashes the cliffs.

Ducked behind a rose bush, I claw into the ground like a madwoman. The hole starts to fill with rain, but I force the jar into the mucky hole and shove earth back over it. My fingers shake. I have Aunt Madeline's hands.

In my mind, I see her hands now: skeletal fingers curled into burnt claws.

Wind screeches so hard it hurts my ears. I raise my eyes from the red-brown earth up to the grey-blue sky over the ocean. A little glass jar filled with almost forgotten beliefs will be no match for Lettie.

Too late to change that. I'm out of here.

In my race through the gardens and back to the woods, I think I glimpse bright red between the trees—those rubber boots maybe—but frig that. Just need to get myself to my car and break the needle back to that Carmel hotel parking lot.

At the front gate, I stop. Take a last look back at little house and the land and the plants around it. No more the fairy tale from my childhood. Not even the dead-still wasteland I found on my return two days ago. It is walloped and whipped and absolutely doomed.

Still. The spirit of Madeline Luck is firmly rooted in this land. It always will be.

I place my hand on the earth, grab a handful of dirt, and I run.

CHAPTER THIRTY-THREE

Inside my car is mercifully still. It rocks now and then, tipped by the wind. The only other movement is the vibration of my exhausted limbs and my shivering teeth.

I try starting my car again. Dead.

Frig.

My fist still clutches the dirt from Aunt Madeline's garden. The rain tried to take it from me, but I didn't let go. I've kept my fist clenched so hard, I can't release it right away. I cradle my fist to steady it and let my fingers slowly open. There it is. A soft teaspoonful of unremarkable earth.

I need to put it somewhere safe. My travel mug and scraped-out pudding cups aren't proper safekeeping for something so important. There is one container that will work.

Aunt Madeline's teapot. Cold, but in one piece. I lift the lid. A delicate whiff of wild berry tea escapes and snaps me back in time. I am six years old and sitting at the table in her kitchen. The morning sun shimmers in the steam of the kettle. I wriggle with anticipation as the teakettle starts to whistle. The shrill note rises up, and my heart rises with it. I lift the teapot lid so she can pour the water in. My small but cherished job in helping Aunt Madeline make tea.

The kettle tips. Crystal-clear water pours into the belly of the teapot, sending rich waves of mayflower-scented steam into the air all around us, filling the kitchen, filling me with warmth from head to toe. Teapot full, I replace the lid. Aunt Madeline closes her eyes and inhales the warm and wild scent as it steeps. I close my eyes and do the same, copying her. Wanting to be just like her. My warm and wild Aunt Madeline.

When a memory like that is buried deep down inside, we never know when it will be snagged and jigged to the surface again. When I was six and waiting, my fingers folded patiently, for that pot of tea to steep, little did I know I would leave that beautiful moment and move farther and farther away from it for twenty-seven years—only to be transported back, in the middle of a hurricane, in the middle of the woods, in my broken-down car, holding that same teapot, now empty and cold. And Aunt Madeline isn't boiling water for tea now, because she is dead. Murdered and burned and gone, and I abandoned her for all those years, didn't even get the chance to say, "Thank you. I love you. I miss you. I remember you."

I release my handful of dirt inside. My shaky fingers put the lid back on.

The car windows are blurred by rain and caked with seaweed and broken leaves. Beyond, the forest is cold and black. Broken branches and pieces of wood thud the roof and ping off the hood. Hurricane Lettie must be done with my aunt's house by now and clear-cutting her way through the trees toward town.

Right through here. I try to start the car again.

It catches. Yes.

I ease the car over swells of moss and old logs, axles groaning. At the crest of what I am sure is dead needles and mulch, the slow screech of metal rips into my car and scrapes the underside, hanging it up. My tires spin and spit up gushes of red muck. I try to power forward, then power backwards, but nothing gives.

It's not a bit stuck. It's impaled.

I turn off the engine and watch the evergreens sway narcotically on every side.

Maybe I can shift the car free of whatever it's jammed on. I get out of the car. An earthy groan splits the air as a monolithic spruce uproots and crashes to the ground, sending a volley of spruce needles hissing into the air. Cheeks stinging, I retreat inside the car. Spit out the turpentine taste of spruce. Pluck green needles from my eyelashes with shaky fingers.

Something black darts past the car.

My eyes snap from window to window, peering through the veil of rain and dead leaves.

Flashlight. I pry it from my backpack. It shines cold white light out my windshield.

Nothing.

I shine the light out the passenger side window.

I see it.

A wolf.

A rattle-boned beast. Heaving. Massive. Crouched low. Fangs gleam in the beam of my flashlight. Pink tongue dangles like a bloody ribbon. Its legs nearly buckle against the battering wind. Thunder cracks.

The wolf's desperate eyes find me.

The wind pries at my car with aching creaks, threatening to rip off the doors and smash out the glass.

The pure violence of the moment sends thrills through me. Thrills only a natural-born scrapper would understand. But the odds are against me in this brawl. Me versus hurricane versus wolf. Better just get out of here.

Eyes locked with the wolf, I keep my body still as I slide a hand down to touch the car floor. I recognize the smooth curves of my travel mug. I grab it.

The wolf watches me. I watch the wolf. I keep the flashlight beaming hard in its eyes. The teapot rests in my lap, fragile and cold. It's coming with me. The spring inside the door handle stretches coil by coil as I move the handle in millimetres. I want to ease the door open, without the wolf knowing, just enough to get a leg out. Then I can shove myself out of the car and run like hell. I make a mental note to sacrifice a second to close the car door behind me. But only a second.

The door is open no more than two centimetres and the wind hooks into the gap, rips the door from my grasp, and flings it open. I fall sideways out of the car. My skull hits the ground first, but I remember to protect the teapot, curling around it like a worm. I roll myself right side up and biff my travel mug as hard as I can at the wolf.

It careens off the wolf's head but doesn't faze it. I just made it mad.

The wolf is on me. Jaws sink into my thigh and yank. My leg explodes with pain.

BOOM.

Thunder. Or a gunshot.

Fangs yank out of my flesh with the shock of the sound. The wolf bolts. Gone.

My vision is blurred by concussions and needles and mud.

But I see her.

She leans, shivering and soaked, against a tree twenty feet from me. She has wild white hair. Apron full of pockets. Rifle in her hands. Red rubber boots.

I swipe the mud off my eyes, desperate to be certain what I am seeing is real.

Thunder shakes the trees. Lightning spikes the sky. In the brilliant flashes, I see her face.

Unmistakable.

Aunt Madeline.

CHAPTER THIRTY-FOUR

Her face is tired and sunken deep with hollows and shadows. But it is her.

It is Aunt Madeline.

She is alive.

Before I can suck in enough oxygen to yell her name, Hurricane Lettie steals the air from the moment. Lettie bombs the forest with bales of thunder so loud my ears crack. Bolts of lightning streak white across the whole sky, hurting my eyes. I swear I taste the acidic spark of lightning on my tongue.

Unaffected by the violence of the thunder or the wind, Aunt Madeline and her wild white hair and red rubber boots are there in one flash of lightning—and gone in the next.

"Aunt Madeline, it's me! It's Fade!"

I blink to clear the black lines the lightning burned into my eyes.

"AUNT MADELINE!"

But she's gone.

As if she was never there.

The rain pelts my face like nails. I'm bleeding quite a lot from my leg and my head. My mouth is full of blood. I spit it out on the forest floor. That fall must have given me a wicked concussion. My heart sinks at the thought.

She wasn't there. She was just a hallucination, a wishful thought, summoned by my broken brain.

I saw her bones. I smelled the scorch of them. I found them.

I look again at where I had seen her. Or someone. Or something. Or nothing. There is nothing there.

Somewhere in the distance, a bone-chilling crack. Maybe a massive tree has snapped in half. A matchstick against the strength of the storm. Hurricane Lettie is going to decimate this forest. She is going to grind these tall, ancient trees into splinters under her boots.

If I stay here, I will die.

For a second, I consider taking cover inside my car for the rest of the storm, until I realize the seaweed stuck to my windshield isn't crunchy stiff tangles of dried seaweed plucked from the shore. It is living seaweed sucked up from the middle of the Atlantic Ocean, carried across the sky, and tossed in the middle of the woods. Hurricane Lettie has uprooted an ocean. My car is a pinch of loose atoms to her.

I clutch the teapot against me. Kick my car door shut and lock it. Look around for any sign of that wolf changing its mind, coming back for another bite of me. But there is no wolf. There is nothing keeping me here.

So I run.

CHAPTER THIRTY-FIVE

The old highway hasn't been hit by Lettie yet. The trees that line the highway creak softly, only grazed by the storm so far. Out of breath, bleeding hot blood, I clamber on hands and knees up the side of the steep ditch, over the guardrail, and onto the crumbling pavement. Not a car in sight, either way. I'm on my own.

Hurricane Lettie is not far behind. Her distant whistle cuts ominously through the woods. I feel the charge of her lightning build-up in prickles across my bloody scalp.

Even with the shaking of my legs and the chattering of my teeth, I feel my phone vibrate in my backpack pocket. My exhausted hands find it.

Nish.

"You have the timing of the devil," I tell him.

"Sorry to bother you, Fade, but Corporal Quill called me to ask where you are," Nish says. "She must have figured out you're not staying at the Grand Tea motel like you're supposed to. I didn't tell her anything, of course. But I thought you'd want to know she's looking for you."

Sure enough, my phone screen loads up with a mass of missed calls from Quill.

"Thanks, Nish," I say. "I just—"

A slap of wind knocks the phone out of my hand into the middle of the road. Frig. I scramble to grab it. I flick mud off the screen and hold the broken glass to my ear.

Nish chuckles softly. "You're not in any hotel or motel, are you, Fade?"

"Not even close," I say.

"You have your car?"

"Nope." I laugh this time. "I think I just gave my car to Hurricane Lettie."

"Do you need a lift?"

I squint up the old highway. Not a headlight, not a passerby, not a storm chaser in sight. Seems no one is brave enough to welcome Lettie personally to shore but me.

"Where are you?" he asks.

Through the phone, I hear the unmistakable chime of a car door opening. I smile to myself. Nish is already getting in his car to come get me. Storm of a century be damned. Nish is a good friend. I don't have any of those.

Maybe that protection jar had a little luck in it, after all.

"Thanks, Nish. I owe you one."

Through the phone, I hear the zip of a seatbelt. Click of a buckle. "No, you don't owe me anything." I can hear Nish's smile when he speaks. "Not even close."

With Nish on his way to pick me up, I shove my cold fists into my hoodie pockets and walk along the old highway. I can't stand still. Thunder rolls. *One. Two.* Lightning strikes. Lettie is not far off.

I stare at my boots as I walk. They're red with blood.

I think about the red rubber boots I saw. Imagined I saw.

What did I see?

The signs of a serious concussion, that's what.

My brain is so preoccupied with diagnosing itself, it takes me a second or two to realize the crunch of gravel under my boots is now the only sound in the world.

Absolute silence surrounds me. No wind. No air. I stop.

The feeling of . . . something. Under my feet. The ground vibrates. The woods fill up with shadows.

The screaming starts.

Voices. Bawling. Hoarse screams. A chaos of terrified voices.

Deer.

Thirty or more whitetail deer bolt out of the woods, bleating breathy screams of terror. Stuck in place like a scarecrow, I stay still as I can as their tan bodies and swift legs hammer past me. The warm blast of leathery musk and salty fur curls against my face. Their bodies flood around me. They leap over the old highway and disappear into the woods on the other side. A few fawns straggle by, screaming in distress as they hop awkwardly, frantic but determined to follow the herd. They are too scared to stop. Then they are gone too.

Awesome.

They were so close to me, I could have touched them. But I kept my hands to myself. Being a human means I'm as dangerous as a storm to them. No need to be a second horror to the poor animals. Better to be a scarecrow.

WRAA-AAA-AAA-AAA-AAA.

Wind slams into my back like a moving car. I hit the pavement before I can get my hands out of my pockets to protect my face.

BOOOOM.

Thunder. The road rushes with blowing leaves and branches. The storm is so loud, I can't even hear myself spit blood.

I see two tiny lights in the distance. Headlights? Coming my way. Please be Nish. I'm down to the last pixels on my health bar. I hobble hard toward those lights.

BANG.

A tall evergreen explodes in a flash of lightning. It tips like a second hand on a clock face and wallops the road. Those oncoming headlights fishtail, barely avoiding being crushed by the tree. Nish leaps out of the car, hands on his head. A deadly close call.

I recognize the tree sprawled across the highway. It's the old jack pine. The one with the scars of two lightning strikes.

Three scars, now. Lettie took the old warrior down.

The jack pine blocks the highway. Nish can't drive any closer to me. He crawls under the trunk and runs toward me.

"What did you do?" he says, seeing my busted face. "Come back to pick a fistfight with Lettie?"

"Yep. And I lost. Bad."

The inside of his car is so clean. I pull off my soaked hoodie and wind it around my thigh, in case it starts bleeding again. "There."

Nish stands next to his open car door, staring at the sky, eyes wide.

Power lines whip and flail. Sparks hiss and fly off them in every direction. Starting fires. Fires in the trees. Fire in the broken wood and leaves littered all over the road. A constellation of tiny fires dotting from here off to the horizon. As far as we can see.

The old trees will make their last stand but probably won't survive a fire. It was my mother's worst fear, all these years, that her sister would get trapped in a forest fire in these old woods and burn alive.

Oh.

Thick black clouds roll over us. They flash, full of lightning. Our breath turns to cold smoke until wind shoves it back down our throats.

Lettie's black clouds crack open. Her gale winds lash and coat the earth with crackling ribbons of rain. Her next crack of thunder and lightning is so violent and so close, it rattles my eyeballs in their sockets and threatens to loosen all my teeth. Nish and I scramble into his car. He pounds on the gas, screeches back from the fallen jack pine, and races us out of there.

Driving away, safe inside Nish's car, we look back at the storm. The deer were smart to run. By the looks of it, Lettie is making her way straight to Grand Tea. They are in for a beating.

"I assume they evacuated everyone out of Grand Tea, just in case."

"No."

What.

"The people of Grand Tea refuse to leave," Nish says. "They believe the storm won't hurt them and the rock won't fall on them, because the Old Witch is dead so the curse is lifted. And to prove their loyalty to their belief, they're staying under the rock through the hurricane."

Holy frig.

"That's a level of delusion I hadn't expected," I admit.

"Indeed."

"What about that annoying Mayor Davish guy? He's staying under the rock too?"

"The mayor claimed he had to leave town for work reasons."

Right.

"Do you think Hurricane Lettie will do it?" I look at Nish.

"Do what?"

"Tip the Grand Tea rock over and smash it on the town?"

"I don't know."

"I thought you said the Grand Tea rock won't move in our lifetime."

"You're right. I did say that. But I didn't realize how powerful hurricanes have gotten here." He shivers. "There's no way to stop it. Lettie will destroy whatever she wants."

BOOK EIGHT

Tea

CHAPTER THIRTY-SIX

The wipers on Nish's windshield worked hard, and he's driven us past the centre of the storm. The road to the hotel in Carmel is rainy and dark, but the wind isn't ripping through here with the same force. Nish eases to a complete stop at a stop sign and looks both ways before proceeding, even though there is no traffic in sight and won't be for hours.

"Fade, I have to be honest with you," he says. "I saw something about you in the town database."

"I shouldn't be in any Grand Tea records," I say. "I've never lived there."

"Grand Tea has no government offices. No municipal services. No police detachment. Unions consider it too dangerous to work under the rock. Access to records resides in the only government database that exists in Grand Tea."

"The archives."

"Fade, I promise I wasn't researching you without your knowledge," Nish says. "I wouldn't violate anyone's privacy that way. It was just there."

I believe him. "What dirt did you find on me?"

"Fade, are you a police officer or something like that?" Nish says in a quiet voice. "You think like a detective. And your name is associated with a whole lot of police files."

"Not a cop, but I did work for law enforcement," I tell him. "But I had to stop."

"Why?"

"I worked for Cybercrime." I take my time with words I still struggle to say out loud. "In the child protection division."

"Oh," he says.

"At first, I was fired up about the job. *Yeah, let's get these psychos. Let's bring them all down.* But after years hunting after the most evil monsters on earth, I realized they're everywhere. They look like anyone. They're nothing special. And there's no end to them. On my last day on the job, they handed me some human trafficker's laptop. I couldn't even open the lid. I walked out. I don't remember leaving the office building, but I did. Never went back. When I came to the next day, I wasn't home. I was standing on the sidewalk, standing in front of a window of an empty store in a part of the city I'd never been to before, looking into the window at nothing. Still in my work clothes from the day before. My brain just broke. Or my heart did. Or both. I fell into a black hole inside my head, and my whole life fell apart. Lost my home. Lost everything I'd worked so hard for. By the time I climbed back to the land of the living, there was nothing left for me. I'll never be right in the head again. I'll never fit back into normal society because I feel that evil everywhere." I turn to stare out the passenger window. "I brought down a lot of monsters, but I feel guilty I can't fight that fight anymore. I still want to help."

Nish pulls his car into the hotel parking lot. Hardly any cars in the lot. Lights in the lobby shimmer through the rain. It looks warm in there. Warm and dry.

"Your socks never dry," I say it out loud, though I didn't mean to.

"Pardon?" Nish says.

"Being homeless in Nova Scotia. Your feet are always in pain. They're always wet and cold. Your socks never dry. It's the second-worst thing about being homeless here."

Nish is too polite to ask about the first.

Rain drums the roof of the car.

Nish insists on getting me a hotel room for the night. Before I can protest, he's already inside the lobby on his way to the front desk.

As we ride the elevator up, I'm so grateful, my throat locks up. "Thank you, Nish." My voice breaks.

If Nish notices, he doesn't let on. "You're welcome."

When we get to the hotel room, I swipe the key card. *Bzzt-click.* The door opens, and I step in. It fills me with light and warmth. I feel human.

Nish doesn't follow me into the hotel room he paid for. He stands politely, if awkwardly, out in the hall.

"You are out of the storm and safe," Nish says. "Your room service meals—a hot dinner tonight and full breakfast tomorrow—will be along. My journey ends here."

It takes me a few seconds to figure out what's happening. That Nish is too much of a gentleman to come into my hotel room, behind a closed door. He hovers in the hallway like an old ghost. A remnant from a lost time.

I kick off my mud-soaked boots and jam them under the door, propping it open.

"Please, come on in, Nish," I say. "Even just till the hurricane passes. If people come by the door and are nosy enough to look in here, all they're going to see is a hobbit and a half giant reading some old scrolls."

His head snaps up. "Scrolls?"

"I went back to Aunt Madeline's house to save her scrolls," I say. "And I did that because you said they're important to her."

The storm, and my adventures in it, have left the scrolls in pretty fragile shape.

"I need your help to save them," I say. "Or at least figure them out before they fall apart."

His eyes keen on the scrolls, Nish nods. Jaw set. I know that look. It's the same look programmers get when it's time to sit down and write some code that will quietly change the world.

"A hobbit and a half giant," he says. "Which one am I?"

"You are hilarious for a nerd," I say.

He chuckles at my boots as he steps over them into the room. "It looks like the Wicked Witch of the East crushed under Dorothy's house, but with realistic blood and gore."

"It does. I always thought her death scene should've had way more gore." I unwind my hoodie from my thigh. Not bad. Hurts like hell, but stopped bleeding, at least. I toss my hoodie in the bathroom sink to soak.

"Speaking of blood and gore," Nish says, "what happened to your leg?"

"I got attacked by a wolf."

He blinks at me. "Pardon?"

"A wolf tried to eat my leg."

Nish sits down in the armchair. "Well, that is unexpected."

"Because my life is the worst-ever fairy tale come true?"

"Because," Nish says, "there have been no wolves in Nova Scotia for over a hundred and fifty years."

CHAPTER THIRTY-SEVEN

There are twenty-eight scrolls in Aunt Madeline's collection. Most are too rain-soaked and fragile to open yet. We decide we can safely unroll a few. Each scroll is tied with a different kind of twine or thread, and each binding holds different dried leaves, tiny twigs, or dried fruit inside its knots. Some scrolls are one piece of paper. Some are thick with many pages rolled up together.

While I would have immediately yanked all twenty-eight ties open like bows on presents, Nish doesn't even think about untying a single thread. Instead, he handles each scroll with painstaking care. He jots his observations on hotel stationary, roughs out quick pencil sketches, takes photos with his phone from every angle. His patience is otherworldly, and his respect for Aunt Madeline's work is breathtaking. I learn a lot by watching him. Not about archiving, but about honour. Honouring her. Honouring the knowledge she curated over a long life.

"They don't look like regular paper," I say, rubbing my fingers across the thick, rough surface of one of the scrolls.

"These papers are made of rags," Nish says. "It's a very old way of making paper. It seems Madeline Luck made her own paper, by hand, by recycling old pieces of cloth."

"She had to make paper out of rags?"

"No, she didn't have to," Nish says. "Paper has been made from wood since the 1850s. Madeline Luck could have purchased paper anywhere quite easily. So she must have chosen to make her own. These scrolls, here, look like her early attempts. But those scrolls, there, show she mastered papermaking. And all this skill was likely honed to create these scrolls. Honestly, Fade, the paper alone is extraordinary. Madeline Luck was brilliant."

She was.

"And Fade, you are brilliant to have gone back to save these. Brave. Crazy, perhaps. But definitely brilliant."

"I wish you could've met her . . ."

Nish waits for me to finish my thought, but my words dry up in my gut and nothing else comes out.

"I will be deeply privileged to meet Madeline Luck through her writing in her scrolls," Nish says. "And through the memories of her niece."

"Go 'way." I smile at him.

"I shall not." He mirrors my sad smile back at me.

"Which scroll is the oldest one, you think?"

Nish lifts a fragile roll with two hands and offers it to me.

Even though I didn't think twice about jamming all these scrolls into my saturated backpack not an hour ago, after watching Nish, I'm nervous to even touch this one. The cream paper is wound and tied with cooking twine. A dried rosebud and a rosemary sprig are knotted in the twine.

The twine crumbles to dust when I tug its frayed ends to release the knot. The dry rose petals and rosemary needles scatter.

I understand Nish's work now. Catalogue the details as well as you can, because everything eventually turns to dust.

The scroll doesn't want to be opened. It wants to stay curled up. Uncurling it and holding it open is nerve-wracking work, but the rag paper is strong. Tucked inside the scroll is a very small piece of normal-looking paper, about the size of the palm of my hand. A delicate page of old stationary, folded in half.

"Shall we open it?" Nish asks.

"You can," I say. "Your hands are way steadier than mine. You're like some kind of history nerd surgeon."

"That is the nicest thing anyone has ever said to me."

The handwriting on the small paper is a fancy cursive writing, as delicate and old as the paper itself. Every word on the page ends with a long, curvy flourish.

"That's the fanciest writing I've ever seen," I say. "But it doesn't look like Aunt Madeline's writing."

"I agree, it's not hers," Nish says. "I would date the handwriting and the paper at the mid to late 1800s."

The paper is titled "To Make Wonders."

"What does that mean?" I ask.

"It's a recipe," Nish says. "Wonders are a type of homemade deep-fried bread."

"Deep-fried bread?" I say. "Nice."

"Families have their own traditions for secret ingredients in their wonders recipes and unique methods of twisting shapes in the dough. A secret recipe passed down through family lines."

Nish holds the paper open so I can see the recipe for myself.

To make Wonders. Take 2 pounds of flour, half a pound of butter, 10 eggs, and some rosewater. Handful size in rosebud twist. Dust with rose petals.

"Would rosewater and rose petals be the secret ingredients?" I ask.

"I would guess so," Nish says. "Rosewater would make for quite an elegant wonder, I should think."

On the inside of the rag-paper scroll that protects this handwritten recipe from two centuries ago are Aunt Madeline's own handwritten words.

This is my paternal grandmother's recipe for Rosewater Wonders. For many years, this bread was the most popular item sold in her family's Rose Tea Bakery, 10 Fivepenny Point, Blueberry Brook, Nova Scotia. My grandmother was quite special. She was born with a caul and was therefore believed to have been gifted with second sight. People lined up at her house on Sundays to see her, to have their tea leaves read and their fortunes told. She had mahogany-red hair that never turned white. Her name was Isobel Myrddin.

"Do you know much about your grandfather Silas's mother?" Nish asks.

"Nothing, not even her name," I say. "My mother never talked about her at all. I'm really glad to know her name."

"Which scroll would you like to open next?" Nish asks.

There's one scroll I've had my eye on because it's tied with teabag string and the knot holds sprigs of dried berries. I recognize the berries. They grow wild in the woods around Aunt Madeline's house. Whenever she and my mother wanted to get me out of their hair, I'd be sent out with a birch basket to pick those berries.

Nish helps me unfurl the scroll. He holds it open. In silence, we read the words written on the scroll in Aunt Madeline's handwriting.

Fade's Tea

Late blueberries. Early foxberries. Mid-March black willow bark. Butterfly pea flower petals. Green fruit from the forget-me-not tree. Equal parts each. Sun dry berries and fruit under glass three days. Serve with ginger snaps and apple jam.

This is my recipe for my niece's favourite tea. Even though she's a child, she is my favourite person in the world to share tea with. Her name is Fade Luck.

My heart fills and breaks. My head drops like a woman hanged. I sob instead of breathe for who knows how long.

I let myself cry.

CHAPTER THIRTY-EIGHT

Nish makes us tea. Not wild berry tea with crystalline stream water steeped in a blue betty pot. Two stale hotel teabags with water from the bathroom sink boiled in a scaly kettle.

But it's just right. It's the second-best tea I've ever had.

Because it's not about the tea.

We pull our chairs to the window and sit together, our feet up on the windowsill. Steam curls from our cups, unaffected by the storm outside.

The power goes out. All the background hums and buzzes of the hotel stop. Hurricane Lettie whistles and screeches outside. Lightning flashes as we make our way back to the table piled with scrolls.

"Let's open one more scroll before we call it quits." I balance my lit flashlight on the table. "Which one do you think?"

"I think there is one we should open," Nish says. He sounds reluctant, for some reason. He selects a scroll from the middle of the pile. As soon as I see it, I know why he picked it. It's nothing like the other scrolls.

The knots in the yarn that tie it closed are gnarly and sloppy, with nothing—no twig or sprig—tied in them. Just an ugly, unravelling mess.

"A messed-up thing that doesn't fit in," I say.

"Exactly what I was thinking," he says.

My hands tremble as I work the ugly knots apart. They loosen enough for us to slide the yarn off. The scroll unfurls itself in my hand; the paper is soft and feathery, but blotched and stained in places. The handwriting is, again, Aunt Madeline's. A fragile sachet the size of a teabag is pinned to the paper, a handful of dried and faded bits of plants inside.

Lightning flashes. We read the title of the recipe on the scroll: "Tea for a Quiet Death."

Serving for one.

CHAPTER THIRTY-NINE

Water hemlock. Deadly nightshade. White snakeroot. Wolfsbane. Death cap mushroom.

"This tea is the Grim Reaper in liquid form," Nish says.

"A murder tea?" I say. "Was Aunt Madeline a . . ."

My brain gallops away with a hundred horrors. Nish shrugs, but I see the look in his eyes. He looks intrigued. And worried.

"Why did my aunt want to preserve her recipe for the world's most murdery tea?"

"Maybe it's not murder."

"Nish. It has five deadly poisonous plants in it. How is it not murdery?"

"Maybe," he says, "it's a suicide tea."

I hadn't thought of that.

"Either way, Fade, I think this scroll was opened not that long ago."

"And tied back up by someone with messed-up hands. Or a messed-up brain. Or both."

"Indeed."

"And this is just one more of these messed-up, frigged-up, horrible things that don't belong in Aunt Madeline's tidy and well-kept world. The handwriting on the back of that one photograph. That chain in the shed. The knots on this scroll. The suitcase. That frigging door."

"I agree."

Something else occurs to me. "Nish, I think there might be one more messed-up, out-of-place thing I didn't think of before."

I grab my phone and find the email my mother sent me on my first morning in Willow Sound. I point out the part of the email I'm thinking of, where my mother typed:

Madeline sent me a card for my birthday last month. And she has never, ever sent me a birthday card in all the years before. Not one. So she's getting soppy and sentimental in her old age. Maybe she finally realizes she was wrong. I'd say she probably has dementia, now, or shaky hands.

"Shaky hands," Nish says. He gets it.

"Maybe my mother meant the handwriting in her birthday card was messed up. Really messed up, compared to Aunt Madeline's normal handwriting. Maybe . . ."

I dump out the photos I saved from Aunt Madeline's cabinet and shuffle through them until I find the black-and-white photograph of the little girl with the long black hair standing next to the toboggan.

"Maybe the handwriting on the birthday card she got"—I flip the photograph over—"looks like this."

iZi pasi Wollo wuNDrs 187x

The deranged scrawl on the back of the photograph is even worse than I remember.

"How long did Corporal Quill say your aunt had been missing?" Nish asks.

"Three months," I say.

"When did your mother receive this card?"

"One month ago."

Ugly knot. Ugly writing. Ugly door.

The teacup next to Aunt Madeline's body in the cellar.

Someone murdered her. Someone poisoned Aunt Madeline by using the recipe for this murder tea, hacked a hole in her floor, dumped her body in her cellar, burned her, and wrote a birthday card to her sister.

They did it all with their messed-up hands.

I hope that person's hands hurt them all to hell.

When I find them, I'm going to make them hurt even worse.

BOOK NINE

Red Rubber Boot

CHAPTER FORTY

The morning after a storm is a special kind of quiet. You survived the storm. Now, you get up and face what the storm destroyed while you took cover in the dark. Sift through the rubble. Gather the scraps. Bury the dead.

I stare up, lying on my back on the hotel bed. Grey light softens the white walls. Distant chainsaws rip and roar. Outside the big window, the sky shimmers like grey glass and swarms with seagulls, orbiting feasts of freshly tossed garbage and guts.

My heavy eyes move to the table where the scrolls used to be piled. Early this morning, just before he left, after the worst of Hurricane Lettie had passed, I handed all of Aunt Madeline's scrolls to Nish. Entrusting him with the work of reading and recording them and whatever else he wants to do with them. Maybe it was naive of me to hand them over to anyone, but honestly, I can't unroll any more scrolls right now. No more old memories. No more new regrets.

My thigh shoots with pain as I force myself out of bed to limp to the window, to look out from the fifth floor. The forest that had run uninterrupted to the horizon yesterday is flattened in huge swaths. The gathering of trees that had shaded this place for who knows how long is all gone. From up here, it's as if a giant boot plummeted down from the cosmos, stomped down everything, and walked away. Leaving a broken province in its wake.

I wonder what, if anything, is left of Aunt Madeline's house. My scabby boots drip by the door. They dare me to screw my feet into their crusty holes, lace up, and go find out.

Maybe the psycho who murdered and burned her would go back to her house for a peek. For a second little thrill. Psychos do that kind of thing.

Maybe I'll get lucky and catch the psycho in the act.

Get my hands on him.

Yeah.

Frig it. I grab my wet jeans and hoodie and those bloody boots. Close my eyes. Click my heels three times.

The woods of Willow Sound are now a graveyard for trees. They lay over each other in heaps like broken bones. Some half fallen, half alive, they still creak and groan. I feel the trees dying all around me.

When I reach the little hole in the stone walkway where Aunt Madeline's protection spell jar had been buried before I arrived, I nearly fall over. Not because I tripped over anything. Because of the pure shock of what I see beyond it.

Aunt Madeline's house.

It is still there.

Aching thigh be damned, I run to the house as hard as I can. To touch it. To inhale the wet wood smell. To get splinters from the rough slats. To convince myself it's real.

It is real.

The stained glass windows. The roof. Even the sieve by the door. All there. All fine. The gardens are mostly gone. The rotted garden boxes and dead plants must have been yanked from the earth and flung into the sky. But not the house.

Lettie had not destroyed Madeline Luck's house. It's almost as if Lettie protected it.

I look east to where my apple tree should be. The tree is gone. Just a cracked-off stump left. A sherry-red skirt of apples spreads on the ground around the stump.

Apples . . . and something else red.

A red rubber boot.

CHAPTER FORTY-ONE

Mud sucks at the boot as I pull it up from the ground. Poppy-bright gum rubber that must have been worn a long time and a long way. It reeks of sea salt and swamp water.

This is the boot.

This is the red rubber boot I *imagined* ran out of the house with Aunt Madeline's rifle. The rubber boot my banged-up brain *hallucinated* on the foot of my dead Aunt Madeline as she shot her rifle and scared off a wolf that hasn't existed in this province for one hundred and fifty years.

What messed-up looking glass have I stepped through?

And where is the other boot?

The police tape that had been wrapped around Aunt Madeline's house is long gone, but Constable Quill and her flock of fools will be back. Ten bucks says they'll claim witchcraft kept Aunt Madeline's house safe from the hurricane. Five bucks says I'll tell them to go frig themselves when they do.

Stumbling through mud to see what's left of the back garden, my foot skids on something silver pink and so slippery it sends me sliding into the backyard feet first on my rear end.

A dead fish. I stepped on a dead fish and slid on its guts. The severed head of what used to be a mackerel gapes up at me from the tread of my boot.

The back garden is a strange, alien landscape. Gobs of silver-green sea slime and scores of dead fish are pooled and strewn everywhere. The whole back garden is coated with sludge and corpses. Dead fish reeking of salty, fishy burps. It is going to be a nightmare here when they rot.

The fog of my breath tickles my face. It is cold back here.

The fog stops. My breathing stops.

I see red.

I see the other red boot. On the foot of a delicate pile of sticks in the shape of a woman lying dead-still near the cliff's edge.

A woman with one red boot on.

And wild white hair.

She moves.

Lying on the ground before me is the most fragile thing I have ever seen. Aunt Madeline. I can't tell if she is moving because she's alive or because she's just a pile of bird bones and moth wings trembling in the wind. For some reason, she's wearing an apron covered in pockets filled with strange things, like a penny-pockets lady. All the pockets look full, except one.

"Aunt Madeline!" I say to her. "Aunt Madeline, it's me. It's Fade. I'm here. I found you. I got you."

Don't touch her too much. Don't move her.

Please work, phone. Please.

My shaky thumb dials 9-1-1 wrong three times.

Her eyes are sunk so deep inside her head, she looks like a skull wrapped in tattered paper. She is so old. So small. But it is her. It's Aunt Madeline. I recognize her face under the hollows and wrinkles. I know that face. I love that face. Her toothless mouth quivers. Trying to say something. I lower my ear to her lips. Her breath smells like blood.

"I dint die . . . in the fire."

"Yes," I say. "The rain put out the fires. You're alive. I'm so glad you're alive."

Her coughs are bloody. She struggles to speak despite the blood in her throat.

"Wss."

"What did you say, Aunt Madeline? I can't—"

"Wesh."

"Nine-one-one, what is your emergency?" the voice in my phone says.

Aunt Madeline winces. "Wass." Her bloody lips try to pucker. She blows two little puffs of air. *Uff-uff.* She tries again. "A wiss."

I know I have to get my brain together for this phone call, but this may be Aunt Madeline's last word on earth.

"Nine-one-one. Hello? What is your emergency?"

"Please wait, please," I say into the phone. "I can't understand her. Aunt Madeline, a what? A wash? A kiss? I'm so sorry I don't understand what you're saying—"

Then I do.

She moves her left hand so I will notice it. In her thin hand of paper bones, covered in mud from gardens that are gone now, Aunt Madeline holds a single dandelion, its seeds long gone, by the stem.

I say the word for her. "Wish."

She nods. "Wiss."

I understand now. She releases the dandelion into my hand, but she may as well have reached in my chest and dropped it inside my rib cage.

"What do you wish for?" I say.

"Don't . . . forget . . . me."

"I won't," I say. "I won't forget you."

"I dint . . . die . . . in the fire."

She closes her eyes, and everything about her goes still and soft. All I can do is hold her bones together to keep her from falling apart.

CHAPTER FORTY-TWO

Ground Search and Rescue comes through fast for Aunt Madeline. Probably because they're volunteers from another community. They don't ask me if she wears a pointy hat or if she has a black cat. They only ask her age, which I don't know, and her medical history, which I don't know. The rescue team quickly realizes I don't know anything useful, and they stop asking me things.

They whisk her away, alive, through the woods on a stretcher and leave me behind in a graveyard of rotting fish, clutching a dandelion stem and a red rubber boot.

Where has she been for the past three months?

Inside, the house is a wreck. Water and broken glass twinkle on every surface. All the treasures and tools of her life are smashed beyond repair, spilled like the contents of a thousand shattered snow globes. The purple cabinet still stands but has lost most of its contents. My aunt's rifle rests next to the cold stove.

If Aunt Madeline is still alive, then who on earth is the person I found burned to death in her cellar? Whoever that dead person was, there is no doubt in my mind that suspect number one for that burned person's murder will be the Witch of Willow Sound.

That Dillweed Davish guy will be thrilled. He'll charge extra for admission to the museum of a notorious killer witch.

Over my dead body.

A random thought trickles into my racing brain. Were the fish still alive when Aunt Madeline came home? Did she have to make her way through a frantic and macabre dance of death? Did she stand in her kitchen, where I am now, to see the shattered remains of her lifetime of hard work, drop her rifle, give up, and walk out to her back garden, covered in gasping fish, to fall down with them and make a last wish alone?

But not alone.

It won't be long before word reaches Grand Tea that Madeline Luck has been found alive and that her house survived the storm. Quill and her pack of bloodsuckers will be back, scavenging for evidence or, rather, witch souvenirs.

I have two choices. I can stay here and protect the house from the parasitic bloodsuckers, or I can go figure out what happened. The truth of the fire. So, I can tell the truth for her.

Aunt Madeline is not a killer.

I grab one last thing from Aunt Madeline's house before I go.

If I was a witch, I would cast a spell to protect the house. But I'm not.

I am a woman who raised herself on the dirt roads of Nova Scotia. Instead of a witch's broomstick, I've got a two-hundred-year-old hunting rifle and a reason to use it.

Same damn thing.

BOOK TEN

HH-040

CHAPTER FORTY-THREE

Turns out Hurricane Lettie didn't budge the big rock. The town of Grand Tea is still there, but it's in rough shape. Power lines sag. Downed trees criss-cross roads and rest on rooftops. Generators rumble. A cluster of twenty-some massive boulders have been dumped along the main road. One crushed a car. Another smashed the porch right off a house. All look like they got cracked off the Grand Tea rock by the wind and dropped on the town. Lettie sure put the pucks to this place on her way through.

Good. I hope they all break their backs yanking broken trees out of their sump pumps.

The pain in my thigh slows me down a bit as I make my way along the main road. I limp over busted shingles and tattered Halloween decorations.

The archives survived. No trees landed on it, but it looks like the flagpole fell and yanked the power line right out of the archives' wall. It's dark inside the front of the building, and darker still around back where Nish's shelter is. I knock on the small green door.

Nish opens it. His eyes dart to the rifle on my shoulder and back to me.

"I'm not here to shoot you," I say. I enjoy putting the emphasis on the *you*.

"Well, don't let me stand in the way of your premeditated—and wholly justified, I'm sure—homicidal plans," Nish says.

"Thank you."

"But before you head off to rampage and pillage, et cetera, I have something quite extraordinary to tell you."

"Of course you do."

"I found out what the HH stands for, on the old chain in the shed."

"Really?" I say. "What does it stand for?"

"Havenwood Hospital."

"A hospital with chains?"

"Yes," he says.

"That can't be good."

"No," he says. "Please come through."

It's on the tip of my tongue to tell him about Aunt Madeline being alive. Or just barely alive. But the words won't come out. Something inside me pushes the words way down.

Nish offers me a flashlight. I follow him into his tiny hideaway home. Small bed, small fridge. Smell of cold coffee and old paper. No windows. The floor and walls are lined with books. Old and new. All of them riddled with ribbons and bookmarks and neon sticky notes.

"Someone with a Ph.D. in history should be living in a historic manor." I hunch down under the low ceiling. "You should be sending butlers to fetch books off massive shelves with mahogany ladders. This place is smaller than a prison cell."

"Historians still want to do research here, but there is nowhere for us to stay since Nova Scotia became gentrified." Nish sighs at the map of Nova Scotia on his wall. "Unless an uncontested mayor presiding over an understaffed archives is willing to slap together an unauthorized shanty for the most desperately devoted historians to stay temporarily, such as yours truly."

"Why did you come to Nova Scotia, of all places?"

"Not just anywhere in Nova Scotia, but specifically right here." He taps his finger on the map. "The oceanside area along the cliffs right here. Fade, there are more recorded sightings of witches here over the last eighty years than anywhere in the world."

"Really?"

"It's true! The Witch of Willow Sound is one witch of many here."

"Go 'way."

"I shall not! I've collected the names of all these legendary witches. I hope to research each one in turn."

"Do they all have weird names?"

"They have wonderful names. The Hag of the Bite. The Old Lady with the Kettle. The Black Lake Witch. The Hammer-Nailer. These women may have been very much like Madeline Luck. Women who lived apart from the rest of society, and for some reason, they are all seen in woods and swamps in the area. Maybe they gather together, here. Maybe they are witches of a coven."

"A coven, Nish? Really?"

"I'm serious, Fade. I have never heard of any place like this in the whole world. I just had to come here and study this land of uncanny women called witches. Even if it means living in an uninsulated tin box attached to the rear-end of an underfunded archives under a giant rock."

"Maybe you'll meet one of them someday."

"That would be a dream come true," he says.

Nish leads me through his room and into the archives building. The stuffy building is thick with silence. Our flashlight beams slide along the brick walls as we walk. Down a dark set of stairs to a heavy steel door marked Authorized Staff Only. The door yawns and scrapes open to reveal a suffocating, massive vault.

"Why is the archival stuff all relegated to the basement?" I lean my head inside the vault. No musty smell. The air is dry as a bone.

"Not all," he says. "There is a public collection upstairs. All copies of originals, or photocopies of photocopies. Scans. Microfilm. Hand-picked records for public use."

"Then why are we down here?"

"Because the Havenwood Hospital records I found are not available for the public to see. They're only down here, locked away in the closed stacks."

"That can't be a good sign," I say. "Is this like some old-time archival dark web?"

"I had my suspicions about it since my first week here." Nish holds the door for me. "Technically, I am not allowed to access these closed stacks without special permission. No one is. They say they're 'too fragile.' There's only one electronic access card to this vault, and Mayor Davish has it. When Hurricane Lettie knocked the power out, the vault door unlocked itself. I couldn't resist taking a peek." Nish beams about his quiet rebellious act.

"So, what's Mayor Dillweed hiding in the basement?"

"This is less a basement, and more of a bunker," Nish says. "About a hundred years ago, the provincial archivist petitioned to move the historical records of Grand Tea to a secondary location outside the town, in case the Grand Tea rock fell and destroyed not just the town but its history. But the townspeople spat on the idea and petitioned right back to keep it here, under the shadow of the rock."

"Big shock."

"Indeed. As his plan B, the provincial archivist quietly decided to store everything in a reinforced steel vault underground. No petition. No permission. That way, if the rock fell, the records would be entombed and, some day, excavated. They would not be lost forever."

The vault is stuffy and pitch-black inside. My flashlight roves over tall shelves of well-organized archival boxes and a few books. Nish pulls on white gloves. He shines his light into an archival box on a work table, already open. The box is labelled Havenwood

Hospital Fonds. He lifts an old book from the box and eases it open to a page marked with the book's own red ribbon.

"Henry the Eighth House was one of the original poorhouses in Nova Scotia," Nish says. "It had room for twenty residents and operated until 1858, when the government opened a larger facility called Mount Hope. At that time, the last three residents of Eighth House were packed up and relocated across the province, from here to Mount Hope. The Eighth House building was sold and renamed Havenwood Hospital and Asylum."

Nish removes a photograph from the book and places it on the table under my light. The black-and-white photograph is labelled "Havenwood Hospital and Asylum, 1901." The photo shows a dark building looming over a field of nothing. No grass. No trees or paths. Just flat dirt, compressed and lifeless, around a lightless big house. Bars on the windows. Every last one.

"Was this building in Grand Tea?" I ask.

"No."

"Then why are the records here in the Grand Tea archives?"

"I wondered the same," he says. "Officials required hospitals to keep records for posterity, but there were no requirements about *where* those records had to be kept. This archive is unofficially known among Nova Scotian bureaucrats as the place where records go to die."

"Because someday the big rock will fall and bury everything forever," I say.

"And until that day, very few people are willing to come in here and spend time under the rock sifting through papers. These records are already dead."

"Perfect set-up to hide bad secrets," I say.

"Indeed."

"So, Havenwood Hospital had things it wanted to hide, then."

"Very bad things," Nish says. "The building itself was purchased by a doctor from Ontario named Willard Havenwood and his wife,

Honoria, in 1859. They turned the bedrooms into wards with thick metal doors and named it after themselves."

"I hate it already," I say.

"The Havenwoods had no interest in running a hospital to help the poor." Nish continues to sift through the files. "They were here to do business with the wealthy class."

"Do business, how?"

"By providing a discreet location where people of means could quietly and permanently place the secret members of their family."

"What does that mean?"

"Anyone in the family who was considered different, and therefore undesirable and unwanted. A physical difference or disability or illness. Any unwanted children. Children of affairs. Children of rape. Mixed race children. Anyone whose existence would inconvenience the elite's reputations could be hidden away in Havenwood."

Oh.

"Before Havenwood, the rich kept these children locked away in attics and back rooms. People would suspect, perhaps, but never ever ask. It was understood. Then with the founding of Havenwood Hospital, for a very high price, families had a new option. Send their unwanted relatives to Havenwood forever. Clear out their attics, and sometimes clear out their family tree. No price was considered too high to allow socialites to host parties and high tea without the cries of hidden human beings interrupting the party."

"History gets dark, doesn't it?"

"I wish it was only history, Fade, but still to this day, people with mental health conditions are shackled and chained in sixty countries in the world."

That fact makes me feel sick.

"What did they do to the children who lived at Havenwood?"

"There aren't a whole lot of official records about what happened to the residents." Nish turns the pages with a delicate touch. "Which is sinister, in and of itself. Most of the resident records are in this strange code. However, other Havenwood records are in plain English, and they're even more sinister. I found no shortage of requisitions for coffin materials, yet zero recorded deaths."

"Were the children forced to make coffins to sell, maybe?"

"No orders of sale. No county requests. They made all these coffins that disappeared along with any dead. There had to have been deaths at Havenwood, Fade. The 1918 influenza epidemic alone wiped out entire rural communities in this province. I promise you. People died at Havenwood."

"Where did they go?"

Nish moves his sad eyes across all the darkened stacks of boxes of records packed into the vault. Hidden from the light. "I don't know," he says with a heavy sigh. "Nova Scotia already has such a dark history of heartless cruelty toward its most vulnerable people. Especially children. The Shubenacadie Indian Residential School. The Nova Scotia Home for Colored Children. The butterbox babies. Havenwood Hospital was one horror of many. A horror story that, it seems, was never written down."

"And Davish holds the only key to these horrors."

"Indeed, Mayor Davish stands watch over this vault of dead records like a prison warden." Nish lowers his voice. "As if he's the one with something to hide."

Nish turns the old Havenwood Hospital book to me. The open pages are neatly handwritten in old brown ink. Down the left side of the left page is a tidy column, a list of letters and numbers starting at HH-001 and running in sequence down the page to HH-025. HH-026 to HH-050 are on the facing page.

"The code."

My spine shivers. Nish gently taps the only number I care about. The number engraved on the shackle in the shed. HH-040.

"Does the code correspond to something?" I ask him.

"Yes." With more care and patience than I would ever have in this moment—or any moment—Nish eases the old book open to another ribbon-marked page. HH-040 written in the top left of the page. Written next to it:

Female. Five. Eyes: green. Hair: black. Insane.

I stare down at those seven words. With my eyes: green. With my hair: black.

Insane.

That awful, heavy, filthy chain was used to shackle this girl. *Female. Five.*

"No name," I say.

"No names in the Havenwood records," Nish says. "Just numbers."

"Do you think this five-year-old girl was Aunt Madeline?" I say. "She was definitely considered odd by her parents. For sneaking out into strange places and climbing on roofs and not socializing like normal girls. Would that be enough to classify someone as insane?"

"Back then, yes," Nish says. "I presume your aunt never mentioned her incarceration to you."

"Not once. But maybe that's not the kind of thing you tell a child. What do all the dates down the page mean?"

"It's hard to tell," he says. "Everything is in code. I haven't come across a guide to the code yet, though I'll keep looking. I did figure out that ESC means escape and RET means return."

Next to HH-040, a long list of dates coded with ESC and RET. Over and over.

"Aunt Madeline ran away. Again and again. Year after year. She escaped."

"Yes," he says.

"And was brought back."

"Yes."

"Does Havenwood still exist?"

"No, the records seem to end in 1967."

"Was there ever a fire there?"

"A fire? At Havenwood Hospital? No. No fire. According to property records, the building was abandoned and eventually condemned. A farmer bought the land in 1994 and tore the building down. Today, it's a blueberry field."

So, Havenwood Hospital didn't have a fire. Someplace else did, though.

"Nish, I have two questions for you."

"I'm ready," he says.

"Can you find out the street address of my grandparents' house? Silas and Jia Luck. They owned two houses, and one of them burned down in 1968."

"Yes, I can. No problem. What's question two?"

"Do you have gas in your car?"

CHAPTER FORTY-FOUR

On our way to Nish's car, we run into trouble. The faces that usually watch from behind windows are outside now. Scraping the remains of their life back together. Even Davish is with them, though he's not doing any actual work himself. Just standing around and shaking his head at the damage.

The Grand Tea townies stop raking debris and chopping fallen trees when they see us coming. They drag their shovels and axes behind them as they slowly clot into a mob and block our way. A familiar black pickup truck is parked nearby.

For some reason, Quill is there.

An angry mob with axes and shovels and a Mountie and a mayor. This should be interesting.

"Hey, Nish," I say. "You know anything about antique rifles?"

"Yes, a little."

"Good." I hand the old rifle to him to defend himself. Or, at least, to keep townies out of his face.

On our way past the familiar black pickup truck, I reach into the bed of it and grab the baseball bat I'd tossed in there two days ago. I rest it on my shoulder, nice and casual. "This town loves a mob."

"You need to keep her out of the archives, Mr. Chaudry!" Davish crosses his arms. "She has no right to be snooping in our town records."

Quill elbows past him toward me and speaks in a lowered voice. "Miss Luck, I have news about Madeline Luck."

"I know," I say.

"Ground Search and Rescue brought her in to the emergency department at the hospital this morning," Quill says. "They admitted her."

"I know," I say.

"Madeline Luck is not dead," Quill says.

I sense Nish straighten beside me.

"I know," I say.

Quill glances back at the mob behind her. She winces. Maybe with a touch of regret. Maybe it's my imagination. "News about the DNA got out, and I apologize for that, Miss Luck."

"What news about the DNA?"

Davish elbows past Quill, nudging the cop back, placing himself squarely in the spotlight of this surreal scene. He clears his throat to speak. "The DNA," Davish says with drama to rival Nish's, "is an exact match."

"Match for what?" I ask.

"For Madeline Luck," Davish says. "She has the same DNA as the burned body in her cellar."

"What?"

"They are both Madeline Luck," he shouts in my face. "We've captured not just one . . . but two Madeline Lucks!"

"What?"

"The Grand Tea ancestors were right!" he shouts to the mob this time. "The Old Witch is dead and alive—at the same time."

My brain can't understand what Davish is rambling about. Nish's hand clamps on top of his head. Seems like he's figured it out.

"That's not funny, Davish," I say. "There's obviously something wrong at the lab. Bad handling. Bad labelling. Bad intentions. Redo the DNA."

I look past Davish at Quill. Right in her eyes. And I say it again. "Redo the DNA, Quill. Before these people do something you can't undo."

Davish moves toward me again. Too close now. His breath is hot. "They've said it for generations—haven't they, Mr. Chaudry?—that the Old Witch that lives out in Willow Sound made a deal with the Devil long, long ago. Now, we have definitive, indisputable, scientific proof that it's true!"

I want to punch Davish's smug face right into his spine, but I keep my arms rigid. I can tell the townies are eating up this deal-with-the-Devil nonsense. And Davish knows it. The townies start to pile on their own escalating nonsense, yelling out theories.

"The Old Witch got the Devil to raise her from the dead!"

"The Devil resurrected her!"

"She resurrected herself!"

"It's proof she's a witch!"

"We were right all along!"

Davish smiles at me with his self-satisfied mug. I crack my knuckles. Crack my neck. Tighten my grip on the baseball bat. Quill—who has been easing away from the crowd—shakes her head at me, one hand on her shoulder radio, one hand on her belt. Her face is stony.

Nish taps my arm. He flashes his car keys concealed in his hand. He's sticking to the game plan way better than me.

Every part of me wants to stand here until one of these townies gets so frothed up, they step up to me for a fight. I really want an excuse to brawl and lay these suckers out. Knock some teeth out of them and some sense back in.

Instead, I spit on the ground. Right between Davish's pointy shoes.

We head for Nish's car. I walk slow. Chin out. Like I made a deal with the Devil too.

"Madeline Luck is alive?" Nish squeaks in shock as I drive us down the old highway toward Blueberry Brook.

"I went back to check on her house this morning," I say. "I found her there. Alive."

"Amazing!"

"She's alive, but in bad shape. She was lying on the ground in her back garden."

"Will she be all right?"

"I don't know. I hope so. She's injured pretty bad. They said it's like she had been lifted up by the storm and dropped from the sky."

"Did you get to speak to her?" Nish says.

"No." It hurts to admit it. "Nish, I'm sorry I didn't tell you. She was in bad shape when I found her. She felt like broken feathers. When I saw her last, she wasn't awake. I didn't know what she'd want me to say or not say to people, because where was she all this time? Was she hiding? What happened to her?" I rub my palms over my face. "This town hasn't made me any better at trusting people."

Nish's voice is kind. "Protecting the people you care about is nothing to apologize for. I admire it."

I shrug and feel Nish's eyes on me a few seconds longer than usual. Like he's making sure I'm all right.

"Do you think Davish is lying about the DNA?" I ask. "To make the whole thing more Halloween-ish, more profitable for a town betting its financial future on occult tourism?"

"Very possibly. Especially if Corporal Quill is involved. Mayor Davish has a talent for firing those people up. Though it didn't take very much."

"Is there anything in old folk stories about witches that exist in two places at once?"

Nish thinks about it while I drive. "Yes. If you consider the myth about the portal in Madeline Luck's cellar."

"The nightmare sleep paralysis thing?"

"Yes. Some people believe the night hag is the astral projection of a witch whose physical body is safely elsewhere. Others believe you can summon the witch on command by reciting the Lord's prayer backwards."

"What do they believe back there?"

"In Grand Tea, they believe the Old Witch uses the portal in her cellar to transport herself anywhere she wants to go."

"Wait, do they think astral projection means she technically has two bodies, then? One back by the portal, one floating out there wherever?"

Nish's hands fly up to his head again. "Fade, do you think—"

"Nope."

Nish drops his line of questioning. Out loud, at least.

"It makes more sense to me that Davish and Quill are lying about the DNA," I say. "People want someone to blame for the hurricane. He's giving them what they want."

"They are getting dangerous, Fade."

"They're not the only ones."

CHAPTER FORTY-FIVE

The summer house property of Silas and Jia Luck is enclosed behind a ten-foot-tall brick wall that extends around the whole property. The wall seems excessive for the Nova Scotian countryside, because there's no one around here to keep out. Nish and I passed a handful of far-flung farmhouses on the drive here. That's it.

The front gate is huge. Regal. Wrought iron bars curving at the top. A big cursive L welded to the middle of the gate. A faded No Trespassing sign zip-tied to the iron bars. A silk wreath—the kind you see at funerals—dangles from the L.

"L for Luck," I say.

It's strange to see my own initial on a gate this palatial.

"Fade, does the shape of that L on the gate look familiar to you?" Nish says. "Because it looks familiar to me."

"It looks like the L on this key." I pull the iron key from my boot. The second key Nish and I had found, hidden in the satin lining of

Aunt Madeline's suitcase. Since then, it's been soaked in mud and rain and blood from a wolf attack.

"Fade, have you been carrying that key in your boot all this time?"

"Maybe."

"That must've hurt."

"Maybe."

The key slides into the big gate's lock. Takes some effort to turn it, but the whole thing unlocks with a deep *clank*. A sound right out of a castle gate in the Middle Ages.

I heave my shoulder against the iron bars. Masses of needle-sharp weeds poke through the gate and into my hoodie. They've grown, unopposed, against the walls and through the metal bars for decades. Digging my boots into the dirt road helps me force the wall of weeds back enough so Nish and I can squeeze inside the gate.

"A gate this wide would have been quite grand," Nish says. "Wide enough to allow motor cars and carriages through. It must have been a very impressive Victorian garden, in its day."

"Silas and Jia Luck were extremely materialistic, but apparently it was a survival tactic."

"How so?"

"Material wealth kept them safe," I say. "They were a mixed race couple in Nova Scotia before that was even close to being socially acceptable. Money and business influence kept them safe. It made them valuable, even to the most racist elite. They had to put on enormous shows of wealth. Big parties. Big gestures. Suddenly 'foreign' becomes 'exotic.' They played the game well."

"That seems like a lot of pressure on a family," Nish says.

"Very true."

"And seems very much the opposite of your aunt and you."

"Very true."

The crumbling remnants of the Luck mansion slump about four hundred feet from the gate. No roof left. No glass in the two remaining windows. It's a hollow shell of a house, weathered and beaten and smothered in moss and trailing vines.

"Do you have any memories of this place?" asks Nish.

"Not one," I say. "The house burned down years before I was born."

We push our way through the weeds. The sharp scent of mint is everywhere. Goldenrod and ragweed tilt and whip around us. Weather-worn life-sized statues lurk in tall grasses, their haunting faces marred by moss. Stone cherubs reach up with severed arms, their heads crowned with dead beetles. Headless muses hold broken harps and busted urns. Two stone lions with no ears and no fangs guard the house. Their lion bodies are strangled with ivy. Their stone coats crawling with ants.

"I guess nature is reclaiming this place," I say.

"Nature always does," Nish says.

The house is no longer a house, but a single defiant wall that has refused to fall. A distressed facade welcoming us to the yellow front door with no home behind it. Like a set on a stage with no players. No hums or smells of a home. Just silence and insects.

The doorknob is so corroded it falls apart in my hand, and the door falls open. On the other side of the wall, I half hoped there would be wallpaper, pictures on the wall, a rug on the floor, a fully adorned living room standing, unbothered, in the middle of a field. But no. Just scorched wood, bare wires, and empty bird's nests.

Shards of ceramic and glass poke from the ground here and there, like little bones. We don't stand on solid earth, but a sagging floor struggling to hold itself together. Even so, it's easy to tell the house was once a palace, massive and sprawling.

"It's crazy to think my mother grew up in a house this big," I say. "She said this place was haunted, that she was raised by ghosts."

"Do you believe in ghosts, Fade?"

"I believe in the ghosts of my grandmother's lies. My mother inherited this bizarre obligation to distant family in China who devoured Jia Luck's lies for decades. Jia, the wealthy and angelic mother raising Canadian sons. On her deathbed, she made my mother promise to keep it up forever. Keep sending them money. Keep sending them lies. It's too late to tell the truth anyway, she said. It would cause the whole family too much pain. So, my mother does it, and she expected to pass on the obligation to me, but I said no. Which means all the lies will unravel on the day Doreen Luck dies. She'll take the blame for it. She knows it. It'll be her only reward for a lifetime of trying to be the good daughter. It's half the reason my mother and I cut ties."

Nish gives me a moment to breathe. "What's the other half?"

A sluggish breeze crawls across the neglected ground, tugging at our sleeves. Stale sighs of chalk and loam and dust dry our eyes.

"I was an accident. I wasn't supposed to exist, and my existence ruined everything. My mother was a travelling nurse, trekking to the most remote locations in Canada. When she wasn't working, she'd drop everything and fly off to any place with sunshine and palm trees. She had to quit travelling to have me and took jobs she hated to raise me. She should have been flying off to glamourous places. Instead she was handwashing diapers in the toilet and wiping my nose. When I was in grade eight, she married a guy with a yacht and three houses and enough bank to send me away to boarding school and finally set my mother free again. She was giddy. I felt like I'd been dropped in 'Salem's Lot. I saved them both the money and frigged off on my own. I didn't need school to teach myself hacking or coding, anyway. She never came looking for me. She says it was because she knew I'd be fine."

"Were you fine?" Nish asks.

I don't answer his question.

"Your family haunted too?" I ask.

"By me, I suppose."

"How's that?" I ask.

"To them . . . I am dead."

Something about the way he says that flicks on every protective instinct in me. Like lights flicking on in a dark hallway, one by one.

"I was supposed to marry a woman once, but it was a mistake. I didn't know her very well, and she definitely didn't know me. That was my fault for trying to be what everyone else wanted. My parents adored her, especially my mother." Nish stands so still as he speaks, he's like a statue in the overgrown garden. "On a research trip to the Netherlands, I met a man. His name was Lio. We met in the Van Gogh Museum near *Sunflowers*, and we fell in love. Lio was brilliant and kind and he knew all the lies I'd lived and he loved me anyway. I spent three beautiful months in his arms." Nish is almost whispering now. "When my work visa ran out, I came home and told my family the truth. My parents said I was dead to them. Lio did his best, but I let down everyone I loved, and I lost him too."

Nish unconsciously rubs his left thumb across his left ring finger where a wedding ring would sit. "My father died suddenly from a massive heart attack. Nine years ago, now. I asked my mother if I could speak at his memorial. She said I should feel lucky to even be allowed to attend. I wrote a speech anyway and held the paper in my hands the whole time. Just in case she changed her mind. But she wouldn't even look at me. At the end, I placed my speech by my father's photo and I walked out. Emotions were high but I was so ashamed. The next day, I left England and never went back."

"I'm so sorry, Nish," I say. "You didn't deserve any of that."

"My brothers are still in England. Oncologists, both, with big, beautiful families I've never met. I don't exist to them. Sometimes I wake up and think I'm a ghost. Maybe that's what ghosts do. But I haven't had that thought once since the day you appeared outside my green door. You seem like an outsider, too, but you don't seem to mind it."

"I don't like people." I kick at the weeds in front of me. "But I like you."

He smiles at me. He looks a bit more like himself already. "I like you too."

We stand there, looking around. Letting the quiet last as long as it needs to.

Through the quiet, what's left of the floorboards groans underneath us.

"This place seems dangerous," I say.

"And spooky," Nish says. "Feels like we're being watched."

"Let's get this over with. The house is gone, but maybe there's still a basement."

"Hm." Nish thinks for a moment. "Typical Victorian layouts would place the cellar entrance at the back of the house, where the servants work. Approximately . . ." He takes his time, stepping gingerly all the way back to the far edge of the sagging floorboards, then lifts the corner of an old door lying in the dirt. "Here."

We heave the old door aside. Millipedes scatter. The bare bones of a staircase go ten steps straight down. I place my foot on the first stair. The wood squishes.

"Don't go down there. Please, Fade. It's not safe."

"You don't know me at all yet, do you?" I skip the first stair to lean down and test the second. Same squish.

"How will you get back up?"

"You and your sensible questions," I say.

I scan the debris for an idea. Something to brace the wood. Something to land on without breaking my neck. My pocket hums. I grumble at the word *Doreen* on my screen and jam the vibrating thing back in my pocket.

"It's just my mother calling. I'll call Doreen back in a minute. I just need to find a board or . . . something."

"Your mother's name is Doreen? Wait. I thought— Wait." He holds up his hands and waves them like he's sorting through invisible pages of invisible books in the air. He looks so intense and deep inside his own brain, I stop what I'm doing to watch him.

He opens his eyes. "Fade, does your mother go by any other names?"

"Nope. Her middle name is Leta, if that helps. Doreen Leta Luck."

"No, no, no." He closes his eyes again.

"Are you reading archival records stored in your mind palace or something?"

"Yes."

"Cool."

"In the directory records for Blueberry Brook," he says, "I found your grandparents' family listed at this address for this house, right here. Listed as residents living here were your grandfather Silas, your grandmother Jia, and their two daughters. Living here."

"Right."

"There was no Doreen."

"What?"

"Nobody living in this house was named Doreen." Nish opens his eyes. The grey of his eyes looks white.

"You're wrong, Nish," I say. "Doreen did live here. My grandparents had two daughters. My aunt and my mother: Madeline and Doreen. No sons. My mother is sixteen years younger, but they were both here."

"No, they weren't." Nish's hands fold together, as if he's closing his invisible book. "If your mother, Doreen, is sixteen years younger than Madeline, then that is the problem. I'm referring to the county directory of 1943. In 1943, your mother was not born yet."

Nish takes out his phone and quickly swipes through his gallery. Photos of documents. Downloaded scans. "Here, look!" He zooms in on the handwritten county directory entry for the Luck family, residing in very same place he and I are standing now, over seventy years ago.

Luck, Silas	*31, m. Head*	*Surgeon*
Luck, Jia	*29, f. Wife*	*Housewife*
Luck, Madeline	*5, f. Daughter*	
Luck, Maryflower	*5, f. Daughter*	

My eyes burn as I stare holes into that fourth name on the list. Who the hell is Maryflower?

CHAPTER FORTY-SIX

"Who the hell is Maryflower?" I shout the question at Nish, at the world, at nobody. My eyes dart around the gutted remains of the old house, looking for something to tell me anything about Maryflower.

"Perhaps Maryflower passed away as a child, and your mother wasn't told about her."

"But the directory says Madeline is five and Maryflower is five. Even if my mother doesn't know about this Maryflower person, my aunt Madeline sure as hell knows." I feel heat boiling up from my guts. "Do you have any county directories dated after that one?"

"I do."

"Was Maryflower listed in those?"

Nish flicks through more images on his phone. Directory records. Ten years later.

Luck, Silas	41, m. Head	Surgeon
Luck, Jia	39, f. Wife	Housewife
Luck, Madeline	15, f. Daughter	

That's it. Only one daughter listed. No more Maryflower.

"Where did Maryflower go?" I say.

Time to call Doreen back.

Before I can tap her name on my phone, the earth groans. I turn in time to see Nish shoot up in the air over my head. I'm falling. Down through the rotted floor into the basement, dropped like a rag doll in the dirt. It stinks of fusty mud and stale human waste down here.

"Fade!" Nish yells down to me.

"I'm all right. I'm all right." I haul myself into a squat, knees throbbing, and wait for my eyes to adjust, to find a way back up.

But that's not what I find.

Little rooms. Concrete. Very narrow. Some with metal tables. Barrels and buckets. A wall with small doors. Two feet by two feet. Stacked. With wheels for handles. Refrigerators, probably. All just rusted-out bakery equipment.

All the little rooms have their doors open, except one.

What's in there? The closed door creaks at my touch. Unlocked. It opens into the crumbled remains of a small room. Hardly bigger than a bathroom stall. Scorch marks and mould blacken every surface. The stink blowing out is fierce. I fumble my phone light on and fill the little room with cold light. Even through watering eyes, I can tell it's a bedroom.

The metal bed frame jammed in the back gives it away. Filthy blankets rest on the springs, though it looks like they were folded with care. A metal bedpan gapes shamelessly in the corner, spilling over with withered spores. Death-white coral-shaped mushrooms have sprouted across the blankets and up the walls. Fungi shaped like butter-coloured brain matter swell out of every crevice and crack. Piles of tiny animal bones cover the floor.

Things are nailed to the wall. Strange things. A man's shoe. A doll. A knitted grey mitten with white stars. A pair of reading glasses, nailed through one of the eyes.

"What do you see down there?"

Hell, maybe.

This awful little room has a door, but no windows. Despite the stink, despite the bones, I kneel on the filthy floor. The room cloaks me in shadows. More than anything, the room feels sad.

Under the bed: teacups. Some are broken. I take one. Worms curl where the cup had been. The teacup cradles a handful of pussy willow catkins. The catkins don't seem that old.

Looming over the bed: a metal hoop secured to the wall with heavy-duty bolts so massive, it seems they were meant to hold bridges and skyscrapers together. But here they are, in this tiny room, holding nothing but a length of chain. A familiar chain. I have held its other half. I have smelled its grimy rust.

Even through the dark, I see the chain has a tag. It's engraved.

HH-040.

I turn around, on hands and knees, to leave. I lift my eyes and stop dead.

Oh no.

A mural. Hand-painted and faded. Swirls and whirls of a child's vision of a moonlit sky.

Filled with tiny stick-drawn dandelion seeds.

BOOK ELEVEN

Burn

CHAPTER FORTY-SEVEN

Nish clutches the car door with one hand and the dash with the other because I am driving fast and talking faster. I have a lead foot when I'm worked up, and the road from Blueberry Brook to Grand Tea is all twists and turns. He really shouldn't have let me drive.

I let up a bit, so he can breathe and so I can think.

"What's your take, Nish? Is that room old-timey normal or totally messed up?"

"It is, as you say, totally messed up," he says. "From what you described, it sounds like a strong room. Or a prison cell."

Female. Five. Eyes: green. Hair: black. Insane.

"So my grandparents locked their own kid up like a prisoner?"

"Maybe they didn't know what else to do back then," Nish says. "Especially given the precariousness of their interracial union."

"Maybe," I say.

"Maybe it broke their hearts."

"Maybe."

The sadness from the little room has settled in my clothes and my hair.

"It may well be that this mysterious Maryflower Luck lived down there in that room," Nish says. "Who knows for how long. Maybe she got expelled from Havenwood Hospital for running away too much. Maybe after Havenwood Hospital closed. Maybe even all her life."

"That's what I'm thinking too."

"Perhaps the strange sounds your mother thought were ghosts were, in fact, the sounds of Maryflower."

Something else in my brain clicks.

"'I didn't die in the fire,'" I say. "That's what she said."

"Who said?"

"The old woman I found this morning in Aunt Madeline's backyard," I say. "The woman Ground Search and Rescue put on a stretcher and took to the hospital. The woman who was wearing the red rubber boots. She said it."

My brain is so busy rummaging through puzzle pieces in my head, I don't see the oncoming car right away—

Hooooonnnnk. Nish throws his arms over his head.

It screeches around us.

I veer onto the gravel shoulder and slam the car into park before I get us killed. The car stops, but my brain continues to careen wildly.

"Nish, the old woman in the garden who I thought was Aunt Madeline. Maybe she wasn't Aunt Madeline at all. Maybe she was Maryflower."

"What makes you think that?"

"The fire," I say. "Maybe she was trying to tell me about the fire in my grandparents' house. The summer house burned down while she was still locked in the basement."

"Oh my gosh, Fade!" Nish gasps. "The funeral wreath on the front gate!"

"Exactly! My grandparents didn't die in the fire. Madeline didn't die in the fire. My mother didn't die in the fire. Why would somebody hang a funeral wreath on the gate if nobody died in the fire?"

"Because they *thought* somebody had died in the fire."

"Maryflower."

"Maryflower."

I turn the engine off. "Did they even go back after the fire to check on her? To see if she was alive?"

"Perhaps they had no hope. It would have taken a miracle for her to survive."

"They didn't even send someone down there to gather her remains for a funeral," I say. "Did they even have a funeral?"

"I expect they wouldn't have been so public anyway. She might have been dead to them long before," Nish says, voice thinning.

I close my eyes and make fists and quiet my screeching brain.

Maryflower.

Insane.

I need to get out of the car. Inhale clear air. Think a minute.

Nish sits inside the car, window down, flipping through images on his phone. The car's blinker measures out the quiet. *Tick-tick-tick.*

"Oh, no," Nish says so quietly I almost miss it.

"Oh no what?"

"Fade, what else was down there?"

"I couldn't see much. Bakery stuff. Some narrow rooms. Metal tables. Little doors with wheels on them, like submarine doors. I figured they were old bakery cupboards or some kind of fridges."

"That doesn't sound like bakery cupboards or fridges. That sounds like 1920s airlock doors." Nish taps his thumbs on his phone screen. "Thank the stars! Blueberry Brook has a historical society. And they have a database of digitized historical records online. I love historical societies. They are unsung heroes quietly holding this province together."

"They have records about my grandparents?"

"They do," Nish says. "Just as I thought. Your grandparents' house was not just a house. It was listed as a business."

"A bakery?"

"No. Discreet Ice-Box Delivery Services."

"My grandparents delivered ice?"

"No. Ice-Box. It's a patented box used by undertakers to ice corpses before burial."

No.

Nish flicks through the pictures on his phone again. "Here, look. Silas Luck. In the Havenwood Hospital expense statements. 'On April 30, 1938, a fee of $25.00 owed to Dr. Silas Luck for Ice-Box pickup.' I see at least a dozen expense statements like that in 1938 alone."

I rest my face in my hands, as if I could shut out my thoughts, shut out the world. "What . . . happened to the ice-box bodies my grandfather picked up?"

"Well, your family had a very large and very private garden." Nish looks at me. "I think we just discovered what happened to all the Havenwood coffins."

CHAPTER FORTY-EIGHT

Nish drives me to the hospital parking lot. We don't say much. We sit in his car holding drive-through hot chocolates in paper cups.

"I didn't see any headstones," I say.

"There probably aren't any," Nish says. "Graves for the poor and unclaimed dead often have no markers. Their families were rich, but the inmates at Havenwood weren't. It was common practice to offer no acknowledgement of that person's existence. They were treated in death as they were in life. No dignity. No rights."

"No wonder Aunt Madeline never wanted to give that land to my mother," I say, staring out at the hospital. "Or to me. How many people do you think were buried there? Who were they?"

"Hopefully, we can answer that someday," Nish says. "Maybe from historical records. Maybe from their bones."

Our drinks are cold. Nish shivers and turns the heat up.

"I had a thought about the items in the little room with the mural." Nish's voice is kind. His patience while I get my act together is also kind.

"The stuff nailed to the wall?" I say.

"Yes, and the teacups under the bed."

"What about them?"

"Madeline Luck studies witchcraft as a branch of knowledge," Nish says. "She learned the traditional arts and has practised them carefully. It's evident from her scrolls. Her cabinet. The items in the spell jar. The plants in her garden. The sieve by the door. All these things come from well-known traditions. The books of knowledge I have poured over for my own research, Madeline Luck has studied the same knowledge. Maybe even the same books. She understands it all better than I ever will. She lives it."

"The Witch of Willow Sound."

"She is a real witch practising real witchcraft, Fade. It's not an insult to say it that way. It's an honour. It is a great accomplishment to be a witch of her stature. The title is an acknowledgement of her mastery of the craft. It is a complex skill set with a purpose. That purpose, typically for Green Witches, is healing. However, in that little room in the basement of your grandparents' house, there were no signs of traditional magical knowledge there. But there was magic there."

"Nails through random stuff and animal bones. Please don't say Black Magic."

"Sympathetic Magic," he says.

"What's that?"

"It's the oldest magic. Sympathetic Magic is a magic of correspondence. Of symbols. It doesn't come from books or old beliefs. It comes from instinct. A Sympathetic Witch makes up their own magic according to what makes sense to them and their understanding of the world."

"Example."

"The items nailed to the wall. What if they are acts of Sympathetic Magic? Glasses. A shoe. A doll. A child's mitten. Each nailed permanently in place. The items can't go anywhere. They have to stay there, where she nailed them. She wanted them to stay."

"Maryflower wanted her family to come back," I say. "She wanted them to stay. Like a wish."

"Yes. Her family was gone. The house was gone. She had very little left."

"Even after everything her parents put her through, she wished for them to come back," I say. "That's heartbreaking."

"It is."

"What about the teacups?" I ask. "Is that Sympathetic Magic too?"

"Possibly."

"Maybe it's some kind of spell. Like in the jar."

"Fade, that's brilliant! The teacups could be a vessel to hold the ingredients of a spell."

"So, in that case," I say, "the teacup with the dead frog and the crocus in it. The one found next to the burned body in Aunt Madeline's cellar."

"That could have been a Sympathetic Magic spell."

"What's the Sympathetic Magical correspondence for a dead frog and a crocus?"

"Oh, I have no idea."

"Try, Dr. Chaudry. Dig into that mind palace of yours."

We return to silence again.

Nish snaps his fingers. "Reanimation!"

"That's my history nerd," I say. "Explain."

"Wood frogs freeze in the winter. They look dead, but they're not dead. When the temperature rises in the spring, the frogs thaw out and come back to life. And crocuses. The flowers die off, but they come back every year in the same place, from the same roots. It is as if they come back from the dead."

"So, the teacup placed next to the burned body in the cellar held a magic spell—"

"—to bring the burnt bones back to life."

CHAPTER FORTY-NINE

Through the narrow window of the hospital room door, I see my mother sitting stiffly. Tailored suit. High-end shoes. Designer purse. Old-money updo. She probably smells like roses from France.

Turned away from the hospital bed, she reads a book balanced on her knee. Doreen Luck is not one for proximity or holding hands. There's no question where I get it from. But at least she's in there.

"Hey, Ma," I say to her, holding the hospital room door open a crack. She waves me in. Inside, the hospital room feels hollow. It smells like old medicine and fresh plastic. Lights buzz. Machines breathe.

My mother and I nod to each other as I step into the room. That half second of eye contact is too much for either of us, so we turn our eyes to the frail old woman sleeping in the hospital bed. She looks like a wax doll. Barely real.

"I hear you've been up to your eyeballs in trouble since you got here," my mother says, peering at me over top of her gold-rimmed glasses.

"Hey, you ordered me to come here," I say.

"To be a help to your family, Phaedra, not to wreck the joint."

The old woman in the bed doesn't stir. She barely seems to breathe.

"She's not Aunt Madeline, is she?"

"She can't be." My mother closes her book. "This woman has scars from childhood that—I can tell you right now—Madeline does not have. This woman has had all kinds of strange surgeries, the doctor said. We would have seen marks like those on Madeline. No, this woman is not Madeline. This woman is . . . someone else."

"Ma, have you ever heard of somebody named Maryflower?"

She flicks her eyes around, thinking. "No. Maryflower? No."

"A friend of mine," I say, "a historian, he found old county directory records for your parents' house in Blueberry Brook. The house that burned down. The directory lists two children in the family before you were born. Two daughters, same age. Madeline and Maryflower Luck."

"Twins?"

"Must be," I say. "This woman looks a lot like Aunt Madeline. Identical twins can have identical DNA."

Madeline and Maryflower. Twins. Come to think of it, that old photograph of two girls from Aunt Madeline's cabinet—they could possibly be twins.

I let my backpack fall off my shoulder onto the floor and crouch to unzip it. The collection of photos from Aunt Madeline's cabinet are stashed in a sturdy archival-quality envelope Nish gave me. My mother watches me sift through them like a delicate deck of cards to find the little black-and-white snapshot I had barely glanced at days ago.

Two little girls around five years old. They stand side by side in front of a wallpapered wall. Same black braids. Same light eyes. Both of the girls hold an urn in their hands.

My mother peers at the photograph. "Why are they holding funeral urns? That's so morbid."

At first glance, one girl seems taller and older. But I look more closely. One of the girls stands perfectly straight, arms at her sides, smiling politely at the camera. The other girl is a little slouched, head tilted, foot turned in. Her expression is sullen. She clutches her sister's sleeve and looks at something—or someone—out of frame. I can imagine some adult snapping at her to let go, stand up straight, smarten up, act more like her sister. I immediately relate to the slouching, sullen girl.

My mother is impossible to read. She returns the photograph to me with a soft sigh. "I suppose it must be true."

I turn the photograph over. There's nothing written on the back. Instead of putting the photo back in the envelope, I place it on the table next to the old woman's bed. Maybe we can show it to her when she wakes up.

"What kind of person goes around reading old directories, anyway?" my mother says.

"Not us."

"Certainly not."

"Useful, though. Sometimes."

My mother and I steep in one of our trademark mother-daughter silences.

"Well," my mother says, "if this woman is this Maryflower twin with her scars, then the . . . other . . . the burned body of the woman they have down in the morgue. From Madeline's cellar. That woman who was burned to death must be Madeline after all."

"Must be," I say.

"Who did that to her, then?" my mother says. "Who set my sister on fire?"

"I don't know," I say softly.

My mother opens her book, closes it without looking at it, and opens it again but stares over the top of the pages before softly closing it again.

"Ma, I'm sorry about Aunt Madeline," I say. "I'm sorry for your loss."

"Yes, well. You lost someone, too, Phaedra. And I am sorry for that."

More silence. Softer than usual.

"So, what do we do with this Maryflower person?" my mother says. "I don't even know her. She's a complete stranger to me."

"I don't know, Ma."

"Well. I suppose, if she wakes up, I will just have to be here, and I'll ask her what she wants me to do. No sense in her waking up alone."

"That's a good idea. I bet she'll be glad to wake up not alone."

"And where are you going?"

"Check on my car. Change clothes. I'll be back when I can."

My mother nods. She opens her book. It stays open this time.

CHAPTER FIFTY

Even though my leg hurts worse with every step—and I know I really should have some doctor stitch it up or give me a rabies shot—I am determined to return to Aunt Madeline's kitchen one last time. Turn the kitchen table upright, brush busted glass off a chair, and eat my Half Moons there. Listen to the ocean through broken windows. Say goodbye to the old place on my terms. Close the door behind me and lock it. Let nature reclaim it. Let the ants and the ferns and the mosses have it. Let the stillness of old Willow Sound take it back.

There is no stillness there, though. I come around the understorey at the edge of the property and see people at the house. Three vehicles. Three people.

Quill is one. The other is a uniformed Mountie. The third wears dark blue coveralls with a firefighter insignia patch on the arm. He tapes a bright orange paper sign to Aunt Madeline's front door. I can't read it from here, but I already know what it says.

They don't hear me coming until I roar at them: *"Condemned?"*

The cop steps toward me and puts his hands up to signal me to stop, but not a single cell in my body has any intention of stopping until I rip that orange paper off the door and tear it into pieces. I crumple the shreds of the sign and shove them into the uniformed cop's chest.

Quill's eyes lock on mine, and she holds up a manila folder with a tidy ream of condemned signs inside. She calmly plucks out another orange sign and hands it to the man in dark blue.

"The fire marshal has declared this building unfit for human use, Miss Luck," Quill says. "You can't go in. No one can. It's an eyesore. And a deathtrap."

"You think your little sign can keep me out?"

"It is unlawful for anyone to enter or use this building," Quill says. "And it's unsafe."

The fire marshal, or whatever he is, tapes the new sign up. And I rip it right off. Quill looks me dead in my eyes and hands him another sign.

"Good, Quill. Go ahead. Put it up. Put them all up. It means nothing to me the second you walk away."

"That's why we will be taking the building down."

"What?"

"The mayor has contracted a fleet of construction vehicles to help with hurricane recovery efforts," Quill says. "They arrive today. One bulldozer is on its way here, right now, to demolish this house. Before anyone gets hurt."

"You calculating little—"

"If you have a problem with the plan, Miss Luck, you'll have to speak with the mayor," Quill says. "And here he is now."

Davish comes around the corner of Aunt Madeline's house in his pristine boots. He seems rather pleased with himself, sharing a laugh with the person walking beside him.

The last person on earth I would ever expect to see walking beside him.

Nish.

I feel like I've been punched in the gut.

The second Nish sees me, his face pops open like a can of snakes.

I'm on my back foot. I can't think of anything to say. All I can do is stare at Nish. At the shame on his face. At the bunch of orange signs in his hand.

"Miss Luck," Davish says. "Your family really should have sold this place to me when I offered to take it off your hands, no questions asked. Too late now, because I don't need it anymore. I can build a replica of her house anywhere I want. With a parking lot and a lit-up magical portal exit to the gift shop."

It's time for this guy to shut his face. Or I can shut it for him.

I kick a nice, thick piece of Aunt Madeline's cedar handrail, break it off, and point it at Davish's face like a ball player at bat calling my shot.

"I suggest you get your ass in your truck, Davish, before I crack your—"

I can't finish the threat. My teeth are full of dirt. That uniformed cop kicked the back of my bad leg and jumped on my back like a coward. He grinds my face into the ground, my arms pinned behind me. The gutless wonder jumped me when my back was turned. Not the first time I've been tackled by a cop and cuffed. First time it hurt, though. Mostly because of Nish and his stupid face still gawking at me.

"Don't do that!" Nish waves his orange signs. "Stop!"

Doesn't matter. I lie there, face down, like a pile of garbage at Davish's feet. My mouth is bleeding. My leg howls. My eyes sting with mud. But I don't care about any of that.

All I care about is that my only friend in the world is standing there with Davish.

"Thank you for the research into this woman and this place, Mr. Chaudry," Davish says. "You've given me everything I need to begin work on my museum. You've done good work for me. I'll have my assistant write up a glowing letter of recommendation that will get you anywhere you want to go." Davish joins the man in blue coveralls in one of the trucks. They U-turn over what was once Aunt Madeline's rose garden and drive off.

"Let her up," Quill says. "Would you like a ride into town, Miss Luck?"

I don't answer. I spit dirt and regret ever speaking to any of them.

"Uncuff her," Quill says. The cold metal comes off my wrists. Takes me a few seconds to get the strength to face them.

"Can I help her up?" Nish asks.

"You can go frig yourself, Nishant Chaudry," I say.

"Fade, please—"

"You used me to get to my aunt, didn't you? You're with them. No wonder you're living under the rock. What other Luck family secrets did you sell to Davish?"

"Stop, please—"

"Why the hell did I ever trust you? I never should have trusted you. I never should have told you anything. Go, frig off, Nish. Go enjoy your sick museum. Go enjoy your little witch killer parade."

I sit on Aunt Madeline's front step and act as if they're gone and I'm alone. Mouth still full of dirt. Eyes full of tears. I fix my eyes on the orange sky above the setting sun.

"Fade, please listen to me," Nish says. "Please look at me."

I don't.

"She can't sit there," that uniformed cops says. "The step is technically part of the house."

Quill must have waved him off because they don't say anything else about it. I hear scuffing feet and wind-tousled office papers retreat. In my peripheral vision, Nish shuffles his shoes for a bit but says nothing.

He leaves with them. I don't watch them go.

I don't want them to see me cry.

Not the moment I had imagined. Not the dignified, quiet closure of handing the house over to the woods with the blessing of vigilant crows. The crows have all left, anyway, heading east to wherever they roost at night. I notice a bunch of trees around the edges of Aunt Madeline's property have X's sprayed on them with orange paint.

Who was I kidding to think Nish was my friend. I don't have friends. Nobody can stand me. I smell like the dead. I take up too much space. My knuckles are scarred from winning too many fights. My face is scarred from losing them.

Maybe I am garbage.

The salt air is heavy. The faint smell of burnt flesh hangs over me. Whatever I eat or think here will be soaked in that smell. I wipe dirt from my eyes and suck it out of my teeth.

I'm better off alone. I'm safer alone. It's my own stupid fault for forgetting that.

I grab a plastic-wrapped Half Moon from the grass. I peel the cake out and cram it past the mud in my mouth and swallow it down before I can taste a thing.

My phone rings. Doreen.

"Hey, Ma."

"She's missing!" my mother shouts.

"Who's missing?"

"Madeline's missing. Madeline's gone!"

"What?"

"Somebody stole her body from the morgue!"

CHAPTER FIFTY-ONE

I smell the fire before I see it. The smoke is acrid and everywhere. Chants of "Witch! Witch! Witch!" echo through the town from Harrow Park. At the entrance to the park, I find a pack of townies crowded in a mass of chaotic energy, their backs to me.

A crowd has gathered, like you'd see around a street fight on a Saturday night downtown. But this crowd is gathered around a fire. They must have thrown half the gas in town on the thing. The flames surge and tower at least twenty feet high. The blaze is so immense, it lights up the bottom of the Grand Tea rock way overhead. Bright orange and blinding, it's like looking at the sun.

Am I in a nightmare? Some medieval fever dream? What the hell is happening?

Not everyone from town is part of that mad crowd. A handful of people step out of the occult shops and horror-themed boutiques, eyes wide and keeping their distance.

Rita, too, stands outside her store. Her shaking head and crossed arms glow orange from the firelight. She sees me and points her chin toward the fire.

I have to get in there.

Sleeve over mouth and nose, I punch and smash my elbows through the chaos of thick bodies. People cough and gag on the filthy, bitter smoke they created. The chant is breaking apart. A new one starts up.

"BURN THE WITCH!"

Throwing my weight around harder now, I push through to the centre of the crowd.

"BURN THE WITCH!"

It's not a bonfire.

It's a pyre.

The scrap wood at the base is piled around the bottom of that metal pole. The one I saw on my first day and wondered what the hell it was for. Now I know.

It's not a pole. It's a stake.

They're going to burn something at the stake.

Or someone.

Hunter-orange sleeves on the other side of the fire heave a red gas can and—*SPLASH*. The oily stink of pure gasoline splatters everywhere. *FOOM*. The flames shoot skyward, and these lunatics jump up and down and cheer it on. Chunks of soot flume and spit. It's so hot on the eyes this close to the fire, it's hard to see much.

But I see her.

On the other side of the fire, I see a tarp draped over a wheelbarrow. I see her frail burnt skeletal legs sticking out from the tarp. I see the remaining tangle of white hair.

The monsters. The mob.

They want to burn the Witch of Willow Sound again.

"NOOOOO!" I howl at them like a wild animal. And they hear me all right.

Before I can get anywhere near the wheelbarrow, hands clamp on me from all sides, grabbing every part of me, forcing me to my knees, holding me in place.

Against the chaos, Davish stands out for his chilling stillness. Pinstripe suit. Black overcoat. Collar up. Fire dancing behind him. Shadows blacken his eye hollows, but I know he's looking at me. Smiling.

Maybe they want to burn me.

"Mark your calendars!" He raises his hands. "Mark this night! Because tonight the Old Witch shall BURN and we shall be FREE!"

He is mad. Utterly insane.

The townie mob cheers him on.

He stumbles through the crowd to me and clutches my sweater by the neck. "Her legend belongs to me now."

His breath reeks of rum. I spit in his face.

Behind him, behind the wheelbarrow, unnoticed: Nish. He stands so still, he's like a portrait propped up in the middle of the fire-lit chaos. And then a brief nod of his head toward what he has in his hand.

Aunt Madeline's rifle.

I want that rifle.

These townie scumbags with their hands on me think they got me. But they don't know a lick about me. For one thing, they don't how much I love a fight.

Adrenaline lights me up. All my pain is gone. I throw hook punches at nothing until the townies clamped onto my arms stumble and smack face-first into each other in front of me. More townies scrabble from behind to grab me again. Fine. I plant one boot on the ground. They focus on my pinning my arms. Let them. I get my second boot planted on the ground and rise up with a roar of effort. One thick-ass thigh-driven stomp of my boot cracks one townie's knee so hard it bends the wrong way. He lets go of my right arm, and that's all I need. I yank the shirt over the head of the next guy.

Jersey him and wail on his kidney with right after right till he cries. Two hands freed, I call out.

"Nish!"

That history nerd comes through for me.

That sweet little antique hunting rifle flies from his hand, over the fire, right to my hand.

I catch it. Cock it and level it at every goddamn head in the crowd. I circle round slowly, aiming at them all in turn, deciding which head I'll blow off.

They get real quiet now. The snapping *hiss* of the fire echoes off the rock looming over us all.

"You are all seriously, deeply insane," I say. I glare at Davish. "And you are pathetic." I sidestep to Aunt Madeline's remains in the wheelbarrow.

And level my gun at Nish's forehead.

To do him a favour.

"Dr. Chaudry," I say. "Be a good archivist and kindly take the Witch of Willow Sound somewhere safe."

His bewildered expression flickers with understanding. And trust. A nudge of my rifle and the crowd clears a path for Nish to back through. He drags the rusted-out wheelbarrow, and Aunt Madeline's remains, out of the firelight. Nish and the wheelbarrow and the burned remains grind and creak off into the darkness.

The fire casts the mob around me as ghouls, but my sight singles out Davish's forehead.

"This the exciting psycho circus you've been after, eh?" I say.

"I just want to make the Old Witch famous," Davish says.

"No," I say.

"If we burn her body tonight, the Devil cannot reanimate her again," Davish says. "If we burn her body here, then her legend will belong to this town forever!" Mid-flourish, Davish stumbles backwards. He knocks himself and the townies behind him into their stockpiles of gas cans. A stack of five-gallon cans and two fourteens pitch over and spill their guts into the base of the fire.

FOOOOOOOOOOOM.

Massive fireball.

Everyone scrambles.

The air snaps with a deafening crack.

I am surrounded by human beings raised under the shadow the Grand Tea rock. None of them look down at the rumbling ground. They all look up.

The mountain that holds up the looming Grand Tea boulder moves.

The mountain is *alive*.

Mud clumps. Rocks tumble. Dust flies. Boulders slide down the mountainside.

The fire has done it. The fireball has finished what the hurricane started, woke the giant from its slumber of three hundred million years.

People scatter, choking on heat and screams.

The last thing I see—so high over my head I nearly break my neck to see it—is the massive boulder known to the living and the dead as the Grand Tea rock beginning to tip.

The night sky tips her teacup to read the fortune of the town.

BOOK TWELVE
Wasteland

CHAPTER FIFTY-TWO

After the screaming.

After the falling mountaintop forced the buildings and trees of the town down her stony throat.

After the Grand Tea rock smashed itself into headstone-sized boulders and scattered them across the land.

I wake up to pain. A swarm of chalky skeletons beat me, eat me alive, but they're not skeletons, they're rocks. Rocks pummelling over everything, over me. The ground is rocks. The sky is rocks. One breath fills me with rocks and dust and blood. I can't catch a second breath—

CHAPTER FIFTY-THREE

I am alive. I think. Got my ass handed to me by a mountain. My ears are ringing. My hands are a bloody mess.

The moon has moved. Time has passed.

I've lost the rifle. My phone. A chunk of scalp. My brain bubbles with images. In the chaos, my hair snagged on a black truck. The pickup flipped, carried off by the rockslide. Searing pain. Split-second decision: yank my hair out or lose my head.

I kept my head. I think.

Geologists had calculated if the Grand Tea rock ever fell, it wouldn't plummet straight down and land in one piece. It would flip down the side of Harrow Mountain, hit the earth full force, and explode apart like a bomb on impact.

They must've been right.

Grand Tea is a wasteland of rubble and rocks. No longer a town, but a quarry. Dust-covered zombies stumble across the jagged landscape of sandstone and slate. The broken edges of every rock glint like knife blades and promise more pain. They slice me when I move.

Memories of the rockfall crackle behind my eyes. Nothing like mudslides and avalanches, which slide down. Pull things in and carry them along. No, this had been cannon fire. The rocks leaped and smashed over each other all the way down. It happened so fast. The massive Grand Tea boulder collapsed like a dying star.

Way, way past the end of the rubble, two distant shadows hover. The shadows look something like Rita and Quill. Way over there beyond the rubble. In a field of waist-high grass. I imagine the smell of the grass and the soft earth underneath it. I bet they breathe something other than cracked rocks and dried blood where they are, way over there.

I want to be over there with them. In that field. In that air.

It hurts like murder to move, but I have to try. The rocks are wobbly and unsettled. I take one step and nearly fall. There's no walking through this hellscape. No place for steady footing. No sense of direction in either ear.

Get to the field. Get to a road. Get out of here.

Get to some place that isn't slammed with disaster after disaster, although I don't know if a place like that exists in Nova Scotia anymore. This little province gets dragged through it. Maybe I'll haul myself to the nearest shoreline. Jack an old Cape Islander fishing boat. Run the gas out and let the ocean take me away. Farewell to Nova Scotia.

First thing, though. Get myself out of this hell and rest my battered carcass down in the cool, sweet grass.

Wait.

Where is Nish? And the wheelbarrow? Aunt Madeline's remains?

Wait, wait, wait.

Last time I saw Nish was at the fire. In that moment, I had hoped Nish would wheel that rusty little wheelbarrow away from the fire and straight to the archives and hide himself and Aunt Madeline's remains in the archives' underground vault for safekeeping.

Now I hope to hell he did no such thing.

Got to get my bearings. Where am I? My brain tilt-a-whirls inside my skull. Harrow Mountain is there. The main road would have run along here. The archives would have been at the end of the main road, way back there.

Like everything, the archives is gone. A few sections of brick mark where it might have been. Nish's shabby little shelter is gone.

The wheelbarrow.

There. Tipped sideways. Stuck.

Empty.

Nish did it. He did the most logical, sensible thing he could do at the time, and now he is damned forever for it. Trapped. Alone. Under tonnes of immovable stone.

Buried alive in a vault with the Witch of Willow Sound.

CHAPTER FIFTY-FOUR

"Nish!" His name comes out like a Cro-Magnon's squawk as I struggle to stand on the Cenozoic remains. The rocks teeter and tip on chalky sharp edges under me. *Cloc-cloc-cloc.* Like bones.

Think, Fade, think.

No. Don't think, just dig. Fall on your knees and dig.

My knees are on fire as I fall. My hands drive under rock after rock. Pull them up. Fling them away. Rocks the size of human heads and human hearts. My knuckles split open. I see my own bones through the flesh in my hands. I can't stop.

"NISH!"

There is no one nearby. No one to beg for help.

Every rock I move has more rocks beneath it.

Nish is down there. How much air does he have? How much time?

I can't feel my hands anymore, but they keep moving. Keep digging. Not digging, mining. Moving the earth. Excavating the wasteland. For my friend.

I uncover a rock shaped like a shovel head. I can use this. I lift the shovel-shaped rock over my head and drive it into cracks and spaces between other rocks. *Clank.* A different sound among the relentless, maddening *cloc-cloc-clocs.*

There. Between my gnarled hands. Something other than rock.

Steel. A steel corner of a massive cube. Three edges welded together. A top and two sides. Unmistakable.

"NISH! NISH!" I scream my face off at that little jut of steel. Maybe he can hear me. I press my ear against it. "NISH! IT'S FADE! I'M HERE! HOLD ON!"

I hack harder with my tool. There. Yes. More steel. Thick steel edges. Welded. Rigid. Intact. That old provincial archivist from a hundred years ago did it. The Grand Tea rock fell down, and the vault held up.

"NISH! I'M COMING!"

But how? How do I get to Nish? The nerdy historian locked inside a steel box buried under a tonne of sedimentary rock and Cenozoic ocean floor. Entombed with the records of an absurd and ungrateful little town that didn't deserve his time or attention in the first place.

My useless hands can't break Nish from this tomb. He needs machines.

Where are the lights? Where are the sirens? Where are the bulldozers sent to raze Aunt Madeline's house?

Behind me, I feel rocks move and clack. A lot of them.

Peering through my sweat and tears and blood-soaked mats of hair, I swivel my aching neck to look behind me.

Shadows.

Finally. My hands are rags.

"Help him," I say.

They say nothing. Do nothing.

"You did this to us."

"You witch."

"You made the rock fall."

Understanding creeps into me on needles and pins.

They pick up broken rocks and bring them toward me.

"We used to burn women like you," they say.

They raise their arms to the sky and slam the rocks down on my head.

BOOK THIRTEEN

Code

CHAPTER FIFTY-FIVE

Am I dead?

I can't see or hear anything, but I know where I am by the smell. Dead air. Cold earth. The brush of cobwebs. Even without the nightmarish pang of burned flesh and charred bone, I would know.

Aunt Madeline's cellar.

How did I get down here? Have I been here for one minute or hours?

I hear chainsaws.

Ripping through something in the distance. Not right overhead, but not far away. What are they sawing?

"TIMBER!" a chorus of voices shouts.

"NOOOOO!" one voice protests.

Cracking of thick wood splitting apart—

CRASH.

My arms shield my head on instinct as what feels like the whole world crashes down above me. Everything shakes. Glass jars tinkle.

Pieces of ceiling fall to the cellar floor, but the ceiling holds itself up. For now.

Someone must've cut down one of the biggest trees around Aunt Madeline's garden. Sounds like it smashed right onto the house. Whatever is left of it.

Moving is agony, but I force myself to move. My mouth is stuck. Some kind of thick tape, like duct tape, covers my mouth and around the back of my head. Must be layers of it. Thick as a scold's bridle. All my blood and stifled screams have loosened the glue on the tape enough for me to rip it off. I suck in dizzying gulps of air.

It is profoundly dark. The same dark, maybe, as Nish is in, in his vault. Same solitude, maybe. Same quiet. Nish has to be alive. He has to be. Waiting for help. Waiting for me. He trusts me to save him. I have to get to him.

Lost my phone in the rockfall. No light. I can't tell which way is which right now. If I can find a wall, any wall, I can get oriented. If I get oriented, I can figure out how to get out of here before whoever dumped me down here comes back.

Hands out, I baby-step forward. Nothing. Baby-step. Nothing. Baby-step. Something brushes my right elbow. My hands are numb rags with little feeling left, so I press my forehead to it. Cold. Rough. Hard. Cinder-block wall. Solid and real. Mortar and edges that give some shape to the dark.

Rough mortar grooves lead me. My elbow hits something splintery. Must be the wooden shelf with the six jars.

I know where I am in the cellar now. I remember. I know where the hole in the ceiling is from here. Just need to find the ladder.

Faster now, and steadier, I make my way along the other walls, groping for the ladder. The toboggan gives me a jolt of false hope, but I remember what it is and move on. None of the walls have the ladder against it, so I wade blindly into the middle of the cellar. Arms out, sweeping the dark like radar beams.

No ladder.

Of course, there isn't. Someone dumped me down here and took away the ladder. They want me to die here. They want me to die.

And I could die. I could finally stop fighting. I could lie down here. Let the pain and dizziness have me. Let my blood fill up my nostrils and fill up my duct-taped skull and drown me. Get back to the quiet and dark, where I am happiest. Where I belong.

But I won't. I'll stand here, like a fool, and face them when they come. Face them with whatever is left of me. Glare at them through my veil of dead snakes. And fight.

It's what I do.

Overhead. Muffled voices. Circling the hole in the guest room floor.

"You said you found the Old Witch's cellar?"

"I found it by accident. It was behind this creepy door."

A familiar creaking sound. The hideous door hacked into the library wall. Opened.

"Where's the cellar?"

"It was right there."

"You're useless. You called me here to show me the Old Witch's cellar. So where the hell is it? And where is *she*?"

"It was right there, Mayor Davish, I swear to you it was there! We found a hole in the floor and dumped the Old Witch's niece down the hole. It's the Old Witch's lost cellar for sure. If the niece escapes, she's a witch for sure, too, and the portal is real."

"Well, is there any other way down there? A normal-person cellar door somewhere with, oh, I don't know, some damn stairs?"

"We didn't find anything like that, sir. Just the hole, which I swear was right here. Maybe the Old Witch put a curse on it."

Idiots. The tree they cut down must have moved the house when it fell. Knocked the whole house off its cinder blocks. Two feet. Ten feet. Impossible to tell from down here. But the hole in the earth wouldn't line up with the hole in the subfloor anymore. Not if they moved the house. They're still blaming witches for their own stupidity up there.

I give up on the ladder. Even if I had the ladder, I can't get out that way now, anyway. Sounds of them arguing. Probably about how to kill me. Or who gets to.

Their words spiral down through the darkness: *Evil. Witch. Fire. Burn. Museum.*

Then a chainsaw gnashing right above me. They're carving up Aunt Madeline's wooden floor.

They want to find the hole to the cellar. To find me.

Panic grabs my heart.

I'm not dead yet. And I'm not about to give those psychos the honour of killing me.

I'm getting out of here.

But there is no way out of here. Not even a place to hide. I can fling six jars of rotten food at them. I can swing a child's toboggan at them. But that's all I've got. They'll laugh, shake it off, and burn me alive.

"We used to burn women like you," they said.

I have so many things to tell Nish. So many things that would make him gasp dramatically and clamp his hands on top of his head. But I'll never get the chance. Nish will die alone in the dark, wondering why I didn't come back for him. Alone, with the dead body of a burned witch. Way too poetic for a folklore historian to die that way, without anyone to write it down. Hopefully, he has found a little light from some source, a pen and paper. Hopefully, he will write his final thoughts and file them, alphabetically and chronologically and by keyword, for some future historian to find.

The chainsaw gnaws and rips overhead, gnashing Aunt Madeline's floor. Sparks from the chainsaw flicker bright orange and fade away.

A spark lights in my brain. A data point. *A memory.*

I grope back to the wooden shelf. Last time I was down here, among all the manifest horrors, there was something else. A stray item that slipped itself inside my brain with no fanfare.

There was a matchbox. Sitting on top of one of the jars.

I need to get some feeling back into my hands. Even with the pain, I need my hands to see for me.

I flap my busted hands up and down, forcing blood flow back into them. I screech inside my head. The movement forces pain and life back to my hands.

Above me, the chainsaw rips and snarls through the wood floor, making my whole body shake with the violence of it, as if I am the wood floor being ripped apart.

I'm not dead yet.

My fingers fumble along the blackness until they touch something small. Rectangular. Hollow. Smooth. The matchbox.

My fingertips pick it up and shake it. One wooden match *tock-tocks* inside.

I want to cry, but I can't. I can't screw this up. *Suck it up, Fade. Push the fear down. Focus, Fade. Focus.*

My messed-up fingers pry out the match and feel for the match head. They find the side of the box with the abrasive stripe, line them up. My hands shake so hard, I can't line them up right. *Come on, Fade.* I hold my breath and hold as still as I can. One match. I can't screw this up.

Please, please, little match, still work.

Chirk. Fwoof.

The tiny bright orange-yellow bead glows and shimmers.

I can see.

I hold the tiny flame as steady as I can, careful not to breathe even a little, not even the slightest molecule of air, lest I blow this beautiful, delicate firelight out.

If I lose this little bead of light, the next thing I see will be the last thing I see: the psycho mob and their chainsaw blade and my own internal organs flying through the air and—

Stop it. *Get it together, Fade.*

I try to light the whole matchbox on fire. It won't light. It must be too damp. Frig.

I'll have to light something else on fire. I scan my bleary eyes over every dim inch of the cellar for a glimpse of something to light: a lantern, a piece of wood, a rag.

A candle.

Orange, I think. Broken next to a bent brass candleholder left upside down on the floor by the wall opposite the jars. Covered in dust and cobwebs. Forgotten.

Above my head, the chainsaw sounds like it has changed direction. Sounds like someone is cutting a bigger hole into the floorboards.

Forget them.

Steady, steady over to the dust-parched wick, tipped on its side.

The match's flame touches my fingertips, and I tell myself to embrace that pain. Because I am more stubborn than pain and more hell-bent than fire. I lower to the floor and ease the last seconds of the match flame to the wick.

I let the match go. I drop the match from my fingers, and it goes out.

But the candle burns.

I throw my head back away from the candle and breathe and breathe. Sure, I have no step two in my plan, but at least I have light. I can see.

If I can see, I can fight.

Even though I don't want to fight anymore.

I want to run away.

I remember something.
Chrysanthemum and nightshade
Have a little key
Chrysanthemum and nightshade
Can't catch me
Chrysanthemum and nightshade
Hide a little one
Chrysanthemum and nightshade
Run, Fade, run!

CHAPTER FIFTY-SIX

I remember the song.
 Nish told me, on the day we met, that magic spells are memory devices used to pass down information from one generation to the next. I know now he is brilliant and he is right.

Magic spell incantations are memory devices. They're code.

Run, Fade, run!

I know exactly what I have to do to get out of this cellar, because Aunt Madeline told me what to do in a spell. In the fresh warmth of a summer day in her dooryard garden, when I was five years old, she taught me a silly song, a nonsense rhyme with a chase and tickles at the end, and I loved it. She and I had played and laughed and danced and sang and—without me knowing—the Witch of Willow Sound placed a magic spell inside the safest place, encoded in musical notes and rhyme, in a reinforced vault deep in my brain.

That day, twenty-eight years ago, the Witch of Willow Sound told me without telling me exactly what I have to do right now, twenty-eight years later, to survive this very moment.

Find chrysanthemum and nightshade.

I shield the candle and bring it to the wooden shelf. As a child, I had imagined Chrysanthemum and Nightshade in the sing-song rhyme Aunt Madeline taught me as two little fairies, tiny and fat. Dressed in the petals of their namesake flowers, playing hide and seek in Aunt Madeline's garden. Now, I understand, they are not characters in a child's rhyme.

I look over those abandoned jars, looking for a specific one. There. The jelly in the jar is dark and rotten, but that doesn't matter. What matters is the label on the jar, which—in Aunt Madeline's lovely handwriting, which I know so well now—reads Chrysanthemum and Nightshade.

I tip the jar over. Underneath: a gleam of brass.

Have a little key.

Aunt Madeline told me without telling me how to find this tiny key. There must be a door.

The light from the candle shows me something on the wall directly behind the jar. Something slightly different from all the things around it. A shadow. A crack in the mortar. Not just a crack. A cut.

I ease the wooden shelf away from the wall.

Strobing flashlight beams blaze from the ceiling hole. They must have sawed through. They must have hacked up all the floorboards and the subfloor in desperation, and they have finally found the hole in the earth that will lead them down to me.

"Is she down there?" Davish's voice. "I don't see her down there."

Can't catch me.

"Do I look like I care?" Davish's voice cuts through the muffled protests. "Someone hand me a lighter."

"Why?"

Silence. Seems Davish is not used to being questioned.

"But if you set a fire here, Mayor, it'll burn everything. It'll burn the trees." A different voice. More than one townie is pushing back against Davish. Finally.

"To hell with the trees!" Davish roars.

"Mr. Mayor, stop! Let us cut the trees down first! Then burn whatever you want."

"But the Old Witch's niece made the rock fall on our town!" Davish snaps.

In the dark, I feel all along the cut in the bricks in the wall. Up, over, down, over. It's a square. With a hinge on the side.

It's a door.

Hides a little one. Must have a keyhole.

"This has gone on long enough," Davish's voice says.

"How are you going to get down there?"

"Oh, I'm not going down there . . ."

Something splatters on the cellar floor. Liquid. I can tell by the smell. Gasoline.

"This is."

Davish won't listen to reason. He won't stop.

Run, Fade, run!

Keyhole. There. Fit the key in the keyhole. Force it to grind through decades of dust. The little door opens. Feeling like Alice in Wonderland, I squeeze myself in through the door, into cold darkness on the other side. Room for me to fit inside. So, it's not a child-sized hiding spot. It was made for Aunt Madeline herself. Or, I suppose, for anyone who needs a safe place to hide.

My candle flame goes out. Doesn't matter. I'm good now. I leave the broken orange candle on the cellar floor. Its final curl of smoke slithers up and tickles my nose.

Last thing I see in the cellar: a lighter. Locked on. Flame high. Falling down from the hole in the ceiling. I close the little door behind me.

Clank.

A beautiful sound. The heavy, smooth sound of steel. The sound of a solid, thick steel latch falling precisely into place, locking tight. Is this just a cubby-hole cavity? A temporary hiding spot about to become a cozier tomb?

I reach a hand out into the darkness next to me, expecting to touch a wall or earth or something solid. But I don't touch anything. My hand keeps going off into the darkness beyond. There's nothing there.

Maybe it's not just a hiding spot. Maybe it's a tunnel.

I drag myself away from the door, away from the cellar.

With every inch I creep deeper into darkness, I expect to bump into a wall or something with my forehead. But I don't. Just keep dragging myself deeper and deeper. Somewhere. Maybe it is a way out, after all. Maybe it is a passage, dug way into the earth that comes out . . . where?

Run, Fade, run.

I drag myself further and further away from the date and time of my execution into the belly of the earth. I have spent a lifetime in shadows, alone, working away on dark screens in dark rooms. I love darkness. I love solitude. I am not afraid of nothingness, or the edges where the code ends, so I keep going.

My aunt had reached out to me through time and space to get me safely this far. There is no question in my mind to trust the Witch of Willow Sound all the way to wherever wicked this way goes.

BOOK FOURTEEN

The Wolf and the Willow on the Cliff

CHAPTER FIFTY-SEVEN

I'm not alone in the tunnel.
 There's a sound. Far away at first, then closer.
Hah-hah-hah.
Too close.
Hah-hah-hah.
I feel it. Like hot breath on my face.
Hah-hah-hah.
Panting. Like a person out of breath. Or a dog.
Or a wolf.
 My brain is too burned out to think straight. Have I dragged myself far enough away from the mob in the cellar to yell at a wolf and scare it away without giving myself away? Can you even scare a wolf by yelling at it, or would that just make it mad? I have no clue. I just know I am a weak and wasted and probably delicious assortment of meat and bones.

I've got no fight left in me, anyway. No strength to yell. My head hurts from who knows how many concussions, and I just want to sleep. I hear a break in the panting, and a soft canine whine. It's probably a wolf. A big bad wolf. Huffing and puffing. The better to see this story, my dear, to its fairy-tale ending.

Another whine. Drooly. Hungry.

"I get it, sis," I say. "I'm hungry too. Last thing I ate was a Half Moon a hundred years ago. What was the last thing you ate, eh?"

I am talking out loud. I think. I could be dreaming.

Groan. Slurp.

"Listen," I say to whatever the hell is in this tunnel with me, breathing on me. "Every psycho townie from Psycho Town, Nova Scotia, has tried to kill me tonight. Multiple times. A hurricane tried to kill me. A mountain tried to kill me. A wolf almost ate my leg off. A herd of deer almost ran me over. I even tripped over a jar and fell in a bush. It has recently come to my attention that I might have the worst luck this side of the Appalachians. I am cursed. So, sis, if you want to take a bite off my big butt, then come and get it, because I don't have any strength left in me to fight. Get a bib on and fill yer boots."

Hah-hah-hah.

The breathing seems quieter, as if it's coming from a bit further down the passage. Maybe I won't get eaten alive in this dead-end tunnel right away. Maybe I can just rest here, then. Put my head down. Not to sleep. Just to close my eyes. Just for a second. Just for a teeny half second. Just for a wink.

Something warm prods my cheek. A nose sniffling me. My head snaps up. That was a close one. With the beating my head has taken, sleep is a deathtrap. I have to stay awake.

The snap of my head shakes a thought loose: This can't be a dead-end tunnel. The wolf—or whatever animal is in here with me—didn't get into this tunnel the same way I did, through the secret little door in Aunt Madeline's cellar. It got in here some other way. Through some other entrance.

There is some other way in.
There is some other way out.

CHAPTER FIFTY-EIGHT

We find moonlight at the end of the tunnel, and I see her. My guide is a patient and emaciated grey wolf. Her dandelion-yellow eyes stare down her narrow snout at me. Other than the part where I heard a hot *hiss* in the tunnel ahead of me, after which I was forced to crawl through a puddle of hot wolf pee, she and I are getting along all right.

The tunnel leading away from the cellar ends in a wolf den. A deep hollow carved by wind and time, inside the cliff above the ocean. The wolf sits at the entrance to her den on her throne of vole and weasel bones, watching the wolf-grey waves of the Atlantic roll by just below us. She is majestic with moonlight glinting in her scars. I slump against a wall of the cave. I am no majestic creature. I am a garbage pile of grime and open wounds.

"Hey, sis," I say. "You look familiar. Have we met?"

The wolf snorts. She is skin and bones and silence.

"Did you know there haven't been wolves in Nova Scotia for a hundred and fifty years?"

The wolf seems unimpressed by my fun history fact. She lies down and crosses her grey and white front paws. The markings look like little white stars.

The icy ocean air keeps me awake against my will. Glinting snowflakes shimmer past the cave. Like we're figures inside a snow globe. A wolf and a woman inside a cave. From our snow globe shelter, we watch the snowflakes fall a little while. Until I get enough strength in my arms to pull myself to the very edge of the cave, ease my head and shoulders out almost to the point of falling, and look around.

The blue-black sky that precedes dawn casts a dreary glow along the rockface. Black lashes of wild grass hint at a path, shaped like a lightning bolt. It zigzags along the cliffside, leading almost all the way up to whatever the heck exists on top of this cliff. Just wide enough for a wolf to climb. Or a person. Or what's left of one. "Thanks for guiding me this far, sis," I say. "I owe you one."

The wolf watches me haul my raggedy self out of the den and into the briny wind. Wild grass bends beneath my boots. The path holds. I stand on it, grateful the ocean wind pushes against me, bracing me against cliff face. Salt air stings my skin. Snowflakes dissolve in mid-air before they touch me because I am such a sweaty, feverish mess. I lumber up the crooked path like an ancient beast rising from the depths of the ocean.

The path takes me as high up the cliff face as it can. Almost at the top, I reach up to clutch fistfuls of dead grass and haul my grisly carcass up and over the edge to the top of the cliff.

I made it. There is nothing up here but a frost-bitten, snow-feathered wildflower field and one dead tree. The faint smell of fire lingers in the grass. Someone burned something here.

I lie on my back and breathe and look up the length of the blackened tree trunk to the sky above it. It's a willow tree. Or was, once. When it was alive.

Aunt Madeline used to call willows healing trees. But I always thought of them as warrior trees. Standing up to storms better than other trees. Surviving. Their restless branches whipping around them like wild locks of long hair.

I can't tell exactly where I am, or how far the tunnel took me from Aunt Madeline's house. Far enough that I am hidden by thick forest around the edges of this field. Still close enough to hear the voices shouting near her house. The chainsaw running. The rage.

But here, in this field on the edge of this cliff by the sea, they can't see me. So, maybe if I just stay lying down in this cold meadow, beneath saltwater-soaked night air, among the long-dead lupines and withering goldenrod, they will never find me and I can be still and stay here forever. Food for earthworms and blueberries and some future flowers.

Red and blue lights tap a beat on my eyelids until I open them.

Police car lights whip around, slashing through the trees. The police car must be pulled up near Aunt Madeline's house. The police have gone there to arrest the townie mob. Or cheer them on.

Finding the niece of the Witch of Willow Sound taking a nap beside a tree that looks like a haunted prop from some old-time horror movie and smells of fire would be just too good for them to resist. No way in hell am I letting them live out their half-cocked—and historically inaccurate—twisted fantasy by burning me alive here. Frig that. I have no choice but to drag my gory carcass out of here and get help for Nish.

He needs me.

Through the trees, I hear her voice. Quill's.

She shouts. Giving orders. In anger. Then in fear.

Pistol shots.

Chainsaws roar back.

I can't see what's happening at the house from here. Can't see if there's even anything left of the house. No sign of flames or smoke from here.

Quill might not help me, but she'll help Nish. She has to.

I have almost nothing left in me. Almost. Do I have enough in me to protect what's left of the little house Aunt Madeline made with her bare hands?

Probably not.

But I have promises to keep.

And maybe if I throw whatever's left of me between them and her house, I can make it a little harder for them to tear it down.

CHAPTER FIFTY-NINE

Unnoticed, I shamble to the broken stump of my apple tree at the far end of Aunt Madeline's yard. My lungs wheeze. My blood-soaked hair hangs in red ribbons of gore.

There's Quill. At the house. Talking to the mob. I can't hear what she's saying.

Davish is with her, holding a chainsaw. They're probably scheming. Probably discussing museum layouts. Deciding what shade of green to paint Madeline Luck's face on the effigies.

Apples dot the ground around the tree stump. I pick up the apple closest to me. Bruised. Imperfect. The haze in my head disorients me. I swear I can smell fresh basil and recently unearthed potatoes. For a second, it feels as though I've reached through time and retrieved my first weapon.

I take a bite of the apple. Honey and blood mix under my tongue, but I don't mind. Then I drill the apple straight through the air, right at Davish's head. He falls back on his rear end, chainsaw reeling. His nose sprays blood in every direction. The others scramble back in shock. Heads turn and they find me standing, leaning on the broken apple tree, another apple ready.

Davish scrambles back to his feet when he sees me.

When I see Quill's face, I realize I was wrong.

Her wide eyes dart around. The stony woman looks scared. For good reason. Uniform caked in soot, chest heaving, a fire extinguisher clutched in her fists, foam dripping. Chainsaws still roaring. Threatening. Her collection of unused orange condemned signs flutter around her black boots and blow through the garden and off the cliff like a wild flock of fiery birds.

She stands between the mob and the house. Facing them.

The Grand Tea mob isn't on Quill's side anymore. Or she isn't on theirs. She has become the stand-in for the witch. The new object of the mob's anger.

Now she knows how it feels.

My eyes deadlocked on Quill's, I limp through the mob. Fear contorts their faces as they back away from me and clear my path to Quill. She raises her hands in defence—or surrender—as I come closer to her.

She flinches as I grab her shoulder.

And pull her behind me.

I place myself between Quill and the mob.

Looming over them, chewing my bloody bite of apple. Waiting.

By the expressions on their faces, I can tell I look as monstrous as I feel. A horror raised from the dead. A lunatic. A freak.

Davish sputters and honks through his bloody face and revs up his chainsaw, pointing it at me.

I don't flinch.

"How the hell did *that thing* get out of the cellar?" Davish asks, his head jerking from the remains of Aunt Madeline's house back to me.

"Magic," I say, blood falling from the word. "By the way, they didn't even burn people for being witches here anyway. You should go talk to the historian you hired, Dillweed."

I spit an apple seed at the ground. Lower my stance. Raise my mangled fists. Even this broken, I still have some fight in me saved up, still look him in the eye.

In his hands, the chainsaw sputters and falls quiet in the awkward silence.

Out of gas. Useless. Poetic.

Davish flings the chainsaw away and bolts. Coward.

I don't have the reflexes or the hand strength left to snatch him. Doesn't matter. He's his own worst enemy anyway.

He stumbles to his truck and peels off, tail lights disappearing into the trees.

Something about the silence and the sunlight creeping onto the scene makes the people in the mob hesitate as they face harsh reality. They look at each other. They squirm and deflate. The big bad pack of nighttime hunters is little more than a bug-bitten band of hungover idiots by the stark light of day. The energy drains out of the moment. I'm not the only freak here.

Three familiar silhouettes march up the dead-straight path through the woods and into the rising sun. One silhouette is topped with wild hair.

"Nish!" I say.

Nish is flanked by my mother and Rita. Their faces drop at the sight of whatever the hell I am now. They swoop in to grab me and hold me up, and I let them.

The mob slips away. Walking stiff-legged and squinting, as if they're not sure where they are or how they ended up here, but, oh boy, would you look at the time. They slink off into the trees.

"All those monsters are just gonna walk away," I say.

"No, I'll get them. Hunting monsters is what I do," Quill says to me, and I believe her.

With her jaw chattering and my feverish shivering, in our battle-stained clothes and faces and all our swallowed screams, Quill and I face each other.

"You came to save me," I say to Quill.

"You came to save me," Quill says to me.

I hold out what's left of my mangled hand to her. "Fade," I say to her.

"My name is Cleo." She shakes my bloody hand in her own and smiles at me. First time I've seen her smile. It's a nice smile.

Nish wraps my grisly neck in a hug. I groan as my innards squelch, but he doesn't care. He hugs me harder until I laugh.

"I thought you were dead!" Nish and I say to each other at the same time.

"Jinx, you owe me a pop!" we say to each other at the same time, again.

We laugh until we hear my mother's sad groan. She raises her hands to her mouth, staring at the remains of her sister's house. One side crushed by a massive tree. Lit up by flares of red and blue light. Neon-orange condemned signs flapping around the yard. Roof dangling with rotted vines. Garden carpeted with dead fish.

"That scumbag Davish wanted to buy Aunt Madeline's house from her and make it into a witch museum," I say.

My mother smirks. She turns a sly smile to Rita, who chuckles with her.

"He should have done his research better," my mother says. "This place was never my sister's to sell."

"What do you mean?" I ask.

"Madeline never bought this property or claimed to own it in any way," she says. "The land all belongs to the Mi'kmaq people. To Rita's family. Always has."

"It's true, sure," Rita says. "When Madeline Luck was a young woman just starting out on her own, she came to my grandmother and asked her permission to live in this spot by the sea, make a little home here, and care for the land. Madeline said, 'I'll live a quiet life, and when I die, the earth will grow back over everything I borrowed from it and heal itself. It will be like I was never here.'"

I didn't know any of that. By their faces, I can tell Nish and Quill didn't know either.

"My grandmother could tell Madeline was smart," Rita says. "Smart enough to live by the old ways. So, my grandmother said yes and the earth said yes, and they both let Madeline live here for a long time."

We five stand together. The little house and its gardens rot and crumble in front of us, with no apologies and no regrets.

Five days ago, when I discovered my aunt's house in disrepair, I was heartbroken. I wanted to grab vats of chemicals and clean it and beat the rot and the bugs back.

Now, I understand the elegance of the plan.

Zeroization. Madeline Luck purposely embedded a self-destruct code in the program. Destroy the content to prevent compromise. Reset to zero. Tea for a Quiet Life.

Even as she became labelled a witch. A curiosity. A freak. Even as the people of Grand Tea tried to claim her story from her and twist it to serve themselves—their conspiracy theories, their fears, their bank accounts—she knew they would never have it. Madeline Luck and her life will never be put under glass.

A woman after my own heart. If that's witchcraft, sign me up.

Gravity pulls down every bone in my body as Nish and Quill hold me up by my arms and walk me to Quill's squad car.

"How did you guys know I was here?" I ask.

"I followed the mob," Quill says. "Rita and I saw you get attacked and taken away. Sorry for the delay—Grand Tea is a little short on working vehicles at the moment."

"I went to the hospital and saw Doreen there," Rita says. "Nish was already there."

"I returned Madeline Luck's remains back to the hospital," Nish says. "And while I was there, Doreen introduced me to Maryflower Luck."

"I'm so glad," I say. "For all of that."

"Maryflower told me about a dead tree on a cliff near here," Nish says, his voice quieter than usual. "She said it was a good place for burning witches."

"Did she see a lot of witches burn up there?"

"Just one."

BOOK FIFTEEN
Correspondences

CHAPTER SIXTY

"Fade. Apple."

My stitched-up hands cradle the fragile, crooked hands of the woman named Maryflower Luck as she wakes up.

"Maryflower," I say. "Aunt Maryflower. I'm so sorry I didn't know who you were when I found you. I didn't know anything about you."

Her fiddlehead-curled fingers jab toward the table next to her hospital bed. I pull the table closer to us. Photographs are laid out across it. The ones I rescued from Aunt Madeline's cabinet before Hurricane Lettie hit. My fingers fumble as I pick up the little black-and-white photograph of the twin girls with black braids and light eyes. Snapped eighty-some years ago.

"Maddie, Mary," Aunt Maryflower says as she taps the girls in turn.

I turn the photograph over. The back is blank.

"Mary. Black bread. Wish flower," she says.

I find a pen in the table drawer and scribble it on my arm to make sure it works. With my painful fingers, I write those five words on the back of the picture.

Her ice-green eyes squint and water to see what I've written.

"What about Aunt Madeline?" I say. "What do I write for her?"

"Maddie. Berry tea. Rosemary."

I write those four words on the back too.

Maryflower points to the words. "This. This. Maddie bes there with you. Magic."

I understand. The notes on the backs of the pictures. My aunts were recording little ways to invoke people from the past. A sound or smell or sight or taste or touch, shared across time.

Correspondence Magic.

"I'll bake black bread and let dandelions get their wishes," I say.

"And I bes there," she says.

Her broken bird-feather fingers point to me. "Apple."

"Yeah, apples. Did Aunt Madeline tell you about me?"

"Fade." She points to me.

For the first time, I notice the little dandelion stem—that had been in her hand when I'd found her—is still with her. It's pinned to her hospital pillow with a thumb tack. It looks a little loose, like the pin could slip out of the fabric at any second. But I just leave it be.

Aunt Maryflower and I sift through the collection of photographs on the table.

"Nanny Isobel." Aunt Maryflower points to the very old photo of a girl standing next to a toboggan in the snow.

I turn the photograph over. This is the photograph with the horrible, messed-up writing on the back. Except this time, my eyes see past the twisted writing to the words there: *Izi. Pussy willows. Wonders.*

Written with her painful fingers.

"Isobel was called Izi," I say. "She loved pussy willows. And wonders."

"Rose wonders," Aunt Maryflower says.

"Rose wonders," I say. "Your grandmother. My great-grandmother."

"Gone."

"Yes. I'll remember her, though. Whenever I see pussy willows or rose wonders, Izi will be there."

"You are smart." She pats my hand. "Maddie said."

"Aunt Maryflower, is this the only photo of you?" I say. "This one of you as a little girl?"

That doesn't seem right.

My phone was lost in the rock fall, but I have an old backup phone. The camera on it works, and that's all I need.

"Here, Aunt Maryflower, I'll take a new picture of you," I say. "Just look right here, at the screen."

I lean my cheek next to hers. I take our picture and hold it up for us to see. Our faces could not be more different. Hers, a paper-thin apple-doll face with shiny beads for eyes. Mine, a swelled-up battle-scarred bruiser's mug.

Aunt Maryflower nods at the digital picture of our faces pressed cheek to cheek. "Both same," she says. "Twins."

Surprised, I look at the picture again. Two green-eyed black sheep raised from the dead who knows how many times now. A couple of wood frogs.

"That's a compliment for me, Aunt Maryflower," I say. "Because you are amazing. You're stronger than anyone I know of. You're my hero."

She laughs a little at that. A laugh like a little bell.

I set my phone with our picture lit up on the screen among the photographs on her bedside table. I prop up the old photo of the twin girls next to it, facing us both.

I try to gauge what Aunt Maryflower wants to do now. But she doesn't speak or ask for anything. She just wants to lie still and look at the pictures.

So, we do that. We look at the pictures together. Quiet. Thinking. Remembering.

Until I notice the quiet is too quiet.
The pin in the dandelion has fallen out.
I am in the room alone.

CHAPTER SIXTY-ONE

In the hospital waiting room, my mother holds two bags of flour on her knees, like she's holding two fat paper-wrapped babies. Rita and Nish sit with her. When my mother sees me coming, she pats the empty chair beside her. But I don't sit next to her. Instead, I crouch down in front of her. My mother reads into this gesture and starts shaking her head even before I say anything.

"No, Phaedra," my mother says. "No. Maryflower and I were going to . . . I told her I would take her out around. Get her hair cut. Get her some new clothes."

"I'm sorry, Ma."

"She's scared of hospitals," my mother says. "She shouldn't have to die in a hospital. After all she's been through in hospitals. It's not right."

"I know, Ma."

Tears quiver on the tips of my mother's lashes. The lenses in her glasses fill up with fog, hiding her eyes, like a veil has fallen over the moment, shielding her from the chaos of a busy hospital as it bustles past. "It's not right." Tears slip down her face and roll off her cheeks and chin. They land on the brown paper bags of flour with gentle taps. She looks down at the rye flour. "She didn't even get to have a bite of black bread."

The soft sound of my mother's stifled sobs transports me back in time, back to that summer day in the back seat of her car, my bruised apple in my hand, my eyes fixed on the road behind us. The icy shock of hearing my mother cry for the first time shoots through my veins again. But this time, she can't push her pain down to protect me. She can't pull her breath back to normal and find dignified silence and keep driving.

This time, the walls that have surrounded and protected my mother's heart her whole life all fall down. Sitting there, in a green plastic hospital chair, with no barricade up, no shield, she seems so small. Her face crumples, pulled by too much pain. She is an old woman and a lost child at the same time.

I realize our parents are still children when we are born. We grow up together, with them.

My mother looks at me, through her tears. "I don't even know how to make black bread."

The guilt these words carry is too much for my mother to bear, and her whole body shatters into sobs. Rita and Nish each place a kind hand on my mother. Still crouching in front of her, I hold my hands on hers.

My mother cradles the flours to her body and weeps. Little bundles of dust that will never be made into bread for her lost sisters.

Chapter sixty-two

When Nish knocks on the door to my hospital room, he finds me standing next to the table by the window. The insides of my cell phone dismantled and arranged in neat rows. He carries a thin grey box tucked under his arm and two coffees in a tray.

"Are you hacking it?" he asks.

"Nope, I'm exercising my frigging right to repair it," I say.

"I just knew you wouldn't be resting in bed, Fade. I just knew you'd be upright and up to something."

He joins me at the dirty glass pane, overlooking the parking lot. "How are your hands?" he asks.

"Not bad." I hold my hands up, Frankenstein-stitched but steady. "Lost my middle finger completely and the end of my thumb but the rest is healing fine. I took the mummy-wrappings off because they got in my frigging way. It takes me longer to do some things, but it's not enough to stop me."

"No way it would," he says.

"They say my brain is a ticking time bomb," I tell him. "Too many hits, even for this big old head. But I don't want to think about it. I have too much to do to worry about that."

Nish's eyes fill with tears, but he blinks them away. We crack our coffee lids open and watch cars in the parking lot come and go. A bright grey sky. A touch of snow.

"Fade, I want to explain to you," he says. "I swear to you. On my honour. I had no idea Davish's plan was to take over your aunt's home for his museum. He brought me here on a grant to research local beliefs in general. It was only when I got here that he told me about his Grand Tea museum idea. It felt so sketchy, but by then, I was stuck with nowhere else to live. But I figured I'd do my research and get out."

"I believe you," I say.

"I did start the process with Quill for Madeline Luck's house to be condemned, but only because I thought it would protect the house from intruders and more damage. Instead, it emboldened him. So it turned out to be the worst thing I could do. I am so sorry for all of that. For every last thing I did wrong. My heart was in the right place, but I made it worse. You were perhaps right, in that awful moment, not to trust me."

"No," I say. "I'm not a trusting person. At all. But I should have trusted you."

"When you refused to look at me in that moment," he says, "that hurt. More than I expected. My own mother won't look at me. Nobody else in the world is interested that I even exist, except you. Then even you couldn't look at me."

"I'm so sorry, Nish."

"It felt like, *If I don't have Fade to see me, then I'm not really here.*"

I grab Nish and hug him. I will do whatever I can to keep this wonderful human being from falling apart. He hugs me back. Somehow, it makes me feel safe.

"I will never do that to you again, Nish," I tell him. "I promise."

"I believe you," he says, pulling away. "I'm happy to inform you I've finished documenting Madeline Luck's scrolls," Nish says. "All twenty-eight of them. I've placed them in archival storage containers for you. They're safe and sound in my hotel room in Carmel. No one knows they are there."

"Thank you."

"Thank you for trusting me with them," he says and holds out the long grey box. "I brought you this one, because I thought you might want to read it now. When your mother discovered I was your directory-reading history friend—as she called me—she brought me in to meet your aunt Maryflower. She told Maryflower I was the person who had found her name when no one else could. I had the profound honour of speaking with Maryflower Luck."

"I'm glad she got to meet you, Nish," I say. "I'm sure you were as kind and respectful with her as you were with Aunt Madeline's life, and with everything else you touch. I bet she really liked you."

"She told me I have a head like a wish flower," Nish says. "Which, honestly, may be the single greatest compliment of all time."

I laugh as Nish wobbles his hair and grins.

"Fade, do you remember how I told you I have collected the names of different witches sighted in this part of Nova Scotia?" Nish says. "And how I wanted to learn about all of them and maybe, someday, meet one of them?"

"I remember," I say.

"It turns out," Nish says, "I've met them."

"Really? Which ones?"

"All of them," he says.

"How is that possible?"

He doesn't answer, just hands me the long grey box with a smile.

"So, what is written in this scroll?" I ask. "A spell?"

"A recipe."

Black Bread

To make this most ancient bread, combine whole rye flour, 80% clean water, 20% levain, 2% salt. For levain, soak old dough in warm water. Stretch and fold into loaf shape. Rest 8 hours. Split top. Bake with low fire under cast iron pot. Wait before breaking. Enjoy as is.

This is my twin sister's favourite bread. She is kind and quiet and profoundly misunderstood. Her life has been harder than most. My interest in plants arose from my childhood hope to help my twin sister. She has travelled every wood and cliff of this province, on foot, alone. She has been whispered about in legends by many names: Black Lake Witch. Lady of the Case. Biddy Black Bread. Hag of the Bite. The Hammer-Nailer. Old Lady with the Kettle. No-Fish. (The latter name, her favourite, for she is harder to catch than any fish.) She ran away often and never likes to stay in one place long. Having been confined for so many years in chains, inside small concrete cells, none could blame her for it. Authorities would bring her in each time, but nothing could hold her still for long. Not iron. Not flame. Not death.

Each time she passed through Willow Sound, I offered her a place to stay, but she refused. After the fire destroyed the shameful Luck family summer house, the authorities believed her burned up and dead. The whole world, except me, believed her burned up and dead. Let them believe it, she said. Let them forget about me. Alone is good. Alone is safe. She was free.

I am dying. Somehow, my twin sister knew. As a child, she would escape from her shackles and break out from her strong room prison in the basement and appear in my bed, seeking comfort. Now, in our last years, she has appeared again, this time to comfort me.

Confined to my bed now, I am unable to walk among my beloved plants or watch the moon journey among her beloved stars. They were my life for so long. My twin sister knew this too. She gathered my old paints and gave my life back to me on the walls and ceiling of my bedroom. My last wishes and a final journey with the moon.

I have asked her to make my last cup of tea, when it's time, and to burn my remains when I'm gone. Remember her as wild and forgiving and free. Her name is Maryflower Ley Luck.

CHAPTER SIXTY-THREE

My car bumps over ruts and frozen puddles, carrying me as close as I can get to what's left of Grand Tea. Loose gravel shores up against a row of looming boulders, some of the boulders as tall and as wide as me. Raised from the rubble by government-funded excavators, this barricade of stone sentries will stand here for generations. They might keep human beings at bay, but nature will reclaim the town.

The fate of the remains of Grand Tea will be hashed out by people in suits and wearing lanyards at shiny hardwood tables, in the hearts of other not-yet-shattered towns.

Now the townies who had nowhere else to go are living in a homeless encampment in a field somewhere. In their tents, they'll find themselves with nothing to do but think and do old-fashioned things, like sharpen knife blades on whetstones. They'll watch the lights inside warm houses nearby flick on at night. They'll hear things outside their tent. Sticks snapping. Lighters flicking. Something crawling toward them through the dead grass. Best to keep distracted. Best to fill the silence inside the tent with something else. Something quiet, like steel sliding against stone. Something to keep their new monsters at bay.

Rita's Trading Post and Convenience is still standing. All of the store's insides are piled up outside in boxes. Moving day. A brick props the door open, and the sign is gone. Rita lifts her head at my knock and smiles at me through a cloud of cinnamon tea from behind the empty counter of her empty store.

"I'm glad to see you, Fade. How are you?"

"Good."

"How's your mother?"

"Better."

"Did she get official permission to give her sisters a green burial, like she wanted?"

"No."

"Did that stop her?"

"No."

"Good for her," Rita says. "I heard about the hospital with the children in chains. And that they're finding unmarked graves at your grandparents' home."

I shake my head, eyes downcast. "My mother didn't know. She was forbidden to play in the gardens—now we know why. When Nish told her about the graves, a memory came back to her. When she was seven, she found a bone in the back garden. Her parents flipped out over what she thought was a wild animal bone."

"I'm guessing it wasn't an animal bone."

"Me too."

"I believe that your mother didn't know," Rita says. "She was a child herself. And people who hurt children on purpose lie about it."

I know that to be true.

"But someone always finds out," Rita says. "Things that are hidden aren't forgotten. They're just quiet for a while."

Indeed.

Not knowing what else to say, I rustle in my hoodie pocket. "Rita, I have something for you."

Rita slides her tea aside.

I place the keys to Aunt Madeline's house in Rita's hand. The original house key and the forget-me-not spare. "The walls are half gone, so the keys are symbolic. Still. Thank you to your family from mine."

"Thank you for honouring our old agreement."

"Older than both of us, but still ours."

"True."

"One more thing."

A gift for Rita. A small velvet bag—forget-me-not blue—tied with teabag string. Rita inhales from the bag and closes her eyes. "Madeline Luck's wild berry tea," Rita says tenderly.

"When you have this tea, she'll be there," I say.

Rita nods, tying the string around the cloth bag with care.

"Have you seen Nish around?" I say.

"He's out back, sure. In the rockfall debris."

"Really? How did he get over the big stone barricade?"

"Not over. Through. The back door of my shop opens right into the ruins."

"May I?"

Rita nods at the back door, giving me permission, and returns to the cinnamon warmth of her tea.

CHAPTER SIXTY-FOUR

In the distance, I see Nish crouching near the rubble that used to be the archives, writing on a clipboard. I'd recognize that hair anywhere. A long red scarf wrapped around his neck, its tasselled ends lifted now and then by the wind. Nish is so engrossed in his work, he doesn't notice me coming.

"This is a no nerd zone, sir, please leave the area," I say. "You have twenty seconds to comply."

"Fade!" Nish laughs. "You look half human! How do you feel?"

"Half human."

Thin metal spikes stick out of the ground all around him. Red ribbons wave off the end of every spike.

"Those spikes mark where the vault is?" I ask.

"Yes," he says. "More rock has fallen down the mountainside since the night the Grand Tea fell. They don't know if the rocks will ever stop falling. Surveyors measured and mapped out the location of the archive building and the vault and recorded it on behalf of the national archives. The vault won't be excavated anytime soon. Not in our lifetime."

"Did any buried treasure fall out of the rock?"

"No," he says. "Not a bit."

"The people of Grand Tea were wrong again."

"I have to confess something." Nish looks down. "I removed a book from the archives. The big book from the Havenwood Hospital. Even though it violates archival rules, I stole the book from the vault and I gave it to Corporal Quill."

"Why?" I say.

"I want people to know the truth about the horrors that happened behind those walls," he says. "It's too late for justice, but we can't let them be forgotten."

"No wonder Aunt Madeline didn't want to give the land to my mother."

"Your mother didn't know," Nish says. "About the lucrative deal her parents made with the Havenwoods. About the unmarked graves. Or about her own secret sister who was kept down there and left to die."

"The Luck family has always been good at burying things." My chest tightens with pain as I say it. "My mother included."

"She was a child," Nish reminds me gently. He's right.

"I'm proud of you for stealing the book, Nish," I say. "It was the right thing to do."

"I Indiana Jonesed it."

We chuckle softly. Red ribbons snap between us in the wind.

"That night the rock fell, Nish, I thought you were trapped down there." My throat closes over just saying the words.

"That night, Fade, you gave me a running head start that saved my life."

"I keep imagining you down there—"

"I'm not down there, Fade. I'm right here," Nish says, squeezing my arm. "However, I did leave my favourite pen down there, in the vault."

My throat lets me laugh a little again.

"It was a nice one too. Archival marking pen. Super micro particles."

"Micro particles of what?"

"Waterproof. Archival grade ink. Extra fine point."

"So, a nerd pen."

"Six dollars apiece!"

"You got ripped off, buddy."

"So, if you want to feel bad for something, Fade, feel bad for my pen."

"RIP to that pen," I say.

"Oh, one more thing. A genealogy fact. I found out what the H stands for in the former mayor Dinwald H. Davish's name."

"Hack?"

"Havenwood."

Havenwood. I let that sink in.

The vault. The book. The fixation with controlling the Luck family narrative for posterity. The obsession with burning Luck women's bodies. Even after death.

Distant rumbling. Crows call out a warning. Nish points at the far end of Harrow Mountain. "Rockslide! Small one."

A mass of grey rocks tumbles down the side of the mountain. My bones feel like they're falling with them. Not a good feeling.

"Well, Nish, I vote we listen to whatever the mountain's trying to tell us."

"I second that," he says.

"Look at us," I say. "The hobbit and the half giant, back together."

"At long last!" He clasps his hands together. "Which one am I again?"

We share a good laugh as we walk across the grim remains of Grand Tea, hopefully for the last time. A sea of red ribbons flail behind us, marking lost things.

"Have you eaten?" I ask him.

"Not yet," he says.

"I baked a batch of rose wonders," I say. "For you."

Nish stops and looks up at me, his tornado-coloured eyes wide. "Did you happen to make them from the instructions in the scroll of the Witch of Willow Sound?"

"I did. In the care facility where they let me stay while I healed up. The kitchen there was empty at night, so they let me use it. I even made the rosewater myself. From scratch. All of it from scratch. The bread is in my car. If you have time."

"For that, Fade," Nish says, "I have all the time in the world."

꧁

Somewhere in the middle of nowhere, Nova Scotia, I sit beside my friend on the hood of my car. Our dusty boots planted on the bumper, we tear into rose-flavoured bread together and talk and laugh with our mouths full. Snow covers the ground. Evergreens surround us. A path cuts through the snow along the treeline nearby. It looks like the even-edged trail of a toboggan pulled through the snow. The cold winter air swirls with the warm scent of butter and roses.

"How on earth did you get your car out of the woods after the hurricane, Fade?" Nish asks. "Wasn't it stuck? Impaled on a log or something?"

"Easy."

"How could it possibly be easy?" he says. "Fade? Fade. Did you physically lift this car with your bare hands and move it?"

"Only for a minute," I say. "Two minutes at the most."

"I can't tell if you're joking or not!" Nish gawks at me, his floofy hair waving in excitement. He shoves the last bite of one wonder in his mouth and grabs another from the paper bag. "This bread is amazing. Thank you so much."

"I knew you'd appreciate it."

"I made you something too." Mouth full, Nish hops down from the hood of my car and scoots back to his own car, parked on the shoulder of the road behind mine. He leans into his back seat and pops out again, holding up an armload of hand-knitted socks in every colour of the rainbow, which he piles into my lap.

"Go 'way!" I say.

"I shall not!" he says. "I used the warmest and toughest yarns I could find. To keep your feet warm and dry and safe, no matter where you sleep or how far you go."

"Thank you, Nish. So much."

"I made you one more thing," he says. From behind his back, he whips out a knitted toque. Fog grey and fuzzy and completely over the top.

"Ta-da!" he says. "Isn't it ugly?"

"Nish, it is hideous and I love it!" I jam the fuzzy thing on my big old head. It fits. The huge pompom wobbles. The ear flaps dangle. Nish nearly chokes to death on the side of the road, laughing at the sight of me.

"This thing is awesome, Nish. You should make yourself one. We can wear them together on our adventures."

"Oh, I already did," he says. "But I made mine in my favourite colour."

He retrieves his own handmade hat from his car and yanks it down over his head. His is ivy green.

We sit together, our pompoms bobbling. He breaks another bread apart for us to share. Sighs of butter and roses saturate the air. Raccoon tracks zigzag the snow, leaving breadcrumbs that trail from us into ice-twinkling thickets of blackberry brambles. Chickadees swoop over us. The evergreens creak.

"So!" Nish says. "I feel I now have a fairly good understanding of your family tree on your mother's side."

"For sure," I say.

"I have to ask about your father's side of the family, Fade. Where are they from?"

"Newfoundland," I say.

"Up north?"

"Yep. Way up north. Where Vikings landed."

"Wait, Fade, wait," he says. "Are you telling me that you are descended from Vikings?"

"Yep."

"That makes so much sense!" Nish is so excited at this discovery, he almost falls off the car. I grab him by the coat, haul him back up into place. He doesn't miss a beat.

"Fade, we should go! You and I should leap onto the next boat to Newfoundland and follow old stories all the way north."

"What about you, Nish?" I say. "You ever think about jumping on the next boat to the U.K.? If you had someone with you who has your back and is more than willing to crack a few skulls?"

Nish thinks for a long moment. "Maybe someday. Maybe when I'm old. In winter. If you are with me. Then you could see Old England covered in snow. To me, it's the most beautiful thing in the world. I miss it there." He seems ready to sink back into that dark place again.

Not on my watch.

"Hold this." I heap my socks into his lap and slide off the hood of my car. He watches me rummage through the pockets of my backpack until I find a small crumple of notepaper. Blank. It'll do. "Have you got a pen?"

"Have *I* got a *pen*?" He proudly holds up three pens and a pencil, straight from his shirt pocket, ready to go. I take a black ink pen and press it to the crumple of paper. Nish cradles socks and chews bread and watches me sketch on the paper on the roof of my car.

"Are you writing a strongly worded letter?" Nish asks me.

"Nope."

I scribble harder and bigger and curlier loops then stop to admire my artwork. I hold it up for Nish to see.

"You drew me!" he says, laughing with that trademark delight of his.

"Yep. What gives it away?"

"You've captured my contemplative yet dynamic air."

"As soon as I get my hands on a film camera, Nish, I'll do this thing properly. The way the Luck witches taught us. With an actual photograph of you. But I don't want to wait till then. I want to do this now."

"Do what now?"

I turn the picture of Nish over. "You're my family, Nish. You're a Luck now. So, what should we write on the back of your picture?"

Nish gets it right away. Tears spill down his cheeks. He smiles. He'll be fine now. I got him.

"You're a lot like Aunt Madeline was," I say. "She would have loved you as much as I do. I know she would have added a teacup to her kitchen table just for you to come home to. And now that we know the significance of her cabinet, I know this is how she would have made your place in the family official. Place your picture in the cabinet with the words of the spell to bring you back."

"Oh, Fade . . ."

I write his name. *Nish.*

"We are the last of a long line of outsiders. A collection of curiosities. The Witch of Willow Sound's cabinet belongs to the forest now, so we can't place your picture there. But our aunt Maryflower taught us to travel light. Our treasures can be kept inside other things. Inside the pockets of an apron. Or inside a teapot."

The blue betty teapot saved from the hurricane. Soft *scuff-tink* of the lid coming off. The inside smells like a handful of familiar earth and paper older than we are. Family photos rest inside. Safe and dry. Waiting.

"So, what are we writing?" I say. "Take your time. This is the oldest magic."

Snow falls. A song sparrow calls *sweet-sweet-sweet* from the trees. The things we write down we will never forget.
Sticky toffee pudding.
Bluebells.

CHAPTER SIXTY-FIVE

The gown. The bedpan. The blue jay feathers. The dandelion. The two keys. Locked inside for good and bound for the bottom of the ocean at last.

The contents of the suitcase tip back and forth as I walk. It's heavier than I remember. Snow rests on the heads of dead grass and gleams on the branches of every pine. It hasn't snowed too much yet. Just enough to brighten everything and to obscure the beaten path to what used to be Aunt Madeline's house.

I'm not back to visit or stay. Only back to finish the work of magic Aunt Maryflower started with a spell jar she made from a suitcase filled with meaningful things.

Snowflakes shimmer as they fall past the feathers of vigilant crows. Honeyed sunlight pours over wild apples in the snow, giving a sweetness to the air. Willow trees sway with gentle patience as I walk beneath them. Icicles dangle from the bare willow branches. They tinkle and jingle to announce my arrival, like tiny bells.

Closer to the location of the house, the air rumbles with new sounds. Low growls and grunts resonate, louder and deeper the closer I get.

Across the bright white landscape, there is movement all around the house. Massive shadows lurch and sway. Clouds of breath huff and unfurl.

I get close enough to see and stop in my tracks.

Black bears. Seven at least. Probably more. Lumbering around the dooryard. Snoozing in the bushes. Gnawing on fish. Quite at home.

Behind them, bittersweet nightshade vines smother the fallen tree that crushed part of the house and wind down the remaining walls. The nightshade berries gleam like blood drops. No windows left. The front door looks intact and open. The top of the purple cabinet juts up from its place inside the house. Still standing, for now. The inside of the house must be all snow and scattered curiosities and slumbering bears.

A small black bear is curled up alone at the top of the forget-me-not tree, sound asleep.

Aunt Madeline would be pleased black bears have made their home here. They must have come for the feast of fishes after the hurricane and stayed.

Leaving the black bears be, I tuck the suitcase under my arm and retrace my steps away from the house and back into the woods. I'll find another way to the cliff.

The ocean is quiet today. Cold, grey, and not moving much. Seagulls sit on the surface of the water, just little white dots from here. The horizon is a blue-grey line.

I step to the edge of the cliff. Directly below, the ocean sloshes and laps. I could drop the suitcase straight down from here. But I don't.

Instead, I step back, wind up, and throw that old suitcase as hard as I can toward the horizon. It sails through the air, getting smaller and smaller, and plummets into the ocean like a diving bird. A splash of white marks its place until the foam dissipates. The surface of the water is quiet again, as if nothing happened.

Something catches my eye on the ground, half under snow.

Claw hammer. Old but solid. Wood handle. Steel head. No name or initials on it. No telling how it got here. No telling whose it was. It feels good in my hand.

I have no use for a heavy old hammer like this. Nothing to carry it in. But if I leave it here, it will rot. Seems like it'd be a waste of a good hammer to leave it.

Alone on the edge of a cliff, I consider a hammer. Is it a tool or a weapon? Depends on how you hold it, I guess.

Wind whips off the ocean. Just a gust. Just enough to push snow over the place where the hammer had been. Just enough to lift my hair from my shoulders and nudge me on my way.

I slide the hammer handle in the leg of my boot.

Good.

Salt air blows deep into the forest ahead of me.

Above, the lavender sky blackens. Below, the ocean is beautiful and cold.

AFTERWORD

All stories about Nova Scotia must have some darkness in them, I say. Because of all the bones.

There are lost cemeteries and unmarked graves everywhere here. Many people have no idea. But if you stay in Nova Scotia long enough—and if you don't mind dark things—you pick up bits of truth about it, like broken sea glass on the shore.

I come from northern Newfoundland, but I've lived in Nova Scotia a long time. And I just happen to love dark things. Many parts of this story were inspired by the bits of broken glass I've found that haunt me most.

The graveyard in the city where Fade sleeps rough in chapter one is real. It's the Old Burying Ground in Nova Scotia's capital city, Halifax. A national historic site, this cemetery receives government funding to keep its lovely headstones safe and mended and mowed—and to keep people like Fade out.

A stone's throw away, the Halifax Poor House cemetery receives nothing. Not a cent to recognize or preserve the mass grave of 4,500 poor house residents buried there over two hundred years ago. No names. No stones. It currently lies under a vacant building, under the busy streets and sidewalks around it, and a parking lot.

Tiny unmarked graves fill the ground in the seaside village of East Chester, where the Ideal Maternity Home once provided a place for the discreet delivery of babies of unwed mothers. It also provided "placement" for those babies, which meant selling them on the black market. Only babies deemed "desirable" were sold. Babies deemed "undesirable"—mixed race babies, babies with dark complexions, and sick babies—were killed. As many as six hundred unwanted babies were buried in small wooden grocery boxes called butterboxes. The home kept poor records, likely to hide its crimes, so the true number of "butterbox babies" will never be known. Their little bodies were buried in unmarked graves on the property, burned in the furnace, or tossed in the ocean.

An hour away, in Sipekne'katik, more children were lost. Mi'kmaq, Wolastoqiyik, Mohawk, and Inuit children were forced to attend the Shubenacadie Indian Residential School. Across Canada, many unmarked children's graves have been found at former residential school sites. In Nova Scotia, official records say sixteen Indigenous children died at the Shubenacadie school. However, survivors of the school and elders in the community remember at least 138 children who died there. The search for these lost children continues in Sipekne'katik. Their remains have not yet been found.

From the 1920s to the 1980s, a systematic cover-up centred on the Nova Scotia Home for Colored Children. Thousands of orphaned African Nova Scotian children were placed in this facility meant to protect them. There, they experienced daily physical, psychological, and sexual abuse and exploitation and were forced into silence. Once known as Nova Scotia's Throwaway Children, the survivors' voices were finally heard through a restorative inquiry in 2019.

The broken chain and the basement strong room cell that imprisoned Maryflower are inspired by the true stories of two Nova Scotian women, Louisa Jane Lewis and Lita Saulnier. *The Poor of Digby County Enquiry of 1885* records offer some details of the life of Louisa Jane Lewis—described as a "confirmed lunatic"—who would escape her keepers and "run at large for a few days, before she could be hunted up and brought back" again and again. Louisa had been kept chained in a pen attached to the side of a house. Her only crime was having mental illness. Or being a rebellious woman.

In 1920, Lita Saulnier entered the Saint Mary's poorhouse in Meteghan, ill with diphtheria. Considered contagious, she was locked alone in a strong room in the basement, where she received meals and laundry through a hole in the door of her room and had no interaction with other human beings. She was essentially forgotten. Lita remained locked in that strong room, alone, for forty years. A new keeper, hired in 1960, discovered Lita down there and let her out. After four decades of isolation, Lita had lost the ability to speak. She spent the rest of her years at a seniors' home in Yarmouth. She died in 1983.

The Grand Tea rock itself is not real, but it is inspired by colossal rock formations that have loomed over Nova Scotia for hundreds of millions of years. The Balancing Rock. The Hammer Sea Arch. The Three Sisters. The Ovens. Cape Split. Many more. They are beautiful and terrifying and seem to exist on the brink of collapse. Battered year after year by hurricanes, blizzards, and relentless Atlantic tides, none of Nova Scotia's monolithic stone titans has fallen on us—yet.

Although Havenwood Hospital and the Luck property burial grounds are fictional, they are based on the true history of the poorhouses in Nova Scotia. There were thirty-two. Every county in Nova Scotia, except Guysborough, had at least one poorhouse at one time. Some government funded, some privately owned. Most poorhouses had unmarked burial grounds hidden nearby. These poorhouses closed over time. Some converted to seniors' homes. Some swallowed by fire. Some abandoned to rot.

Their bones are still there.

ACKNOWLEDGEMENTS

Thank you to *you*—dear reader, first and foremost—for finding this little book and for reading it. I hope you got to read it through the steam of your favourite tea or covered the pages with crumbs from those cookies you like. Did it spark you to think up your own spells and write them down? (If so, I'd love to know. I promise your spells are safe with me.)

My deepest gratitude to Jennifer Knoch, senior editor at ECW Press, who found this little book before it was a book at all. Jen is a kind, whip-smart, and wickedly brilliant mentor, editor, and ally who puts her heart and soul into what she does. It is a privilege to work with her. I will never be able to thank her enough.

To the entire team at ECW Press, thank you for your hard work, and for being some of the loveliest, most creative people on the planet. Thank you, especially, to Cassie Smyth, Alexandra Dunn, Crissy Boylan, Jennifer Gallinger, Kenna Barnes, David Caron, Emily Ferko, Jessica Albert, Michela Prefontaine, and Victoria

Cozza. Thank you, Teagan White, for sharing your haunting and beautiful art.

Thank you to my son, Gabe Mifflen, who always looks after his mum. Gabe built, repaired, and maintained the computers this book's manuscript was written on. He went above and beyond to put everything in place so that nothing I wrote down would be lost. I'm so grateful and so proud of him. He is my favourite person in the world to share tea with.

Thank you to Carter Chaplin, who encouraged me to put my writing out there for once. Every shy writer and quiet artist needs a kind-hearted, gentle soul in their corner who makes it a little safer to try that step into the light. Carter has been that for me, and for this book. He's a good man.

Thank you to my parents, Linda and Walter. My love of stories came from them both. My mother, who filled our childhood with love, books, and Buddy Stories and raised us in a home where the walls were literally made of books. My father, who may be the best storyteller of all, regaling us with funny, heartwarming, sometimes heartbreaking tales of life growing up in Newfoundland.

Thank you to my brothers, Jonathon and Jordan, whom I always have in mind when I write. Growing up, we shared our books, made-up stories, and imaginary worlds, and I guess I never grew out of it.

To Kyla Russell, for a lifetime of love, unwavering support, and the most exquisite corpses.

To Roxanne Potvin, for helping me be more creative and brave.

To uncle Gordon Penney, the lion-hearted protector of people and keeper of old stories.

Thank you to Kai Smith, for the author portraits, and for the joy your work honouring Nova Scotia's wildlife inspires.

Thank you to Ara Bentley, whose gift for finding beauty in abandoned places forever changed the way I see the world.

Thank you to Dr. Lauren Quattrocchi, who keeps raising my bones from the dead so I can keep writing. Thank you to Emily

Daley, for her care after an injury that almost stopped me writing this book halfway through. Thank you to Dr. Kenneth Cameron—the humble, Nova Scotian legend himself—for everything.

This story was inspired by many extraordinary, strong women: Jessica Goreham-Penney, Suna Hanoz-Penney, Marguerite Penney, Ruth Freeman, Violet Colbourne, Margie Derbyshire MacDougall, Amber Brown, Nynke Leistra, Jennifer Leger, Kate Snow, Michelle Bumstead, Kim Wolstenholme, Paula Rent, Ashley Mitchell, Jessica Atkinson, Tiffany Christie, Laura Keeping, too many more to name. I admire you all. And with love to my nieces, Meredith, Leyla, and Ela. Your Aunt Vanessa will always have your back.

The magic in this story came from my memories of my grandmothers, Susie Penney and Margaret Snow, and the things they cooked and baked and made with their own hands.

Last but not least, I give thanks to a little, old black cat named Lego, for keeping me company while I wrote every last word of this book, and for nudging me back to the real world, now and then, to let me know that my tea has gone cold and her cookie bowl has gone empty.

KAI SMITH

VANESSA F. PENNEY was born in northern Newfoundland and raised in rural Nova Scotia. The coal-black ocean depths and bone-buried shorelines of the East Coast inspire her writing. Vanessa lives in Dartmouth, NS.

Entertainment. Writing. Culture. ─────────

ECW is a proudly independent, Canadian-owned book publisher. We know great writing can improve people's lives, and we're passionate about sharing original, exciting, and insightful writing across genres.

───────────────────── **Thanks for reading along!**

We want our books not just to sustain our imaginations, but to help construct a healthier, more just world, and so we've become a certified B Corporation, meaning we meet a high standard of social and environmental responsibility — and we're going to keep aiming higher. We believe books can drive change, but the way we make them can too.

Being a B Corp means that the act of publishing this book should be a force for good — for the planet, for our communities, and for the people that worked to make this book. For example, everyone who worked on this book was paid at least a living wage. You can learn more at the Ontario Living Wage Network.

This book is also available as a Global Certified Accessible™ (GCA) ebook. ECW Press's ebooks are screen reader friendly and are built to meet the needs of those who are unable to read standard print due to blindness, low vision, dyslexia, or a physical disability.

This book is printed on FSC®-certified paper. It contains recycled materials, and other controlled sources, is processed chlorine free, and is manufactured using biogas energy.

ECW's office is situated on land that was the traditional territory of many nations, including the Wendat, the Anishinaabeg, Haudenosaunee, Chippewa, Métis, and current treaty holders the Mississaugas of the Credit. In the 1880s, the land was developed as part of a growing community around St. Matthew's Anglican and other churches. Starting in the 1950s, our neighbourhood was transformed by immigrants fleeing the Vietnam War and Chinese Canadians dispossessed by the building of Nathan Phillips Square and the subsequent rise in real estate value in other Chinatowns. We are grateful to those who cared for the land before us and are proud to be working amidst this mix of cultures.

ecwpress.com